THE
TOUCH
OF
Silk

Books by Shannon Page

Eel River
Our Lady of the Islands (with Jay Lake)
I Was a Trophy Wife (essay collection)

The Nightcraft Quartet:
The Queen and The Tower
A Sword in The Sun
The Lovers Three
The Empress and The Moon

Island of Second Chances:
A Taste of Midnight
Love and Lemongrass
The Touch of Silk
Toil and Water (forthcoming)

Collaborations, as Laura Gayle

The Chameleon Chronicles:
Orcas Intrigue
Orcas Intruder
Orcas Investigation
Orcas Illusion
Orcas Intermission

Tales from the Berry Farm:
Orcas Afterlife
Orcas Aliens (forthcoming)

THE TOUCH OF
Silk

BOOK THREE
ISLAND OF SECOND CHANCES

SHANNON PAGE

ALoT
PRESS
A Little of This, Inc.

The Touch of Silk, by Shannon Page

Copyright © 2025 by Shannon Page
Edited by Spencer Ellsworth

Cover art and design by Kathia Zolfaghari
Interior design by Shannon Page

HUMAN AUTHORED™
AG THE Authors Guild
9792314

First Edition

ISBN: 978-1-967168-05-7

ALoT PRESS
A Little of This, Inc.

"Too good to be true? Well, I suppose that depends upon your definition of *good*. And of *true*."

—Countess Lucinda Devonryshireton,
The Countess's Exceedingly Perfect Guide to Love and Romance, Volume I

Chapter 1

LYNNE

Lynne Daniels stood in the back room of the Evintrude Gallery, listening to the crowd on the other side of the door.

A huge crowd. A huge crowd here, tonight. A huge crowd here tonight for one reason: to see Lynne's tapestries, on display, on the walls and tables, *in an actual art gallery.*

Oh god.

Did this room have a fire exit?

The noise of the crowd increased as someone opened the door leading from the gallery's main room. Lynne froze. Kate Evintrude walked in, holding a glass of white wine, which she handed to Lynne. "Here, drink this, and no, you can't escape, so don't even think about it."

Lynne took the glass with a trembling hand. "How did you know?"

"Because the same thing happens with every artist, and not only on their first opening night. So drink up, take a deep breath, and come meet your adoring fans." Kate gave her a winning smile. "We've got a nice turnout."

Lynne moaned. "Why? *Why* are so many people here? Why did I agree to do this? What was I thinking? I'm a doctor, not an artist! I hate crowds!"

"Drink your wine."

Kate stared at Lynne until she took a sip. It was nice wine, dry, tart even, yet fruity—maybe grapefruity. "Is this Sauvignon Blanc?"

"It is. Drink some more."

Lynne obeyed. "From New Zealand?"

"Yep."

Kate watched as Lynne took several more sips.

"All right, that's probably enough," Kate said, when the glass was half-empty. "I think you're ready to head out there now."

"Oh god." Lynne looked behind her for that elusive—nonexistent—back door again. "I've changed my mind. I can't do this."

"I'll go out first and say a few words about your work and your life history, as we discussed," Kate said calmly, ignoring Lynne's panic attack. "You wait just inside the door, behind the screen, and as soon as I introduce you, you come out and give your little art talk. You have your notes, right?"

Lynne lifted up a folded sheet of paper. It had gotten a little creased and sweaty, but she thought she could still read what was on it.

"Great," Kate said, still exuding steady calmness. "Just say your piece, and then open it up for questions."

"Oh my god. Are people going to ask questions?"

Kate patted her arm. "Okay, maybe you're not quite done with your wine yet. Of course they're going to ask questions, and you're going to answer them, because they're about your lovely and fascinating work, and people are going to want to hear all about it—from you."

"No they're not. No one wants to hear anything from me. I'm just an old woman who must have been drunk when some crazy gallery owner convinced her to hang her sewing mistakes on a wall for everyone to see."

"Hush now," Kate said. "Here we go." And she turned and

stepped out of the back room and into the gallery, leaving Lynne alone. A moment later, Lynne heard her tapping a spoon on her own wine glass and calling for everyone's attention. The crowd slowly quieted.

And then Kate was talking about Lynne's work, and her life. How did she learn all those details? Did Steph tell her? Lynne couldn't remember talking to Kate about any of it.

Of course, Lynne couldn't remember a thing right now, her nervous brain freeze was so overwhelming.

But then Kate's spiel was over, and she called out Lynne's name, and the audience applauded!

As if sleepwalking, Lynne saw her feet move, and her feet were attached to her legs so they moved as well, carrying her out from behind the screen and into the gallery. My god, there were so many people here. *Don't think about that.* Kate smiled and indicated that Lynne should step up to the front table beside her. "Lynne Daniels, everyone!" Kate said, beaming at the crowd.

The applause redoubled, every single person smiling at Lynne. She smiled back at them, or at least she hoped it was a smile and not a rictus of terror.

And then the clapping died down and Lynne cleared her throat, unfolded her sheet of notes, and began her talk.

She must have gotten sucked into another dimension for a minute or ten, because suddenly she was done with her talk and slipping the crumpled paper into the pocket of her flowing pants, and the audience was smiling and applauding again, and then a dozen or more hands went up! People actually did have questions!

Lynne looked over the crowd. Who to call on first? Why were there so many complete strangers here? Her heart raced as she scanned the room, desperate for a familiar face. Ah, there was Julie, from soup group. "Yes, Julie?" she said.

Julie smiled and said, "Your work is gorgeous, and so unusual; thank you for sharing it with us." Lynne nodded as Julie went on. "I was wondering, do you take commissions?"

"I, er, haven't before, but…" She looked at Kate, who took over smoothly.

"Lynne would be happy to talk to anyone about what they might have in mind," the gallery owner said. "Though she will make no promises—as I mentioned earlier, the artist Lynne Daniels is also the not-exactly-retired Dr. Lynne Daniels, as many of you know from encountering her at our health clinic." There were nods and smiles around the room. "More questions?"

All those hands went up again. Lynne scanned the crowd. "Yes?" she said, indicating a young woman in the back.

"Yes! Thank you, wow. I'm just getting into embroidery, and your work is *so* inspiring."

"Thank you," Lynne said.

The young woman nodded. "I've been working with floss, and not separating it, because I'm still figuring out how it all works, but I do know you can pull the threads apart for a finer line."

"That's correct."

"What I'm wondering is, how does that work with the various fabrics? I see that you do a lot of work on silk—which, first of all, oh my god. But also, isn't the weave of silk so tight for the thicker floss? How do you get both weights of thread to work together in the same piece—in the same *part* of the same piece?" She pointed to the landscape tapestry she was standing beside, a depiction of the West Sound harbor, at sunset.

Oh, what a good question. Lynne started talking as she walked over to the young woman, so she could point out the particulars of the piece. The crowd parted around her, watching and listening raptly. Her nerves melted away as she explained the process— how she'd stumbled across it by mistake during a moment of inattention, but found she really liked the effect, so she'd started doing it deliberately.

"I eventually had to rig up a larger hoop to keep the silk taut," Lynne finished, adding with a chuckle, "and it wasn't even hoop-shaped. My son helped with the construction." She looked up, finding Ethan's beaming face in the crowd. "Ethan Daniels, everyone."

The crowd applauded both her and Ethan; the young woman looked delighted. More hands went up, and Lynne found herself easily answering all their questions. Who knew so many people were interested in embroidery! It was just something she did in the evenings alone at home, to keep her hands busy while she watched TV or listened to an audiobook.

She had never thought of herself as an artist. Apparently, everyone else did.

After the tenth or twentieth question, there was another sound of a spoon tapping on a wine glass. "I'm going to stop us there," Kate called out, from the front table. "I'm sure Lynne will be happy to chat more with you individually throughout the evening, but we've got a buffet of great munchies ready to eat over by the far wall, and all this wine won't drink itself!"

Laughter filled the room, and conversations swelled as the audience moved toward the food and drink.

"Well?" Kate was suddenly beside her, smiling hugely, and handing her a fresh glass of wine. "How are you doing now?"

"Oh, that was amazing!" Lynne gushed, exulting in the adrenaline and the heavy relief of being off stage. "What a great crowd!"

"You were fantastic, as I knew you would be." Her tone was warm, and not at all smug; she really was just the nicest person. "And I've already had several very serious inquiries about purchasing pieces."

"That's great!" Lynne sipped the wine. "I really do need to make space in poor Ethan's room."

Kate laughed. "Yes, that's one reason why all this is a good idea, I suppose." Then she sobered a bit. "Are you certain you won't agree to sell the anchor piece, though?" She nodded to the long panorama of Crow Valley, stretching nearly the width of the gallery's eastern wall. "We would have a bidding war for it, just from the folks in this room."

"You know darn well it's already been sold, and for an absurdly generous price." Lynne looked through the audience again, and indeed, here came her next-door neighbor Steph—and her shy husband David! He hated crowds! "I doubt you could talk her into letting it go, but you're welcome to try."

Kate pulled her friend Steph into a hug even as she said, "Leave it to you to snap up the best piece before the show even opened."

"There wouldn't even *be* a show if it weren't for my, ah, let's call it assistance," Steph said, laughing. She turned to Lynne. "I bet you're glad we pushed you into this."

"Oh, I don't know about that!" Lynne laughed with her. "But I am glad to be done with the public speaking."

"How does a doctor have stage fright?" Steph asked. "Don't you have to give rounds and seminars, all the way from medical school onward? You give a talk at the senior center here every week!"

"That's entirely different," Lynne said. "I can talk about medical things all day, to any size audience—I could do that in my sleep. Talking about my personal work..." She shrugged, and glanced at David, who was looking back at her with sympathy. "I know it's not rational, but I was waiting at any moment for someone to raise their hand and point out what an utter fraud I am."

"But that didn't happen," Kate said.

"Thank goodness!"

They all laughed as more people she knew made their way through the crowd. Julie and her boyfriend Gavin; Julie's daughter Megan; Matt; and...a vaguely familiar man.

After hugs and congratulations from her friends, Gavin indicated the silver-haired man beside him. "Lynne, you remember my friend Will?"

It took her a moment, but Will smiled and she placed him. "Oh! From pickleball last year—"

"—and beers afterwards," he finished, putting out a hand for her to shake. "It's a pleasure to see you again, and your work is spectacular."

"Thank you, and yes! I mean, the other way around—yes to the pleasure, and thank you for the compliment." She shook his hand; his grip was warm and strong, without crushing her smaller, more delicate hand. Indeed, her hand almost felt cradled, protected in the embrace of his. *What a strange thing to think!* she thought, only reluctantly letting go before the exchange became awkward—well, more awkward. *I must be completely wound up tonight.* "You look different in real clothes," she blurted, before she could stop herself. *Oops. More awkward, coming right up!*

Will laughed, looking down at himself. He was in what might be called cocktail-casual: dark slacks, a striped blue button-down shirt, no tie; his shirtsleeves were unbuttoned and turned up at the cuffs, exposing his tanned wrists. "Well, one doesn't wear sweatpants and a ball cap to an art opening, even on casual Orcas Island."

Lynne wanted to cover her mouth with her hand. *What is the matter with me?* She forced herself to laugh along with him as she glanced at her own outfit: cornflower-blue silk pants and a pale cream top festooned with embroidered flowers. "I thought the same. And now I should probably get something to eat before I make an even bigger fool of myself." She held up her glass of wine, which was more than half gone already.

"May I escort you over to the buffet?" Will asked, offering an elbow. Somehow, he made the gesture seem gallant and comfortable rather than stuffy or old-fashioned.

"Yes, thank you," Lynne said, and took his arm.

"We'll come too," Steph said, taking David's hand and following along. "I love other people's cooking."

"I don't know why that always surprises me," Julie observed.

Their little group moved toward the food, eventually securing plates of nibbles—cheese, rolled meats, crackers, olives. Then, somehow, she found herself standing with Will under the Crow Valley panorama.

"I inquired about purchasing this piece," Will said, "but Kate told me that it has already sold."

"It has," Lynne said. "To Steph—" She turned, looking for her friend, but she and David had vanished into the crowd. As had Matt, and Julie and Megan and Gavin, and Kate. "The redheaded woman who was with us earlier."

Will smiled, like sun breaking through clouds. She hadn't remembered how good-looking he was. In fact, she'd barely remembered him at all; it had been a pleasant afternoon with friends, and that had been that. "Well, then, I suppose I'll need to be one of the people talking to you about a commission."

Lynne felt her face flush with warmth. "I...we would have to talk about that," she said. "I don't usually know, when I start a piece, where it will end up."

"I am comfortable with uncertainty." His smile grew even warmer.

Are we still talking about my needlework?

"Ah, good," she managed. "Well, uh…"

"Hey Mom!" Suddenly Ethan was at her elbow. "You wanna introduce me to your friend?"

"I'm Will Hamilton," Will said, putting out that wonderful strong hand. Ethan shook it.

"This is my son, Ethan," Lynne said.

"It's a pleasure to meet you," Will told him.

Ethan grinned. "Likewise!" He turned to Lynne. "Marie and I are going to head on out—we have that dinner, remember."

"That's right," Lynne said. "Well, thank you for being here for the opening."

"We wouldn't have missed it!"

She pulled her son into a hug. He took the opportunity to whisper in her ear, "Hubba hubba!"

"Stop it," she hissed back to him, though she couldn't help laughing as well as she let him go. "Have fun this evening!" she said brightly, and glanced around for Marie.

"She's already getting the car," Ethan told her. "We had to park, like, blocks and blocks away."

Lynne didn't point out that the entire town of Eastsound barely comprised "blocks and blocks."

After he'd left, she turned back to Will, who was studying the tapestry. "You do have a singular talent," he said.

"This entire experience is going to go completely to my head and I will become quite insufferable," Lynne protested. "It's just threads on fabric!"

Will turned and held her gaze. His eyes were a rich, warm brown shot through with green flecks of an almost jade-like brightness, picking up the silver of his hair and his neatly trimmed beard. Lynne didn't usually like men with beards, but this one... She found herself unable to look away from him, and also, automatically, thinking about how she would depict that play of colors in a piece. "Oh, I don't think so," he said. "It is so much more than that."

The rest of the crowded, noisy room seemed to fall away as she stared into his eyes.

"In fact," Will went on, "I would be honored to buy you dinner and continue this conversation in a quieter venue."

Lynne swallowed as excuses flooded her mind, but she pushed them aside. It was just dinner—and possibly discussion of a commission. Wasn't this the whole reason she was putting herself out here like this? "I would like that," she said.

His smile warmed her to her toes, and put the lie to the 'just business' line she was trying to tell herself.

"Shall we sneak away," he asked, "or do you have further responsibilities here?"

"I don't have any more speeches to make, but I imagine Kate expects me to hang around in case more people want to talk to me." She glanced around, not seeing the gallery owner. "I'll check in with her and see what she thinks about the timing."

Will nodded and pulled a slender cell phone out of his pocket.

"I will secure reservations somewhere appropriate—in, say, forty-five minutes or an hour?"

Lynne smiled gratefully. "That sounds perfect. I can't imagine even the most die-hard of fans will stay longer than that."

He stepped away to make the call as Lynne re-entered the crowd. She finally found Kate in the middle of a group of four or five people about Ethan's age. "Ah, here she is now," she said, stepping back to welcome Lynne into the circle. "Nadia here was just asking about your source for fabrics, and how you decide between a single ground color and some of your more patch-work-effect pieces."

"Yes," said a dark-haired woman, her eyes shining with enthusiasm. "Your embroidery is so lovely, it's all everyone was talking about, but I'm also struck by your use of base color—where do you find such lush silks?"

"Ah, everywhere," Lynne said with a smile. "Online, and fabric stores, and yard sales—you name it. And the best thing about this kind of work is that, unlike sewing clothing or something like that, I don't need any particular quantity or shape of fabric, so I am always on the lookout for interesting scraps. Which, by the way, is the answer to your second question: if I have a bunch of little remnants that seem to want to go together, then that's what I do. If I have one perfect piece by itself…" She pointed at the tapestry closest to them on the wall. "Like this one, for example. I picked this silk up in a little secondhand shop in Cannon Beach, Oregon, at least a dozen years ago. I don't know why they were selling fabric samples, but they had a whole pile of the most luscious things that seemed to beg to be fancied up and tacked to a wall. I snapped them all up, and have been working through them ever since."

She talked to the group for another few minutes before Kate deftly steered her to another part of the room, where more questions awaited; and then, shortly, a third group after that. By the time Will came to find her, nearly an hour had passed, and the gallery was finally emptying out. Even the soup group members had all left.

"I managed to find us a table at the New Leaf, if that is all right?" He looked worried.

Lynne laughed. "I love the New Leaf."

"Then, shall we?" He offered his arm again, and Lynne took it.

Out in the night, she took a deep, grateful breath of air. "Whew. That was great, but also pretty overwhelming."

"I imagine so." He glanced down at her. "I'm parked just down here, if you…"

"Oh, can we walk?" she asked. "It's not that far, and I still think I have some nervous energy to work out of my limbs."

"Then walking it is." He snugged her arm close to his side, and she felt warm all over again.

Their booth at the New Leaf was just before the step down to the corner room, and had the feeling of being both in the center of things and a little removed. She wondered how he'd managed to score it; the restaurant was still hopping, with most of the tables occupied. "Not as quiet as I'd hoped!" he said with a sheepish grin, as they looked over their menus.

"Much quieter in here than out there," Lynne said, nodding to the long dining room they'd just walked through.

"Yes," Will agreed. "This is my favorite table."

"Mine too! Table eighteen." She felt absurdly pleased as they smiled at each other. "I like being tucked against the wall here— and you can see the view better than from any of those supposedly better ones." She glanced at the row of tables against the darkened windows. "In the daytime, I mean."

"Exactly!"

A young waiter appeared and asked for their drink orders. "Ah, hmm," Lynne said. "I probably shouldn't drink more tonight…" she started, but Will laughed and raised a hand to stop her.

"It's your first art opening, and it was a smashing success. If you can't indulge even just a little bit, today of all days, then when can you?"

She laughed as well. *Accepting a spontaneous dinner invitation from an attractive man isn't indulgence enough?* "Okay, since you put it that way…"

She ordered an Orcas Sunrise; Will asked for a Spring and Tonic.

Their cocktails arrived quickly. Will raised his glass for a toast. "To indulgences, now and in the future," he said, with a twinkle in his eye.

She clinked her glass against his, debating whether to ask him to elaborate or to just ride the wave. "Ooh, this is good," she said, after her first sip. "I always forget how much I like this."

"It's pretty too," he said. "Like one of your tapestries."

"Says the man with a purple drink!" she said with a smile. "Yours is even prettier, I think."

He scooted his glass closer to hers and looked at them side by side. "Actually, they go well together, don't you think? A sunset, in two glasses."

"Exactly." She admired the drinks for a moment, then picked up her glass and took another sip, savoring the bite of the vodka and the tang of cranberry and lime. "Ahh. I think I'm finally beginning to unclench a little."

He gave her a smoldering look over the rim of his glass as he sipped. "I am very glad to hear that."

The server appeared again, wondering what they wanted to order for dinner.

"I ate too many appetizers at the gallery," Lynne said, picking the menu back up, "but I think I could manage the sliders."

"And some truffle fries to share?" Will asked.

"Yes!"

He ordered the ribeye steak, medium, and a bottle of red wine; the server nodded and left.

"I know you said you've had enough to drink already, but with steak and burgers, I couldn't help myself." Will gave her a grin.

"I have it on good authority that they'll cork up an unfinished bottle and let you take it home," Lynne assured him.

"Excellent," Will said. "This one won't suffer from being open overnight, either."

Before too long, the truffle fries came out—hot and crisp and salty, with the funky undertone of truffle oil. Lynne kept telling herself *This is my last one*, and it kept not being true. She and Will chatted comfortably as they nibbled, him asking her about her work and her life on Orcas Island.

"And what about you?" she asked, after a bit. "I know you play pickleball, and I think I remember from last fall that you're in real estate?"

"Mostly commercial real estate, though I do some residential, usually branching off from commercial developments."

Lynne was trying to figure out if she'd seen his name on fliers around town when he went on.

"I'm licensed in both Washington and Arizona, though I do most of my work down there."

"Oh! I was wondering what sort of commercial developments we have here on the island."

He nodded. "A few, though you're right, it's mostly residential here. The majority of my business is in Scottsdale and the surrounding areas. I tend to regard my time on Orcas as something akin to a vacation." He chuckled and added, "Or at least, I try to. Business seems to follow me around."

"Sounds like being a doctor and unable to go out in public without being asked for medical advice."

"So you understand!" They shared a smile as the server arrived with the bottle of red wine.

"Just a tiny glass for me," Lynne said. She hadn't quite finished her cocktail.

"Of course," said the waiter, and poured for each of them. "Your meals will be out in a few minutes."

"We're not in a hurry," Will told him.

After the waiter had left, Lynne asked, "Where is your Orcas house? I assume you don't just stay in the inn here when you're on-island."

"No, though their rooms are quite nice. I have a cabin out in Eagle Lake."

"Oh, I haven't actually been out there, though I've seen pictures of the community—and the lake, of course. It looks lovely."

"It's spectacular." His eyes got a dreamy expression that somehow made him even more handsome. "I bought there when the development was just getting going, in the early nineties. Built the cabin myself—I mean, with hired help, of course, though I swung a hammer a time or two."

"What brought you to Orcas?"

He chuckled. "It's funny—my wife at the time had this dream of living here. She'd read about the island in a magazine and just couldn't let go of the idea. It took us a few years to visit, and we both were charmed, so we looked around at some properties. I wanted to live closer in to town, but she saw the parcel out in Eagle Lake and that was that." He shook his head and took a sip of his drink. "So why, you might ask, am I the one who got the cabin in the divorce?"

"I was wondering that," Lynne said with a smile.

"Suffice it to say, dreams are one thing; reality is quite another. Maggie tried, god bless her, but she actually hated living in such a remote place—and I don't just mean Eagle Lake, but Orcas Island generally."

"Island living is not for everyone," Lynne agreed.

"We tried to make a go of it. I thought when the cabin was finished, things might get easier for her, but no. Then we tried the partial-year thing, snowbirding in Arizona and summering up here, and that helped for a while. But then came one year when she just didn't want to head back to Orcas in the spring, and I really did, so she told me to go on up without her. By the time I went back to Scottsdale that fall, it was to start meeting with the divorce lawyers."

"I'm sorry," she said, because that was the polite thing to say.

Will shrugged. "Don't be. We're both happier apart than we ever were together. And we're not enemies; we still care about each other."

"Do you have any kids?"

"No. I would have been willing, but Maggie had her career—she's an interior designer—and she never really had the urge. It made things easier, when it came time to go our separate ways." He leaned forward slightly, setting his empty cocktail glass on the table, but not picking up his wine glass. "And you? I met your son Ethan tonight; are there other kids? And…a husband, an ex?"

"My husband died nearly twenty years ago. He was a doctor as well, and Ethan is our only child."

"I am so sorry for your loss," Will said, holding her gaze.

"Thank you. But, as I said, it was long enough ago that it's just part of the fabric of my life." She gave a small smile. "If you'll excuse the pun."

Will chuckled appreciatively. "Still, I imagine one never gets over such a thing."

"Not entirely. The best way I've heard it described is, the grief never gets smaller, but your life gets bigger around it, so that over time, it takes up less and less of a percentage of—well, everything."

"Profound. And it makes sense. Even lesser losses, like divorce, get smaller in the rearview mirror."

"They do."

The waiter appeared with two plates of food, setting their meals before them. "Will there be anything else?"

"No, thank you, this looks perfect," Lynne said, and Will agreed.

After the waiter stepped away again, Will picked up his wine glass and raised it for a toast. "To a lovely meal…with a lovely woman…perhaps the first of many such evenings? If I may be so bold?"

Lynne raised her glass and clinked with his. "I don't find the notion entirely odious," she said, laughing softly.

Will smiled broadly. "I am glad."

HE WALKED HER back to her car after dinner, since he was parked just beyond hers. At least, that's what he said; Lynne was pretty sure he would have insisted either way.

And she didn't hate that idea either. It had been a long, long time since any man had awakened the kinds of feelings in her that Will had, this evening.

What did it mean? He had "boldly" hoped for many more such evenings. Did she want that as well? Why not?

Lynne had never been opposed to the idea of another relationship, or even of marrying again. She had dated a few nice-enough men in her early years on Orcas, but no one had sparked deeper feelings in her. And the sentiment had clearly been mutual, as none of the men she'd dated had tried to take things further either.

Was it just because she was so raw and open, so vulnerable, right now—on the very night of her art opening? But no, she didn't think so. Certainly this was a huge step outside her comfort zone, exciting and terrifying in equal measures. Will, however, was an interesting, appealing man in his own right: Lynne was quite certain this was true, and not just a side effect of her giddy stage fright, or even of the extra drink or two she'd had tonight.

In any event, she'd see how she felt in the morning. No need to figure out their entire future in this moment.

As they approached her car, he squeezed her arm gently before drawing them both to a halt. "You are certain you are comfortable to drive home?" he asked.

"I am good," she said, "thank you. Not only the sliders and the fries, but all that steak you fed me—I think the wine is well and truly diluted in my bloodstream." Then she chuckled. "Trust me, I'm a doctor."

He laughed softly as well. "I was entirely convinced until you added that last part. Now I'm worried." But he winked. "I will now cleverly suggest we exchange phone numbers, so that you can call me and let me know when you make it home safely."

"Oh, that is very clever," she said, digging in her purse for her cell phone. "I am not seeing through this ruse at all."

"I didn't think you would."

That accomplished, there was nothing further to do but get into her car. "I should be there in about thirty minutes," she told him. "I'll call you as soon as I walk in the door."

"Perfect," he said, flashing her his wonderful smile. "If I don't pick up, it's because I'm in a dead zone on the road. I have good service in the cabin, though; may I call you back if I miss your call, or will you head straight to bed?"

Lynne didn't think she'd ever be able to sleep again. "Ethan and his partner are staying with me for the weekend, and probably aren't home from their dinner yet. I'll be waiting up for them." She smiled up at him. "So, yes."

They wished each other a pleasant drive to their opposite sides of the island, and then Lynne drove off into the night.

Chapter 2

ALICIA

"How are you doing?" Julie asked her, quietly, as they stood gazing up at one of Lynne's tapestries. The hubbub of the crowd around them, oddly, made their conversation feel private.

"I'm okay," Alicia told her, honestly. "It's weird to be at a party, but it also feels good. Sort of. Mostly."

Julie gave her a sympathetic smile. "I understand. When I left my husband, it was like I'd stepped into a new country—or even onto a new planet. One where the air was different, or the gravity. And I couldn't believe everyone didn't know this fact about me, couldn't just read it on my face: *She left her marriage!*"

"I know!" Alicia said, grateful that she got it. "That's exactly it. I hardly know who I am anymore—we've been married eighteen years. Our marriage is old enough to vote."

"That's about as long as ours lasted," Julie said thoughtfully. "I wonder if there's something special about that amount of time?"

"The eighteen-year itch?" They both chuckled.

Julie put a hand on her arm as Steph and Matt spotted them in the crowd and started heading over. "Let me know if you need anything, okay? Even just to talk?"

"I will. Thank you."

Even though she knew Ron wouldn't be here, she still almost hadn't come tonight. It wasn't the sort of thing he enjoyed—a public event celebrating somebody who wasn't Ron, focused on a creative product that wasn't Ron's scholarly writing, with wine Ron hadn't vetted and supplied—but she had made sure, through the friend grapevine, that he had no plans to show up.

She was glad she did come, though now she was ready to call it a night. She looked around for Lynne, not spotting her. "I think I'm going to head out soon," she told her friends, as Matt and Steph joined them.

"Us too," Matt said, glancing over to where Gordon sat parked in a folding chair by the door. "Dad's wiped out."

"Is Lynne still here?" Alicia asked.

"I think she left," Steph said, and there was an odd light in her eyes.

Julie picked up on it as well. "Oh? Is there a story there?"

Steph shrugged, grinning. "I don't know…but she went out at the same time as a *very* handsome gentleman, who was looking at her *very* admiringly."

"Wow!" Julie said. "Go Lynne!"

"I guess I missed that," Matt said.

"Women's radar," Steph said, and she and Julie giggled.

"Well, if the guest of honor is gone, I think it's okay for the rest of us to take off," Alicia said, to general agreement.

After a drive home so short she still couldn't quite believe it, she let herself into her place, dropped her keys on the table just inside the door, and sank down into her easy chair with a relieved sigh.

The last couple months had been…everything, honestly. Awful and wonderful and terrifying and exhilarating and heartbreaking and freeing and—everything.

Alicia had not been back to her and Ron's house—except once, picking up more of her belongings when she knew he would be out—after she had left late that evening back in March. March

14: Pi day. Steph had hosted soup group, and had gone all out, making not just incredible Thai lemongrass soup but also four different savory pies. It could have been a great evening except for Ron, who had been cranky and awful for months already—well, crankier and more awful than his usual, which was saying something—and who for some god-unknown reason had chosen that evening to make the pass at Steph that everyone knew he'd been working toward for at least two years now.

I should have just sent him home by himself then and there, Alicia thought, leaning back in her chair and closing her eyes. But inertia had taken over, like it always seemed to do after Ron had pulled some of his bullshit, and maybe even some stunned disbelief. At the end of the evening, she'd gotten into the car with that miserable troll she was married to and endured him whining and growling at her for the entire drive home. He didn't even stop when they got there; he somehow blamed Alicia for the awkwardness with Steph.

As if!

Alicia took another deep breath and tried to let that terrible evening fall away. Again. It had been two months now, and her life was peaceful. Nobody yelled at her; nobody was annoyed by her; nobody treated her with barely concealed contempt.

She had stayed two weeks at Steph and David's house—not knowing where else to go, she had fled straight back to them that same night, luckily finding them still up. They had given her a brandy and a soft bed, but it was clear they weren't looking for a roommate. Even if they had been, Alicia wouldn't have wanted to intrude on what was clearly a lovely renaissance in their marriage.

Ron had blown up her phone with voicemails in the days after she left, first demanding that she come home, then threatening to fight her for every penny in divorce court, then begging her to come back and at least talk to him, then growing sullen and maudlin. She had not answered any of his calls or returned any of the messages, eventually deputizing Julie to let him know that she needed some time to process what had happened, and that if he were smart, he would stop hounding her. Amazingly, Ron had taken the advice, and had stopped the barrage, only checking in with Julie once a week or so to see if Alicia's position had changed.

Being left in peace by him had only underscored how, well, peaceful her life was now. She did still care about Ron—at least, she was pretty sure she did—but she didn't miss him.

She did not want to go back to him.

So she had asked around, telling everyone she knew that she needed a place to live. Rentals were few and far between on Orcas Island, particularly on a freelance editor's budget; she wasn't sure how long this would take. Only a few days into her search, though, she was playing pickleball with her friend Robin, who told her that they were losing their tenant in the tiny cabin behind her and her husband Greg's house; would Alicia be interested in taking a look? Alicia leapt at the opportunity, even as she felt a little suspicious at the low rent Robin mentioned.

"It's truly miniscule," Robin had said. "Don't get too excited until you see it."

"I don't have much stuff, and I like small spaces."

Robin had smiled at her sympathetically. "I've been to your house; this isn't even as big as your kitchen."

Alicia had shrugged. "Okay, I'll keep an open mind."

But this place was *perfect*. Tiny, definitely, but it had everything it needed: a kitchenette; a main living/dining/everything else room with a built-in desk that even had a peekaboo view of the Sound; an alcove at the back of the everything room with a bed built into it, and a curtain that could be pulled across to make it a dark sleeping cave. A teensy bathroom like you'd find on a boat. And, best of all, a glassed-in front porch, big enough for one Adirondack chair with a small table beside it. "I *love* it," Alicia had said. "Can I move in today?"

She'd been living here for a month and a half now, and she still hadn't gotten over the novelty. Her own space! Such serenity, so much room to breathe.

Alicia had lived alone for years before she married Ron, but this felt different. It *was* different; she had had boyfriends before Ron, one of them fairly serious, but nobody had gotten all the way into her heart like Ron had.

Our marriage is old enough to vote, she thought again. *And it voted to call it quits.*

It was good that she and Ron hadn't had children. They'd be teenagers by now, and divorce was always hard on kids.

Of course, staying in a bad marriage "for the sake of the children" wasn't much better.

Alicia liked kids, and she loved editing children's books, seeing young minds come alive when they encountered a particularly compelling story. She wished she knew more people here on the island with kids; she missed their bright energy. But it seemed like everyone either had no kids or grown-and-gone ones.

Alicia put the kettle on to boil while she rummaged through her drawer of tea bags. It was too early to go to bed; she would sit out on her porch for a while with a cup of something herbal and fragrant. It was a lovely, mild night.

She settled in her Adirondack chair with her steaming cup and sighed happily. The peace and serenity of her new home was just the balm she needed, after living with her shoulders up around her ears for years. Tiptoeing around Ron's moods, always wondering what he was going to be a butt about next. Grabbing what little moments of independence she could—pickleball games, lunches with friends, even sometimes her editing work, if he left her alone in her office to do it—had kept her going far longer than she should have, she realized. Now, with day after day of answering to nobody but herself, the relief was still palpable.

She gazed down over the steam of her tea at the lights on the water below. In the distance, a car went by, its headlights illuminating the treetops for a moment before releasing them back to the darkness. *This is my life*, she told herself. *Just mine.*

So she really needed to move forward with the divorce. The trouble was, she did still love Ron, despite everything. When she remembered how charming and loving and fascinating he was when they were first falling for each other, her heart cracked into a million pieces, and all she wanted was to have that man back, to hold him tenderly in her arms, to listen to him talk, to see his rapt attention as he listened to *her*.

But did that man even exist anymore? When had she seen him last? It was so hard to remember. Of course no couple stays in their heady early days of infatuation. Love was the thing that grew from the embers of those white-hot flames—if you were lucky. Love carried you through the annoyances, the crises, the challenges. The growing older.

Did Ron love her? He must; he wouldn't be so bereft now if he didn't. But if he loved her, how could he live with how he'd been treating her for so long? How could he reconcile loving or even just respecting her with his obvious infatuation with Steph? And what if, god forbid, Steph had returned that infatuation—did he imagine they would have an affair, or leave their spouses for each other? Just what in the world had Ron thought he was doing?

She finished her tea, then brought her mug into her adorable, fantastic, perfect little cottage and set it in the sink. No dishwasher here, but one person didn't dirty many dishes; hand washing was quick and efficient, even pleasurable. She could see herself living here happily alone for a long time. She had even offered to sign a lease, but Robin had gently pushed her to accept a month-to-month option. "You don't know what the future is going to bring, and I'm fine with that," her friend had told her. "I will have no trouble renting the cottage if you patch things up with Ron, or buy a place of your own, or even leave the island."

"I can't see myself leaving the island," she had said, avoiding the other two possibilities. In any event, Robin had been right: it was smart to leave her options open.

She yawned and glanced at the clock. Nearly nine. That was late enough to go to bed and read. She was in the middle of a fun YA fantasy trilogy, that she told herself she was reading for work research, but in truth she was just completely enjoying for its own sake. Time for some mental and emotional escape.

There was always next week for finding a lawyer.

LYNNE

OVER BREAKFAST ON Sunday morning, Ethan and Marie were polite and courteous, telling Lynne about their evening with friends when she asked, but Lynne could see that Ethan especially was dying to know more about her dinner with Will. So she eventually took pity on him and said, "I think I went on a date last night."

Marie leaned forward, eyes shining. "You *think*? Ethan told me about finding you talking with a certain handsome man."

Lynne laughed. "Well, yes. A certain handsome and charming man asked if he could buy me dinner, to talk about a possible commission. Instead, we just got to know each other a bit."

"Sounds very nice," Marie said.

"It was. He walked me to my car afterwards, and insisted on a phone call to make sure I'd gotten safely home. And reiterated, during that phone call, the desire to see me again that he'd already expressed during dinner. Perhaps he does want to talk about that commission after all."

"Or maybe he just wants to see you again," Marie said, grinning.

"Maybe it was a date," Lynne conceded. "However unexpected that may be."

"Mom, you could have tons of dates if you wanted them," Ethan said. "But Will seems like a nice guy. What does he do?"

Lynne filled them in on everything Will had told her.

"Eagle Lake, huh?" Ethan asked. "That place out past Deer

Harbor? That does seem on brand for a rich real estate dude."

"It does," Lynne said. "I know there's a lot of spiffy homes out there, but he says his is a cabin."

"Cabins, cottages—that's the kind of thing rich people call their second homes," said Marie with a knowing smile. "You'll have to tell us all about it after your first overnight at that charming man's house."

"Marie!" Ethan cried, giving his girlfriend a playful swat on the arm. She laughed.

Lynne chuckled as well. "You youngsters, always rushing ahead with things. What happened to the thrill of the chase? The joy of slow discovery?"

"We totally had slow discovery," Ethan said, turning to Marie. "I hung out at your restaurant's bar forever before I asked you out."

"It was the second time you ever showed up there, and you did not 'ask me out,'" Marie said, rolling her eyes. "You waited till my shift ended and said you and your friends were going to check out a band at a club in Fremont and did I want to go with you."

Ethan gaped at her. "I invited you to a concert! That's totally asking you out."

Marie shrugged. "Whatever. It all worked out, didn't it? I'm more interested in your mom and Mr. Handsome and Charming." She turned back to Lynne. "So, what's the next step?"

"Well, he did say he was going to call me soon…"

Marie was already shaking her head. "Nope. Don't wait for him to call. Figure out what you want and go for it." She put her hand out. "Where's your phone? Let's call him right now."

Lynne's phone was probably still beside her bed, but before she could tell Marie that, at that moment, it began to ring.

"Ha!" Marie said, delighted. "We've manifested him! This is clearly meant to be."

Lynne got up and hurried to her bedroom, catching the phone before it went to voicemail. It wasn't Will, though; it was Alicia.

Poor thing. "Hi," Lynne said, sitting on the bed. "Thank you so much for coming last night."

"Oh, I wouldn't have missed it. I already knew your work was gorgeous, but seeing it all lit and displayed in the gallery was amazing."

Alicia sounded pretty good, Lynne thought; she had looked a bit pale last night, and she hadn't mingled a whole lot with the crowd, but it seemed like she was holding it together. Not that Lynne was surprised: Alicia was resilient. You'd have to be, to tolerate living with Ron Alderson for as long as she had. "I thought so too," Lynne said. "Every now and then, I suppose I am forced to admit that all you people had a point about my work."

Alicia laughed. "Aha! It worked!"

"I guess it did."

"Anyway," Alicia said, "the reason I'm calling is that I'm putting a kind of last-minute pickleball game together for noon today, and I wondered if you wanted to play?"

Lynne thought about it. "I don't know," she finally said. "Ethan and Marie are leaving around then, and I don't want to miss any more of my time with them…"

She glanced up; Ethan was standing in her bedroom doorway, wide-eyed. "*Is that him?*" he stage-whispered. "*Go, say yes!*"

Lynne shook her head and mouthed, "*It's Alicia.*"

"Okay, that's fine," Alicia said. "I can try someone else—"

"How many more players do you need?" Lynne asked.

"Two; it's just Robin and me so far. I tried you first."

"Don't call anyone else just yet—I'll call you back in five minutes."

She hung up and looked at Ethan. "Do you also think I should not wait for this man to call?"

Her son shrugged. "Whatever, Mom; I want you to do whatever makes you happy."

She only needed to think about it a moment more. "All right then." She punched Will's number as Ethan tiptoed away, grinning.

"Well, good morning, lovely lady!" came Will's pleasant voice. "I was just wondering if it was too early to call you."

"I'm an early riser; it's safe to call me most any time after about seven."

"Ah, good to know. So...did you sleep well?"

Jeez, even his innocuous comments sounded sexy. "Very well," she said. "And you?"

"Excellently. And I had the most *interesting* dreams, as well."

Whoo, she thought, wanting to fan herself. "I'll be interested in hearing about them...if you want to tell."

He gave a low, warm laugh. "I always like to tell. Especially *interested* parties."

"Um. Okay. So," she said, forcing herself to focus, "I just heard from a friend who's trying to put together a pickleball game at noon today. Are you up for that?"

"I'd love it," he said without hesitation. "And refreshments afterwards? Doesn't have to be beer."

"I think refreshments are a distinct possibility," she said. "And you know I like beer."

"Wonderful!" She heard a rustling on his end of the line before he added, "I should probably get my morning chores done around here, then; it's a long drive to town."

"Sounds good. Just meet at the courts at noon?"

"I look forward to it."

Back out in the kitchen, Lynne rejoined Ethan and Marie at the breakfast table. "Well?" Ethan asked.

"Is it a date if you invite other people along?"

Marie laughed. "A double date, maybe."

"What if the other people are two girlfriends—and no, not a couple."

"You invited two chaperones?" Ethan said, giving her a mock-disgusted look.

"Pickleball with Alicia and Robin." Lynne sipped her coffee; it had gotten cold while she'd been on the phone. She got up and put it in the microwave for thirty seconds.

"I just don't see the appeal of hitting a little plastic ball around on a carved-up tennis court," Marie mused, "but anything that gets you out in the company of a charming new man the day after he buys you dinner sounds like a date to me."

"Mom has a second date! Mom has a sec-ond da-ate!" Ethan sing-songed.

The microwave beeped; Lynne pulled her coffee out and sipped. Much better. "Shouldn't you kids be getting ready for your ferry or something?"

"Why?" Ethan asked, looking wicked. "Do you need to spend the next few hours figuring out what to wear?"

Oh god. She did! She couldn't possibly wear her shabby old exercise clothes...

"Mom!" Ethan said, looking at her face. "It was a joke!"

"Come on," Marie said, getting up from the table. "Let me see what you've got in your closet."

FEELING BOTH FOOLISH and weirdly pretty in a pink polo shirt and gray culotte shorts she hadn't even realized she still owned, Lynne drove to town. When she pulled in and parked at the pickleball courts, Alicia and Robin were already there, dinking a ball back and forth on court one. She didn't see Will anywhere. *Oh no, what if he changed his mind...*

Then there was the rumble of tires on gravel and a sleek black Audi sedan parked beside her car. She couldn't see the driver through the tinted windows, but a moment later the door opened and—yep, it was him.

Lynne got out and gathered her gear from her trunk, as Will did the same. "Good morning again," he said, his smile bright in the sun. "You look marvelous."

"So do you," she said, taking him in. He wore longish white shorts with a sort of tennis vibe to them, and a bright turquoise shirt that set off his silver hair and beard spectacularly, and picked up the jade flecks in his eyes.

"Why, thank you." He gave her a small bow that somehow seemed adorable, not mocking. "Shall we?"

"Let's."

She pulled on her gloves and they joined Alicia and Robin on the court, making introductions—or re-introductions, in the case of Alicia, with whom Will had played last fall. Will brought out a second ball and they started warming up as well; after a minute, Alicia said, "Are we ready?"

"Ready as I'm going to get," Will said, glancing at Robin beside him, then back across the net. "These teams to start, then rotate?"

"Perfect," Lynne said, stepping back to serve.

She had thought she'd be too nervous to play well, but after only a slight bobble on her third shot, she found her groove. Lynne really liked pickleball—not as much as Alicia, who adored it; Lynne found it just challenging enough to be good exercise while also being just silly enough to be great fun.

The teams were well matched, too; the first game went to "extra innings," as Will called it, and he and Robin finally pulled it out, thirteen to eleven.

"Shift!" Alicia called out, and rotated over to play with Robin, leaving Will to cross over to Lynne's side.

"Here you are," he said, reaching out to hand her the ball.

She shook her head. "No, your serve is much stronger than mine."

"I find it easier to keep track of the score when I'm the second server. Besides, your serve is excellent. The way you drop it just past the kitchen line is impressive."

She wanted to deflect the compliment, but Alicia and Robin were waiting, and Will was still holding out the ball, so Lynne took it and got into position. "Zero-zero-start!" she called, and gave it a good whack. Of course *now* it went well past the kitchen, nearly to the baseline; which turned out to be a good thing, catching Alicia off guard as it skittered past her feet.

"Great serve!" she called, lobbing the ball back across the net as Will and Lynne switched sides.

"Thanks." She smiled at her friends. "One-zero-start!"

The game was nearly as close as the first one, and about twice as much fun. Lynne and Will played very well together. He was the stronger player, but not by much; and, unlike many men Lynne had played with over the years, he was very good about sharing the effort. He didn't jump in and poach her shots, and he was clear about calling "I go!" or "Yours!" on shots anywhere near the middle.

"That was great!" Lynne said, as everyone tapped paddles at the net after her and Will's victory.

"Now I get him on my team," said Alicia with a grin.

Lynne had to stifle an entirely inappropriate reaction. *NO HE'S MINE*, her inner dragon growled, catching her quite by surprise. "I, uh, need a quick sip of water," she said, making herself smile at the group.

"Actually, me too," Robin said, heading over to the sideline with her.

Alicia and Will stayed on the court, talking quietly. Strategizing, most likely: not planning anything nefarious...or romantic. Lynne pulled her water bottle out of her bag and took a deep draught. The cool liquid helped calm her down.

"He's really good, but not *too* good, if you know what I mean," Robin said, dropping her bottle back into her bag and pulling out a little towel to mop her forehead. "Why hasn't he played with us before?"

"He's only a part-timer here," Lynne told her. "And yeah, I do know—it's nice to play with someone who challenges you to step up."

"Exactly." Robin dropped the towel into her bag as well. "Okay, partner: shall we show them how it's done?"

"You bet." They tapped paddles and took the court.

Alicia and Will had the starting serve, and for a scary few minutes it looked as though they might pull off a Golden Pickle—achieving eleven points without ever relinquishing the starting serve. But Lynne managed a line drive right between them that they both muffed, and then Robin put her trademark spin on enough deceptively simple serves to confound both Alicia and Will. Soon the game was tied at six-all, and Lynne began to feel as though there was hope.

Robin served; Will hit a gentle lob back into Lynne's court; Lynne gave the ball a good bat, aiming for that middle ground again...but the ball caught the net, rolled right on top of it for an agonizing half-second, and dropped back into the kitchen on Lynne and Robin's side. "Oh no!" Lynne cried.

"That's all right, we'll get it back," Robin assured her.

Alicia scored two quick points on her serve, but on her third serve she set Robin up. Robin slammed the ball at Alicia's feet. "Dang it!" Alicia said, laughing as she tossed the ball to Will.

He served to Lynne, not holding back; she felt lucky just to get it back over the net. Then he tapped it right into the corner of the kitchen, where neither Lynne nor Robin could get in time.

"Nine-six-two," he called, hitting it hard and spinny toward Robin. She stumbled a little getting to it, got a paddle on it, but her return fell short.

"Yikes," Lynne muttered, planting her feet and getting ready for Will's serve.

He took pity on her, handing her an easy one; her return blew between Will and Alicia. "Fiddlesticks!" Will cried, fetching the ball and batting it over the net to Lynne.

"Fiddlesticks?" Lynne laughed. *How cute is that?* she thought, tapping the ball twice with her paddle as she prepared to serve. "All right, six-ten-one!" she called, and gave it all she had. Will was already moving in, and he shouldn't have; she served long again, confounding him as it came in low at his ankles.

Lynne quickly got them tied up at ten-all, then blew an easy shot. "I always do that," she groaned, handing Robin the ball. "Too much time to think."

"Don't worry," Robin reassured her. "I told you, we've got this."

And she was right. Robin sailed another long serve past Will's feet, though he made a valiant effort trying to reach it. For a moment, Lynne was worried he'd fall, but he kept his balance.

For her game point serve, Robin grinned across the court to Alicia. "Here it comes, ready or not."

"Oh, I was born ready," Alicia taunted back.

Not ready enough: Alicia flubbed her return, whacking it hard into the net, and the game belonged to Robin and Lynne. "Woo-hoo!" Robin cried, hopping up and down. "World champions!"

"Mix it up and go again?" Will asked.

They played three more games before everyone agreed they didn't have anything left. "Well, I certainly worked up a thirst," Will said, as everyone gathered by their bags, drinking water and wiping their brows. "Lynne and I were thinking about stopping by the Island Hoppin' Brewery; do you ladies want to join us?"

Yet again, Lynne had to fight down a sudden irrational possessiveness. *All right, here's where we have two chaperones on our date*, she thought, smiling at her friends.

"Sounds great to me," Robin said, glancing at Alicia, who also shrugged and smiled.

"Sure, I'm in," she said. Did Lynne see something pass across Alicia's face, once her smile faded? Or was she just looking for signs that the younger woman was doing all right, so soon after leaving a long marriage?

They caravanned to the brewery, ordered their beers, and grabbed one of the outside tables under an umbrella. The day was spectacular: sunny, and well over sixty degrees—crazy-hot for the Pacific Northwest, particularly in May.

"This is juuuust right," Robin said with satisfaction after taking a healthy sip of her ale.

Lynne picked up her IPA and sipped; the hoppy bite was indeed completely perfect. "So much better than water," she laughed.

Will tore open the big bag of chips he'd bought to accompany his lager and laid it in the middle of the table. "Enough for everyone—we need to replace our electrolytes, right, Doc?" He grinned at Lynne.

She nodded. "Indeed, the salt will be important for replacing what we sweated out. This is practically medicinal." She grabbed a handful of chips and bit into one. Okay, potato chips were definitely not health food, but they had to be worth something; otherwise, why did they taste so right at a moment like this?"

Lynne was pleased to see that Alicia also took a big pile of chips. It was good to see her eating more; Lynne had sometimes worried about her, nibbling on salads and taking tiny portions of everything at their potluck soup group dinners. Alicia had not an ounce of fat on her, and Lynne had always wondered if this was something she did to herself, or something Ron demanded. Evidence seemed to suggest the latter.

The four of them chatted comfortably for a while, and the talk soon turned to current events. "Actually, I'm a little worried too," Robin said, after Lynne mentioned some changes at the clinic that were going to be implemented as a result of new federal legislation. "We were in line for a renewal of our grant, but everything coming through the HHS is frozen. I've contacted our agency representative, but she can't tell me anything—she's just as out of the loop as everyone else. At least she still has a job... for now, anyway."

"That's terrible about your grant," Alicia said, looking indignant on Robin's behalf.

"What exactly does your—company?—do?" Will asked. "I'm afraid I'm pretty out of the loop around here."

Robin leaned forward and took another quaff of her beer. "I run the Junior Center." At Will's puzzled expression, she went on. "It's modeled after the island's senior center, but for kids. We have activities and programs, and meeting rooms, and a big playground. It's also a place where they can get a hot meal, whatever their ability to pay—or not. Most of our funding comes from the ACF—the Administration for Children and Families—but of course…" She shook her head, as did everyone around the table.

"Most of your staff is volunteer, right?" Lynne asked. She'd done some stints there herself, vaccination clinics and well-baby visits for parents without insurance. Even though Washington State had a decent Medicaid-funded health insurance program, some people, particularly in the migrant community, either did not qualify for the program, or were leery of coming to the attention of immigration authorities. Lynne had never believed that some official government document was needed in order for a person to deserve quality health care. Perhaps this made her a radical, but she felt that the position was entirely in line with her Hippocratic Oath.

"The folks running a lot of the programs, yeah. I take a salary, as does my chief admin, and we pay a few of the teachers a stipend when we can. And of course the cook." She chuckled. "It's hard enough to get a good cook on this island, when we're competing with the likes of New Leaf and Matia and all. If we then tried to ask them to work for free, I shudder to think."

"And then there's all your expenses above and beyond staff," Lynne noted.

"What's going to happen to the Junior Center if the grant doesn't come through?" Alicia asked.

Robin shook her head again. "I don't know, honestly. We've got a little money in the bank, and Greg and I can pitch in if needed—we've done it before, when the feds were being slow to release funds. I can appeal to the community; Orcas is very generous and giving. But everyone's already being asked to give so much, to so many different places…"

"We should do a fundraising event, something fun," Alicia said, her eyes shining. "Not just ask folks for money, but tie it to something." She glanced around at her sweaty companions. "A pickleball tournament!"

"Doesn't the club already do one?" Lynne asked.

"They're not having it this year," Alicia said. "I went to sign up last week and couldn't find anything, so I asked around. Apparently the guy who usually organizes it is away, and nobody else wanted to take over, but a lot of people want to play." She went on, her excitement visibly growing. "We should do one! It would be great—the teams can get sponsors, and there can even be a competition about who can raise the most money! What do you guys think?"

Robin was nodding, though she didn't look entirely convinced. "It would be a lot of work…"

"I'll do it!" Alicia said. "I'd love to do it. I already owe you for giving me a place to live—"

"*Renting* you a place to live," Robin interrupted with a smile.

"—at well below market rate. And I can get the mailing lists and everything from the pickleball club, ooh and see if they want to co-sponsor the whole event. Oh, and I can go around to local businesses and see if they want to donate prizes. We can do a raffle too. This will be so much fun!"

Lynne was pretty sure that she agreed with Robin: this would be a lot of work. But she hadn't seen Alicia so excited in so long, she couldn't even remember when. "I think it's a great idea," she said. "Let me know how I can help."

"Play in the tournament, obviously," Alicia said. "And raise the most money!"

Lynne laughed. "I'll see what I can do."

"You and Will should partner up—you play great together," Alicia added.

Lynne turned and looked at Will, who smiled back at her. "Sounds good," he said. "Assuming I'm on-island for the event." He turned to Alicia. "When is this tournament held?"

"Mid-August, usually, but we can choose whenever works for the most people, since it's not part of the official pickleball club events."

"Mid-August is perfect for me," Will said, and everyone else nodded.

"Oh this is great!" Alicia was practically jumping up and down in her chair. "I'll get in touch with the club again and get started, and then I'll send some proposed dates around."

"This is very generous of you," Robin said. "Are you thinking only mixed doubles teams, or do you want to partner up with me?"

"I don't know," Alicia said. "The regular tournament is one day mixed, and one day not. Probably we should see what kind of interest we get and then decide." She grinned at her landlady and friend. "I would love to play with you."

Lynne was startled to notice that her beer was nearly gone, just as Will put his own empty glass down on the table. "Another round?" he asked.

"One is enough for me," Alicia said. "At least on a nearly empty stomach." She looked sadly at the deflated chip bag on the table between them, and the crumbs on her napkin.

"I actually need to get home," Robin said.

"And I'm your ride," Alicia said. "I guess we're going to shove off, then. Thanks for coming out today—and thanks for being the first team to sign up for the Great Junior Center Benefit Pickleball Tournament!"

Will laughed. "Our pleasure."

Lynne nodded, agreeing with him, and feeling a warm happy sensation in her belly at his use of "our". Or maybe that was just the beer and chips, and the lovely sunshine?

They all walked out to their cars together. After Robin and Alicia drove off, Will stood beside Lynne's car. "I'm so glad you called me this morning," he said. "I truly was intending to call you, but you beat me to it."

"I believe you," she said. "And I was going to let you be the one to call—except time was of the essence."

"I hope you will not think me too old-fashioned if I express the hope that I will be able to phone and ask you out for a proper date, sometime very soon?"

She grinned at him. "That sounds lovely. And just the right amount of old-fashioned."

He gave his little bow-nod. "Then, until we meet again..."

"I look forward to it."

He waited until she got into her car, strapped on her seat belt, and started her engine before he unlocked his own car, and then he waited for her to pull out before following her onto the road. Lynne of course turned right at the corner of Lover's Lane and Mount Baker Road, while Will went left, so she could stop watching him in her rearview mirror.

Though she did think about him during her whole drive home. How nice it felt to have—what? Not a boyfriend, not yet, not exactly; they had just met last night, if you didn't count that brief encounter last fall.

But maybe he would be a boyfriend? Someday?

Lynne was not at all opposed to the idea.

Chapter 3

JULIE

D espite the official-looking letter from the Eastsound Historical Character and Beautification Commission that Julie and the rest of the town's business owners had received back in the spring, threatening an inspection of everyone's properties to root out "inappropriate storage, manufacturing, or residential facilities," no inspection had been forthcoming. Leslie Magnas, the longtime well-connected owner of the Island Cottages out in West Sound, had made a few phone calls, and the whole issue had quieted down. "And the next time you want to go beard that man in his den—or in the Lower Tavern—you let me know first and I'll come with you," Leslie had said.

"It wasn't like I'd planned ahead," Julie had told her. "It just… happened."

"Well, no harm done, I suppose," Leslie had said gruffly.

"I guess not."

Not that Julie believed the problem was solved—not by a long shot. No, the stupid commission had been approved by the voters, and the sneaky underhanded vacation rental developer Sam McLeod was certainly still moving ahead with his nefarious scheme to…to somehow take over Eastsound and reshape it for his own benefit, though Julie could still not figure out what exactly he stood to gain from this power grab.

In the meantime, she had protected herself as best she could, finding her records from when she had bought her shop and the house behind it. There was no mention of zoning in her purchase documents, but the use of both buildings was clearly laid out. The house had always been a residence; the shop building had originally been some kind of outbuilding, a barn or storage shed, until a prior owner had converted it to a small store. Both buildings had then slowly fallen into disrepair before they were finally put on the market. Julie had done a great deal of work over the years to make them the sweet and sturdy structures they were now.

The very idea that Sam would want to take her home and livelihood away from her! It steamed her, galled her, pissed her all the way off.

The bell over her shop door rang, signaling another customer, and Julie let her expression of anger fall away as she donned a welcoming smile. "Hi, let me know if you have any questions," she said to the young couple who walked in.

"Thanks!" said the woman, gravitating immediately to Julie's new line of oversized blank books. "Ooh," she said to the young man, "this would make an amazing sketchbook."

Of course it would, Julie thought, still smiling blandly at them. *That's what I designed it for.*

They didn't spend much time lingering over her more creative products: the handmade bound books (including handmade paper!) that contained Julie's "pithies," clever or humorous quotes often attributed to the good, and fictional, Countess Lucinda Devonryshireton and following a theme. Julie was currently, in her small slivers of spare time, working on a volume of pithies about the perils and pitfalls of small communities, though her books with quotes about love and romance were by far her best sellers.

But could she help it if small-town politics was much on her mind these days?

The young woman chose three sketchbooks, and her boy-friend-or-husband picked up a few fridge magnets that Julie's friend Karen made. Karen ran the jewelry shop just next door, but she didn't want tourist items like the magnets to bring down the tone of her gold, pearl, and precious gem offerings, so Julie had offered to sell them here. "I'm all for the tacky tourist stuff," Julie had told Karen, laughing.

"Oh stop that. You know what I mean."

But it was true that, although Julie's wares were an abundant expression of her personal creativity, they were also the sorts of souvenirs that tourists didn't mind spending money on. Julie found herself more and more often these days leaning into the items that sold well, rather than things that sparked her interest, and feeling guilty when she tried to focus on anything else—like small-town drama.

"Did you find everything you were looking for?" Julie asked, as the young couple set their items on the glass counter next to the cash register.

"Oh yes," the woman said, smiling. "You have such a nice shop."

"Thank you." She began ringing them up.

"The whole island is great," the young man said.

Julie nodded. "Is this your first time visiting?"

"Yes!" the woman said. "We'd heard about it from friends at work, and just knew we had to come and check it out."

"We needed to wait for a special occasion, though," the young man said, and as his girlfriend's gaze was down in her purse, searching for her credit card, he gave Julie a wink. "It's our one-year anniversary of dating."

"Happy anniversary!" Julie said as she stole a quick glance at the woman's left hand: a bare ring finger. *Ah*, she thought, and reached behind the counter for one of Karen's business cards. If they were making their way up the street going into every shop, they'd get there anyway, but just in case... She bagged up their purchases, then slipped him the card with an answering wink as soon as the woman turned toward the door.

The morning stayed fairly busy after that, so she had very little time to stew over her and Leslie's (and her boyfriend Gavin's, though he was less emotionally invested in the whole issue) next move: figuring out whether the commission had been legally created in the first place. Yes, it had been passed by the majority of voters who had cast ballots in the spring special election—a very small number of people—but had it been legitimately placed on the ballot in the first place? Leslie's initial digging, and discreet inquiries among friends who worked in the San Juan County Courthouse, had revealed some questions. First and foremost among those questions was why a special election had been authorized in the first place. Surely the issue of whether or not Eastsound needed to be Beautified and have its Historicity Preserved could have waited a few months for the next regular election?

Sadly, answering those questions was going to take some time, and probably a trip or two over to Friday Harbor, to look through the records of the county council's meetings. The minutes which were published online were summaries at best. Unedited, full minutes were not made available to the general public...a fact which had never stopped Leslie Magnas in the past.

At about twelve thirty, during a lull in the ebb and flow of customers, Karen walked in, carrying a very intriguing, and very fragrant, box with a picture of a dragonfly on the side.

"Hey," Julie said. "What's that?"

Karen was grinning from ear to ear. "It's our lunch, and a thank-you from me, and a celebration all packed into one... big...assortment...of..." She opened the box with a flourish. "Baked goods!"

"Oh wow," Julie leaned over the box, taking in the many items. "From the Dragonfly Coffee House?"

Karen laughed. "What was your first clue? Try the turnover

first. It's savory—and still warm."

Julie was already picking up the steaming morsel. "I didn't know they made cheese turnovers," she said, around an insanely delicious mouthful.

"Cheese and onion, and they don't usually. It's an experiment."

"I hope you got one too." Julie wiped crumbs off her face and glanced at the door. Fortunately, customers were staying away for the moment.

"Oh, I did. How did you think I knew to get you one?"

"So what is this a thank-you for?" Julie asked. "Did that cute young couple come by?"

"Did they ever! She oohed and aahed over everything, and bought a garnet bracelet and matching earrings. Then he came back ten minutes later, after he'd parked her at the Dragonfly with a big latte and texted her sister to call her—which was all pre-arranged, and guaranteed to keep her occupied long enough for him to buy that one-karat engagement ring I showed you last week."

"Wow! The one with the scrollwork and the fleur-de-lis?"

"The very one!"

Julie took another bite of the turnover. "That's wonderful!" she said when she could get words out again. A flurry of crumbs filtered down; she grabbed a paper napkin from the box and brushed them onto the floor behind the counter. "I think that's the most beautiful ring you've ever made. If I wasn't so opposed to getting married again…"

Karen laughed. "You are well on your way to getting married again, and I've already told Gavin that I'll make whatever you like—*and* for a friends-and-family discount."

"You are too kind, and nope, never gonna happen." Why was this so hard for people to believe? Everything was perfect between her and Gavin. Why screw it up?

Karen just kept laughing and shook her head.

Julie finished the turnover and went back through the box.

"What are these?" she asked, picking up an interesting cookie.

"Lemon-lavender shortbreads, and I'm a believer in love, so I'm not listening to you." She was still grinning, so obviously pleased with herself. "Stephan—that's his name—isn't going to propose until dinner tonight, but I had to go and at least look at the happy couple after he'd made the purchase. That's how I ended up with the avalanche of pastries—I couldn't decide, so I just bought some of everything."

"I can't possibly eat all this," Julie said, biting into the short-bread and rolling her eyes with delight. "You did say this was *our* lunch, right?"

"Yep." Karen plucked a small round chocolate cookie from the corner and popped it into her mouth. "But I might have already tried a thing or two before I got here. Anyway, you just keep what we don't eat now. It'll still be good later."

The bell over the door rang and a family of five started making their way in. The mother, at the last moment, noticed the PLEASE ENJOY YOUR ICE CREAM ON THE PORCH sign and herded her small kids back out, settling them on the bench that Julie provided for just this reason. Julie smiled gratefully at the father, who seemed at loose ends in a shop filled with lovely handmade books, stationery, and note cards.

"I'd better be getting back," Karen said, glancing out the window. "I put a 'back in five minutes' sign on my door."

"I hate doing that," Julie murmured to her.

"Me too. But after that sale, I felt I could afford it."

"Thank you for the lunch!" Julie closed the box and set it behind the counter, not bothering to try to convince Karen to take some pastries back with her. Julie had never been able to get Karen to do something she didn't want to do.

"My pleasure! Thanks for the most excellently good deed!"

"What good deed did you do?" her customer asked, making polite conversation as Karen closed the door behind herself.

"Nothing much," Julie said. "She owns the jewelry store next door, and I sent a young couple her way. It was her designs that convinced him to buy an engagement ring, though—she makes all the pieces herself, and they're exquisite."

"Oh, that's great." The man looked thoughtful. "We have an important anniversary coming up…next door, you say?"

Julie pulled out another one of Karen's cards and handed it to him. "On second thought, if this keeps up, perhaps I should ask for a commission."

STEPH

SO MUCH PLANNING! Steph had thought that putting together the occasional community meal in their back yard would be a piece of cake, so to speak. She already threw a big Christmas party every year, for all her friends and neighbors and anyone else they wanted to bring; as well as a handful of smaller events over the course of the year—along with whenever it was her turn for soup group, of course. She loved entertaining; she loved cooking; she totally had this down.

But she had never charged people for her parties before. Somehow, this was making all the difference.

Any number of times, she had wanted to cancel the event—or, rather, cancel everyone's payments for the event, and give the dinner anyway. Unfortunately, she had made the mistake of mentioning this to her next-door neighbor Lynne, who was the one who had convinced her to charge for these meals in the first place. Predictably, Lynne would not hear of her backing out like this.

"People don't value what they don't pay for!" she'd reminded Steph.

"Everyone loves my parties, and I don't charge for them," she'd said.

Lynne had shaken her head. "You know that's different, and I'm not going to keep having this argument with you. Listen: just get through the first one and see how it feels. You don't have to do any more after that if it doesn't work out."

"Do you think it won't work out?"

Lynne had only shaken her head more vehemently.

So now Steph was sitting in her study with a gigantic pile of menus on the low table before her. She'd changed her plans easily a dozen times by now, juggling the items, trying to choose courses that went well together, that were easy to make (but not *too* easy), that she could be certain of getting the ingredients for—oh, and that everyone would find delicious and unusual (but not *too* unusual), and worth the price they were paying for the experience.

And then of course there were potential allergies! She couldn't serve shellfish—too many people couldn't eat it. She would have regular bread and gluten-free bread, plus sourdough; dairy and non-dairy options; she'd keep peanuts right out of the entire meal. There would be a vegan option; paleo people could just double up on the meat and veggies and leave off the carbs. Everything would be listed on the menu, and she'd asked her customers to let her know of any food sensitivities she might not have thought of.

She sighed and leaned back on the couch, staring at the ceiling. This inaugural dinner wasn't for another week and a half; Steph was neglecting her own soup group gathering here this Sunday. But soup groups were easy! All she had to do was figure out what kind of soup she wanted to make, and let the others know in time to bring something to go with it. Easy-peasy.

She leaned forward again and reshuffled the menus. What about a bunch of marinated pork tenderloins—she could grill them—and a spicy chutney to serve over the meat...hmm, not even every carnivore ate pork these days...but she was tired of chicken, chicken, chicken. Duck? Duck was fancy and technically poultry, even if it was twice as fatty as pork tenderloin. Could she get her hands on enough ducks to feed a crowd of twenty-five? Of course that would blow her budget right out of the water...though of course she wasn't doing this to make money...

but she also didn't want to just lose money...

I can do some duck, some pork, some pressed tofu; plenty of grilled vegetables...

But were vegans sick of tofu?

Did she even *have* any vegans signed up for the meal? Was she overthinking this? She tapped her laptop and brought up the guest list. Yes, darn it, one person was vegan and another was "mostly vegetarian but white fish is also okay if it's not the majority of the dish."

Fish, hmm? But now she'd had her heart set on grilling, and she could grill fish, but it never turned out quite the way she imagined. The grill was a bit of a blunt instrument, and fish really needed to be cooked perfectly. She could grill salmon, salmon was sturdy and forgiving...but salmon wasn't white.

She sighed again and closed the laptop lid.

David appeared in her study doorway. "Still working on that?" he asked her, with a sympathetic smile.

Ugh, he could probably hear her sighs from all the way down the hall. "I didn't realize it would be so complicated!"

"It's not too late to cancel."

"It is! And—I don't want to cancel. I just want to have it all figured out and then have it happen and be wonderful. I want to be excited about it like I was when I first had the idea to do this."

He came in and sat beside her, taking her hand. "You will be. I promise."

She looked into his sky-blue eyes. "How do you know?"

"Because you always get overwhelmed at this point in planning any big thing. When none of the decisions are made, so the possibilities are endless. As soon as you start narrowing things down, it all falls into place."

"Really? I always get like this? I love entertaining."

"You do. You get a huge thrill out of successfully pulling off an event—which you always do, in case you were wondering." He squeezed her hand. "You get the biggest thrill out of pulling off the more complicated events—just like this one. And before you protest," which she was opening her mouth to do, "yes, I know you've never charged money for events before, but you've totally done dinners this big, this complex, and with all sorts of people you don't know. Remember the year when that little repertory theater company had their caterer cancel at the last minute? You put together a whole huge fancy dinner with like three days' notice, and it was the best fundraiser they'd ever had."

"Well, people felt sorry for them…"

David only laughed, but kindly. "You tell yourself whatever story you need to, love, but I have full faith in you. I've seen you do this a million times. It's your superpower."

She squeezed his hand back. "Thank you. I don't feel very superpowerful right now."

"I could help you, if you'd like."

She just stopped herself from saying *What could you do?* Her sweet, loving, broken-but-healing, deeply introverted husband. "Um…" she started.

"You're stuck in the planning phase right now, yes?" He nodded at the clutter all over her table.

"Yeah. There's too many parameters, too many moving parts—"

"Exactly. Remember what I do for a living?"

She looked at him, bemused. "You invest in foreign and domestic stock markets, and analyze investments for other people—for brokers, mostly." Which had nothing to do with tofu versus pork versus white fish versus boring old chicken…

"Yes, but to do that, I compile data—vast amounts of it. I keep track of it. I compare it to other data. I look for patterns. I assess portfolios. I apply rule sets to categories of investments so that when I do assess those portfolios, I can recommend a balanced menu, so to speak, curated for each particular investor—or investment group."

She nodded, beginning to get it. "I see. But what can you do for me right now?"

He leaned forward, holding her gaze. "I have *spreadsheets*. And I know how to use them."

Steph laughed, leaning forward herself to catch his adorable mouth in a kiss. "Oh, honey, that's got to be the sexiest thing you've said to me in a long time."

He rolled his eyes faux-dramatically. "Oh god. I had no idea I'd fallen down on my, er, other sheets game." He got to his feet still holding her hand, encouraging her up from the couch. She followed willingly. "Come on," he said, "let's go to my office for a minute and I'll show you what I can do to help. And then we can…see about that other issue."

"With pleasure."

She grabbed her laptop and let him lead her from the room.

Chapter 4

LYNNE

When Lynne showed up at the clinic for a shift filling in for one of the regular docs, the clinic's director said, "Oh, good, there you are. Do you have a minute?"

"Sure," she said, though she hadn't yet checked the schedule, so she didn't know how big her workload was today. Kathy, the doc she was subbing for, had requested this time off several weeks ago; often patients would reschedule routine appointments in order to see their usual physician.

She followed Dr. Leland Park into his office and sat across from his desk. Leland was a young doctor— well, in his mid-fifties— who had moved to Orcas from Lopez Island a few years back. The other docs liked to tease him about his move to the big city. "What's up?"

Leland leaned forward, trying to cover his discomfort with an awkward smile. "I'm afraid I have some bad news."

Oh thank god, Lynne thought. *He's tired of this patchwork staffing—he's going to let me go. I can finally retire for real.* She tried for a pleasant, understanding yet inquisitive look and said, "Oh, I'm sorry to hear that."

Leland nodded. "I am sorry too." He took a breath. "Kathy has given her notice, effective immediately. She's out this week doing orientation at her new job in Sequim."

Lynne could not cover her gasp of surprise. "I thought she was happy here! Didn't she and her husband just finish building a house?"

"They did, and they're putting it on the market. I don't know all the details, but they apparently had a heart-to-heart and finally admitted to each other that island life is just not for them. She began job-hunting on the mainland and the clinic in Sequim snapped her up right away."

Lynne said, "I'm not surprised." Kathy had been one of their newer, and more popular, practitioners—intelligent, empathetic, and (seemingly, anyway) dedicated to the community. She was the kind of doc who routinely ran an hour or more late by the end of every day, because she took as much time with each patient as that person needed, no matter what the official schedule (or the insurance reimbursement) dictated. People clamored to get onto her roster. "This is bad news indeed. What are you going to do?"

Leland looked uncomfortable again. "Well, of course, I've already drafted the position listing and we're putting it out to the networks. We'll begin interviewing as soon as any viable candidate expresses an interest. In the interim, however…"

Oh. Crap, Lynne thought.

"I was wondering if you'd be able to take on her caseload? Just until we can replace her, of course."

"Of course," Lynne echoed, then realized that she had essentially just agreed to this when she hadn't had a moment to think it through…although what was there to think through? She couldn't leave all those patients in the lurch just because she didn't want to work full-time. Her clinic, her community, needed her. "I mean, yes, I'll do it, but Leland—"

"I know, I know," he said, before she could spell it out. "I'm so sorry to do this to you, but I really have no choice. And I know you have other commitments—like your program at the senior center. I'll be taking on some of Kathy's patients as well, and Jason and Marjorie have offered to cover for when you can't be here."

Good, he'd already talked to the other two docs. "Sala and Jilly can probably see a few more folks too," she said. The two nurse practitioners were highly capable. You had to be, to practice in a rural clinic far from any ER.

"Yes, a few, though they're both pretty much at capacity as well." Leland sighed and leaned back in his chair. "It really seemed like at last, we were turning a corner—we were finally fully staffed and working through the worst of the backlog. I just hope we don't lose too much ground before we can replace Kathy."

"Darn that Kathy anyway, letting us down just when we really need her," Lynne said, trying for a kind of gallows humor, but it fell flat. This would leave them without any emergency backup, as well. Yikes. "Did Sequim offer her a huge raise, and a pony?"

Leland chuckled sadly. "I don't even know if they're matching what we pay, but of course, the cost of living is quite a bit less there."

Lynne sighed. "Right."

"She really is very sorry."

"I bet she is. And I don't mean that in any snarky way," Lynne clarified. "I understand trying to make a go of it out here, and not being able to. Island life isn't for everyone, and more power to her and her husband for admitting that and making the change." She sighed. "But still."

"But still."

They sat in mutual sorrow together for a minute. Then Leland said, "Well, that's all—you probably need to get to your patients."

"Yeah." *My patients. Not just my patients today, but my roster of patients.* Lynne got to her feet. "I'll go get signed in."

"Thank you, Lynne." He got up from his chair as she did, and walked around his desk, holding out his hand. "I really appreciate this."

"Of course, Leland." She grasped his hand and held it a moment, then went out to get started.

BY FOUR THIRTY in the afternoon, she had fallen as far behind as Kathy did on her worst days, with seven patients still to see and the clinic officially closing in thirty minutes. She could hear conversation out in the waiting room, as the receptionists explained the situation and offered to reschedule for anyone who was unable, or unwilling, to wait.

Sounded like nobody took them up on it.

The trouble was that Lynne had been taking the time to tell each patient about Kathy's departure, and invariably this had led to lengthier conversations as she got to know more about their conditions and histories than she would have otherwise. Not to mention processing their surprise and dismay about losing a doctor they'd loved. "I really thought she'd be one who stayed," more than one patient had told her.

"So did I," Lynne admitted. "But don't worry: I'm sure we'll find someone just as good, or even better. Orcas Island is a wonderful place to live."

She was just going to keep believing that. Leland would be able to recruit someone amazing.

After ducking into the bathroom for a quick pee, Lynne was heading toward the exam room where her next patient awaited when her cell phone rang. She finished rubbing hand sanitizer into her hands and reached into the pocket of her scrubs, where she almost just clicked the button to silence the phone, but she pulled it out instead.

It was Will.

"Hi," she said, swiping to answer. "I'm at work so I only have a moment."

"Then I will be efficient: may I take you to dinner this evening? I'm so sorry for the short notice, but I just learned that Amara Delancourt is guest-cooking at Matia, tonight only. It's hush-

hush, but a little birdie mentioned it to me and I've managed to hold us two spots at six o'clock…"

"I'm so sorry," she said, and oh, she was. She didn't even know who that chef was, but if she was cooking at Matia and it was a secret, she must be somebody huge. "But I'm going to be stuck here for several hours more at least tonight. I'll be lucky to get out of here by eight."

"No!" he cried, mock-horrified. "They are taking such advantage of you! Walk out of there at once and never look back!"

She chuckled. "I'll explain everything when I see you next, because I am definitely taking a raincheck on your invitation. Can I call you when I leave here tonight so we can make a plan?"

"Absolutely. I will count on it. Eight, you say?"

"Or thereabouts. I *hope* I'll be done by then."

"Then I hope so too. I look forward to your call."

"Thank you," she said, putting more emotion into her words than she'd entirely meant to…though it felt oddly right. "Until then."

"Until then, lovely lady."

Smiling, she tucked the phone back into her pocket and walked to the exam room door, where she studied the chart for a moment before knocking softly and heading in to meet her eleventh patient of the day.

IT WAS A pretty good guess: her last patient left at ten after eight. Lynne relocked the clinic door behind him, and stood for a moment in the dark lobby, letting the overwhelming day settle around her.

Her stomach growled, reminding her of Will's call…and his offer for dinner, darn it. She hadn't eaten a bite since a hastily grabbed lunch in the breakroom—two granola bars and a cup of cold water from the dispenser.

Not that she'd stopped thinking about Will, to be perfectly honest. He was a constant low-grade presence under her con-

sciousness, these days. An awareness. An anticipation, even, perhaps.

She smiled at the fresh thought of him and pulled out her
phone, punching his number.

He answered in the middle of the first ring. "Ah, Dr. Daniels,
there you are."

"Here I am," she said, trying not to sound as weary as she felt.
"Just about to finish up here and lock up. I should be home in
twenty minutes, if you'd like a longer phone call, but I didn't
want to keep you waiting any longer."

"Well, that is very thoughtful of you." He sounded relaxed,
pleased. "I would like a longer visit with you, and to cash in that
raincheck as soon as possible. So you finish up there and, ah,
we'll talk very soon."

"Sounds perfect."

The cleaning service had already come and gone, and the clinic's nonmedical staff were responsible for restocking the exam
and lab rooms, but she made the rounds of the back-office spaces
anyway, double-checking to make sure everything was in order.
Then she spent a few minutes at the computer, typing up a few
quick notes on her final patient, then encrypting and sending all
her notes from the day to herself; she would dictate the patient
charting after she was home and had gotten some food into herself. Oh, and who was she kidding: a big glass of wine as well.

I can't believe I have an entire patient caseload again, she thought,
as she checked the lock on the back door. She tried not to feel
resentment for Kathy, but she found herself at least wishing she
had given proper notice, so that Lynne could have had time to
get used to the idea. *Well, I guess the time is now*, she told herself,
as she let herself out the front door, locked it, and set the alarm.

She started across the parking lot toward her car. Oddly, it
wasn't the only car there...there was a second car parked next to
hers, and...was that a person leaning against the other car?

Her heart rate picked up in a moment of ancient, remnant

big-city alertness before she recognized Will. A breath of relief escaped her in a whoosh.

His chuckle echoed across the space between them. "I truly didn't mean to scare you."

"You're fine!" she said, walking up to him. "I just—this is a nice surprise!"

"I hope so." He reached behind him and picked up a large brown bag that had been sitting on the hood of his car. "And if the pleasure of seeing me isn't a nice enough surprise, I'm imagining that this might be."

An astonishing aroma emanated from the bag. "Ohh," she moaned, as her stomach growled again. "You brought *food*!"

"Not just any food." He set the bag back on his hood and opened it, pulling out a series of takeout containers, followed by paper napkins, plastic silverware, and a sleeve of plastic cups. "I saw no reason to let an Amara Delancourt dinner go unappreciated—by either you or me. So I went anyway, and had her box up your share...and a good deal of mine, so you wouldn't have to eat alone."

Lynne suddenly felt almost lightheaded with delight. Or maybe that was still the hunger? "Wow! Oh, my god. Is it all still hot? Wasn't that hours ago?"

"Alas, a few things would have suffered from the wait, so I'm afraid I had to eat those myself. But when I explained the situation, Amara took pity on you and threw in a few more durable extras." He opened one of the containers, which was packed full of some kind of little dumplings. "These are even good cold," he said, taking one out and handing it to her.

She took it and bit into it, and moaned again. "Oh. My. God." She quickly ate the rest of it; it wasn't cold, rather a perfect room temperature. It sent a flood of flavor through her mouth, caressing her tongue, tickling her taste buds. And just when it seemed like that was the whole story, a second, subtler layer of flavors unfurled. After she swallowed her last bite, she said, "That was incredible. What's in it?"

Will shrugged and grinned at her. "Amara keeps her secrets. She said, 'Oh, a little of this, a little of that' so many times when I asked about the dishes, I finally gave up."

"Wow." She plucked another dumpling out of the container and ate that. It was just as good as the first one. "These are astonishing. My friend Steph needs to meet this woman." She ate a third dumpling, and said around a mouthful, "I would say Steph should try these, but I'm afraid I'm going to eat them all right here in the parking lot."

Laughing, Will said, "That was actually the idea. Hold on." He went around to the back of his car; she heard a click as he popped open the trunk. He returned a moment later with a red-checked tablecloth in one hand and an unopened bottle of wine and a corkscrew in the other. He shook out the tablecloth, laying it over his hood.

"We can't do that!" Lynne cried, mortified.

"Why not?" His white teeth glowed in the late evening light as he smiled, and the silver in his beard glimmered.

She picked up the tablecloth and spread it over her own hood. "Your car is much too nice to be a picnic table. My old beater, on the other hand…"

BY THE TIME they had laid waste to every single container, along with a good deal of the bottle of wine, Lynne was floating on air. They sat side by side on her hood, their feet resting on her front bumper like they were a couple of teenagers passing a bottle of Jägermeister back and forth on a Saturday night. She had told him all about her day, including the why of it, along with some speculation about what this might mean for her time and availability going forward—and how much she didn't want this to get in the way of getting to know him better.

Will had made it clear that he wanted exactly the same thing, and that he was happy to help her figure out how to make it work.

"This is the nicest thing anyone has ever done for me," Lynne said, raising her plastic glass of wine to him in a toast.

He tapped her glass with his. "I will take that as the hyperbole that it has to be. Surely someone must have fed you a surprise picnic when you were hungry and tired from an unexpectedly long day at work."

She started to answer glibly, then stopped and thought about it. Her husband, Charles, also a doctor, had worked at least as hard as she had. They had been overextended even before they'd had Ethan. He'd been a good husband and father, and they'd loved each other deeply. She had grieved him terribly when he'd died of pancreatic cancer—far too quickly, far too young—but he had never been one for the kind of romantic gestures that seemed to be second nature with Will. "No, I can't say that anyone ever has done such a thing," she said at last. "So, thank you again."

"It is my pleasure, lovely Lynne." He set his empty wine glass down on the picnic table and reached out to take her hand. She placed her hand in his, and they gazed into each other's eyes for a long moment before he leaned forward ever so slightly. "May I...?"

"Yes," Lynne said, and matched his forward lean. After the smallest hesitation—was he making sure that she was sure?—their lips met in a kiss.

She felt the tickle of his beard; it was so much softer than she'd expected. She purred quietly, without even quite deciding to, and let her senses drink him in. He tasted of course like the food they'd just shared, and the wine; but also of himself, warm and pleasant and welcoming.

His hand let go of hers and came up to caress the side of her face; she leaned into it ever so slightly, loving the warmth and softness of his palm against her cheek, even as she greedily did not remove her mouth from his. Her tongue darted out of its own accord to explore. His tongue met hers, and they danced.

It was a long moment before the kiss broke and they came up for air. "That was…very nice," she breathed, still close enough to kiss him again. Which she really wanted to do, and also…

"It was," he agreed. "It was everything I'd hoped for and more."

Lynne marveled again that he could say such things, and that they could sound sincere and real. He meant them. He'd been thinking about kissing her, and thinking it would be good, and it was better than good. "Maybe that was a fluke, though?" she asked, giving him a wicked grin. "Should we double-check?"

His deep chuckle was the sound of sexiness itself. "I like the way you think."

When the second kiss ended, Lynne's core temperature had risen into the red zone, and she was trying to figure out if she had ever in her whole entire life been this alive, this awake. Hadn't she been exhausted and overwhelmed not even an hour ago? Now she felt like she could climb Mount Constitution, backwards and in high heels.

Though there was something else she'd much rather do…

"I don't suppose you'd be willing to accompany me home tonight?" Will asked.

Yes yes yes yes yes, shouted everything inside Lynne. And for the longest moment, she couldn't think of a single reason why not. She was an adult, in charge of her own life; nobody was waiting for her at home; Eagle Lake was really not that much farther from town than her own house was…

Oh. Right. Because proximity to town was important, and tomorrow morning was going to arrive very early. "I wish I could—I really, truly, honestly wish I could," Lynne said. "But I have to be back here at seven thirty tomorrow morning."

She could read the mixed disappointment and understanding in Will's eyes. "And you want to be well rested for your patients."

"I do, yes. I mean, right now I feel as though I will never need to sleep again, but I do have to think about tomorrow." She leaned forward and caught his hand again. "More importantly, however: when I do come home with you, I don't want to have any other distractions or obligations to worry about. No deadlines, no competing demands. No early alarm clock. I will want to give you my full attention."

His smile glowed, and he squeezed her hand gently. "Now that, lovely lady, is a reward worth waiting for."

MATT

MATT PARKED AT Steph and David's house on Sunday evening. "You wait there, Dad," he said to his father, in the passenger seat. "I'll be around to help you out."

"I don't need help getting out of a damn car," Gordon said, but he did stay put.

Normally, Matt didn't bring his dad to soup groups, though everyone had made it clear that Gordon was welcome. As Matt had explained to Lynne when she'd brought it up, the occasional respite from caring from a parent with increasing dementia was a vital part of his own self-care.

However, the older woman that Matt hired to stay with his dad when he needed to leave the house, Ramona, had had to cancel this evening at the last minute. "I am so sorry to do this to you," she'd said when she phoned him. "But I just got a call from the hospital, and they're having to reschedule my scan for next week. They've had some staff calling in sick, and are rejiggering everything. Now the only time before September they can take me is tomorrow morning at eight, and with the ferries as they are in the summer…"

She hadn't had to explain *that* to him. "On a Monday, no less," he said sympathetically.

"I've already got a room booked in the Anacortes Inn, and I was hoping to take the eight o'clock boat tonight…"

"Do that," he'd said. "Go, and don't worry about us." Even if she waited and tried for the nine thirty-five sailing, that would still mean she wouldn't be able to cover this evening at Matt's house unless he left the soup group early, and he didn't like the idea of Ramona staying up till all hours the night before a scary medical scan. "Just relax, if you can, and get a good night's sleep."

"I'm so sorry," she'd said again, and he'd spent some more time reassuring her before insisting she get off the phone and get down to the ferry terminal if she wanted a chance at one of the few standby spots.

As Matt walked around the front of the car, he wondered if he should have canceled coming tonight after all, as he'd been tempted to. Gordon had been cranky and obstreperous since hearing about the change of plans, something that was increasingly difficult for him to adjust to. But Matt had already made his baked pretzel dish—his own personal riff on Chex Mix, using only the best things and the right amount of seasoning (if he did say so himself)—and he'd figured Gordon would enjoy the social outing.

Matt hoped he would, anyway.

He opened the passenger door and Gordon made his slow, painstaking way out, muttering under his breath. Matt stood by patiently. It wasn't his dad's fault that his legs were weaker than they'd been when he was younger, and that his mind struggled to keep hold of as much as it could in this bewildering world.

Soon they were slowly climbing the steps, and then Steph was welcoming them in. Gordon's face lit up when he saw Steph, and Matt said a silent word of thanks to whoever might be watching over senile old men and their long-suffering sons. "I remember you!" Gordon said. "And I remember this house—there were some very pretty girls here!"

Matt gave Steph an apologetic glance over his dad's shoulder, but she smiled warmly and took Gordon's arm. "Yes, I think that must have been Julie's daughters, at our Christmas party. You really enjoyed talking with them, I remember. Come on in."

"Are they here tonight?"

"No, they've gone back to Portland, but Julie herself is here. You like her."

"And I like you! You're pretty too!"

Steph just laughed.

Younger Gordon would have been more suave about complimenting his hostess before inquiring about potential prettier guests...but of course, younger Gordon hadn't been such an unrepentant horndog—at least not out loud. Matt shook his head and followed them in, his mind straying to Megan, Julie's older daughter.

Matt never needed much prompting to think about Megan. It had been wonderful to see her when she and Lori had been up for Lynne's art opening, but their time together had been far too short, and far too...not enough. Not what he wanted, what he yearned for. Though they had never acted on it, their attraction was mutual and even acknowledged; the trouble was their lives. Hers was in Portland and his was up here on the island—and almost entirely consumed by Gordon and his evolving needs.

Matt knew this, Megan knew this, and it was fine. Nothing lasted forever, things would likely change someday, maybe even soon; plus, he was still recovering from his breakup from Heather last fall...he told himself all this for the millionth time, and then set it back into its spot in his brain and heart as he joined the group in Steph's big crowd-friendly kitchen.

"Hi," said Lynne from the corner conversation nook, where Steph was already getting Gordon settled beside her. "I'm glad you both could come."

"Me too," said Matt, now even more relieved as he watched Gordon grin around at the room, and then back at Lynne, who was positively glowing. She was so kind; it must be the doctor in her, to be able to be so empathetic toward his difficult father. Surely she must see enough dementia patients at the clinic, yet she looked perfectly delighted to have Gordon plopped beside her.

Julie and Gavin were seated at the island, glasses of wine before them; Steph's husband David, who really seemed to be coming out of his shell these days, stood beside the stove stirring something—probably the soup. He turned and smiled at Matt. "Grab a glass and help yourself," he said, nodding to the beverage station under the big bank of windows looking out over the garden.

Steph was at the fridge by now, filling a tall glass with ice, then getting a flavored sparkling water for Gordon. Matt hoped it would be sweet enough for him...or at least that his dad would be polite if he didn't really like it.

Matt was pouring his wine when the doorbell rang, followed almost immediately by Alicia's voice calling down the hallway: "I let myself in!"

Everyone glanced at each other, silent communication flowing between them. *Is she okay? She sounds okay. Should one of us ask? Or wait for her to talk about it?*

Alicia and Ron's breakup was a couple months old by now, but it had been an ugly one. Ron had been angry, defiant, and impossible. The soup group had closed ranks around Alicia, deputizing Julie to let Ron know that everyone would like him to stay away from their gatherings for the time being.

"I see," Ron had told her. "A sabbatical. Of course." He had sounded bitter but resigned, Julie had reported.

Matt still felt weird about the whole thing, even as he also felt a kind of guilty relief at no longer being the group member with the most recent breakup, the one that everyone was tiptoeing around the way they were Alicia right now.

She joined the kitchen group, breezing into the room and setting her dish on the expansive island. "Sorry I'm late! I live so much closer to Deer Harbor now, I forget it still takes at least twenty minutes to get here."

"You're fine, hon," Steph said, going over and giving her a hug. "How are you doing?"

Matt watched as everyone in the room quietly, but unmistakably, paused and waited for Alicia's answer.

"I'm great!" She grinned around at everyone, either ignoring their careful concern or not minding it. "I've got an amazing new project I need to tell you all about!"

Lynne groaned melodramatically. "Not the pickleball tournament fundraiser."

"Exactly that!" Alicia laughed as she walked to the wine counter and poured herself a glass of Chardonnay. "I bet you and Will have loads of pledges already!"

"We have a few." Lynne smiled.

"I had to hurry to get to our mutual friends first," Gavin said, clinking his glass against Julie's. "We are so going to out-raise you two!"

"That's the spirit!" Alicia cried, raising her glass to the room. "Nothing like a good healthy competition to *really* get Robin's center back in the black."

"Tell me more about what you're doing?" Steph asked Alicia. Matt followed them both over to the far side of the kitchen island, since he wanted to hear too.

Lynne, Julie, and Gavin, clearly already in the know, drew Gordon into conversation.

After Alicia had told them about it, Steph nodded enthusiastically. "That's a really good idea— and very nice of you," she said, as she chopped a big bunch of chives.

"Well, it just seemed obvious. And Robin's doing so much for me. I wonder…"

"What?" Steph asked, when Alicia didn't go on.

"Oh, I don't know. Maybe the group is a good size now, but it still feels a little weird. Unbalanced, maybe. Change is hard. You know?"

Matt glanced over at the other conversation group. Yes, they'd lost Heather and now Ron, but they'd pretty much gained Gavin, who came to nearly every dinner, and here was Gordon as well, not to mention David. But Alicia wasn't wrong. "I like Robin," he said. "I'd be up for inviting her in, if the group wants. Do you think her husband would want to join as well?"

"Greg?" Alicia asked, cocking her head as she thought about it. "I don't know, maybe? He's nice, but I don't know him quite as well as I do Robin."

"This is how we get to know people," Steph said. "None of us really knew each other before Julie invited us to join her book group."

Matt chuckled. He knew Julie and Gavin were making another run at starting a book group. He hoped it worked out better for her than her first effort—or, differently anyway, because this soup group was a delight.

Even with the shifting memberships. Matt was suddenly startled to find himself not missing Ron, exactly, but…noting his absence, in a not entirely happy way. Ron was a strong spice, so to speak, but he had been a part of the group since before Matt and Heather had joined—so he had always been here, from Matt's perspective. He hadn't always been as disagreeable as he'd been for the last while. Matt had had some really interesting conversations with him over the years; he was intellectually stimulating, and very smart.

He wondered how the man was doing, now that all the couple's friends had rallied around Alicia—and for good reason, of course. Should Matt reach out to him, just to check in? Would that be disloyal to Alicia? He would ask her, before he committed to anything. But if she was okay with it, maybe he'd give Ron a call, ask him out for a coffee or something.

Steph and Alicia were still discussing the merits of inviting Robin (and maybe Greg) into the group. "I'd be happy to run it by her," Alicia said, "see if she's interested. I can tell her that the group would need to all chime in before we made any lasting decisions."

"That seems like a good approach," Steph said, sweeping about half the chives up and sprinkling them over the soup pot on the stove. "Okay, gang," she said, more loudly, "soup will be ready in about fifteen minutes. Do we want to sit down in the living room for a bit, or is everyone comfortable here?"

"I'm comfortable!" Gordon sang out, grinning between Julie and Lynne.

Matt felt himself unclench the rest of the way.

Chapter 5

STEPH

The menu was set; the shopping had been done; everything that could be prepared ahead of time had been cooked and stored. David had helped her set up the tables and chairs for a test run of how the back yard would look, and it had been beautiful, and plenty spacious enough. Her first community dinner party was in two and a half days, and Steph was beginning to think that maybe, just maybe, it was all going to come off all right.

She was about to head to town to pick up the printed menus and ingredient signs from the Office Cupboard when her phone rang. She didn't recognize the number, but it was a local area code, so she answered it. "This is Steph."

"Ms. Hancock?" said a man's voice on the other end.

"Yes. Who is this?"

He cleared his throat. "Fred Forte, Ms. Hancock, from the San Juan County Building Department. We have received notification that you are in the process of opening up a restaurant on your residential premises. Is that correct?"

"I…no…" she stammered, trying to make sense of what the man was saying. "No—not a restaurant. I'm just—having some people over for dinner." Who in the world had sent notification to the *Building* Department? She wasn't building anything!

"Oh? That is not how the word came to us. You are not charging customers for this dinner?"

Steph felt her face flood with color as her stomach sank. "I did my research!" she cried. "I have a food handler's license, and enough bathrooms, and my kitchen meets the code for—"

"Answer the question, please, Ms. Hancock," the man interrupted calmly.

"I am charging, yes. But...just for reimbursement of what the ingredients cost, honestly." It pained her to admit it, but it was true. "And it's only for one night. Not a restaurant, not a new building, nothing like that."

On the other end of the phone line she could hear the rustle of papers. "I'm looking at one of your fliers," Mr. Forte said. "It quite clearly states that Saturday's dinner is the *inaugural* event of an ongoing series of such dinners." He gave a prim little *ahem* again. "Correct me if I'm wrong, but inaugural means the first, does it not?"

"I...have been kind of hoping to do a few of these a year, yes," she said. "What is this about? Is there a permit I failed to get, or something? Is this a problem?"

Now he sighed softly. "Why yes, the county generally appreciates it if people starting up businesses apply for—and receive issuance of—a business license. And we at the Building Department specifically find it to be a kindness if county residents making infrastructure changes to any premises run their ideas past us first. Just to be sure everything is safe and healthy for the paying public, you understand."

"I'm not building anything!" she nearly wailed, then forced herself calmer. "Nothing at all. Folding chairs in my back yard, and two long folding tables."

"What if it rains?"

"It's June. It's not going to rain." Before he could contradict her (it was the Pacific Northwest, it *always* could rain), she went on.

"And if it does, I have two large greenhouses we could move the tables into. *Permitted* greenhouses."

"I don't suppose those greenhouses have been inspected and cleared for human occupation?"

"Well, no," she admitted. "They aren't going to be occupied—we're just going to have dinner in them. Or not. Probably not. Because it's not going to rain."

"I see. So—"

"So what do I need to do?" she interrupted. "If you're looking at my flier, you know that this dinner's on Saturday. It's too late to cancel it. How do I make the Building Department happy?"

He chuckled, without humor. "It is not a question of making the Building Department happy or unhappy. It is a question of undergoing the proper inspections and obtaining the proper permits. And I'm afraid that, short-staffed as we are, we do not have an inspector available to take a look at your site until…let me see…" There was another sound of paper shuffling, and then keyboard clicking. "The twenty-seventh of October, at eleven fifteen in the morning."

"October?!" Steph cried. She was still holding her car keys; she dropped them on the front table and sank into the small chair where people sat to take their shoes off. "That's after the entire summer is over!"

"I am aware of that. Would you like me to put you in the calendar then? These appointments fill up quickly."

"Uh—yes, I mean no—I have to think about this." Should she just take the appointment? She could always cancel it later, when she figured out what the hell was going on here anyway. "No, yes, I'll take it. Put me down."

"Very good." She heard the sound of keys clicking again. "You'll be receiving an email confirmation with further instructions."

"Great," she said, flatly.

"And I am required to inform you that if the department determines that you went ahead and inaugurated the business prior to such inspection and approval of your premises, and the issuance of a business license, you will be found to be in violation of county code and that will be grounds for an automatic disallowal of your proposed business."

Of course. "So, I have to cancel Saturday's dinner."

"Indeed you do, Ms. Hancock, if you want to legally hold these events at all in the future."

Holding back tears, she simply nodded, though of course he couldn't see her.

"Do you have any questions?" he asked, after the silence had stretched a few more seconds.

Steph had all sorts of questions: where had this come from, why in the world was it illegal to have a dinner in your own back yard, just who had alerted the Building Department anyway, did someone have it in for her? But she just said, "No, I don't."

"All right, then. Thank you for your time."

She bit her tongue in order to stop herself from automatically saying something stupidly polite like *You're welcome* or *Thank you back.*

After Forte hung up, Steph sat there in the front hall for a long while. Then, she got up, went into her office, and began making calls.

LYNNE

INSTEAD OF GOING to Will's house for the very first time (with a carefully packed overnight bag), letting him cook her a fine and fancy dinner, and then seeing what delightful things might happen next, Lynne was bringing him to dinner at Steph's house on Saturday night, along with everyone else in the soup group, a handful of their neighbors, and Alicia's friends and landlords Robin and Greg.

"I can't just throw all this food away," Steph had said, after telling Lynne a very exasperating story about a last-minute call from some officious jerk from the county. "And there's too much that won't keep, and I'm all ready to give this party—so I'm going to give a different party instead, for almost as many people as had signed up. Free of charge, too. Let that noodle-head come and try to bust me, I'll show him."

"Are you sure we can't contribute anything to help defray…" Lynne had started, but Steph interrupted.

"No, I very specifically may *not* charge for this dinner, or I'm in trouble and I'll never be able to do these the way I want to." She'd laughed ruefully. "Listen to me! You had to talk me so hard into this, but now I'm all convinced, and suddenly they won't *let* me!"

"It does seem a little odd," Lynne had agreed. "Small-town politics, I guess."

"I just wonder how anyone found out about it? Who did I offend?"

Lynne had wondered that herself, but she said, "Well, your fliers were up all over town, and the bookstore was selling tickets for you. It wasn't like it was a secret."

"I know, it wasn't supposed to be. I did all the research!"

Be that as it may, something had gone wrong, and so Lynne was helping her friend make the best of a bad situation. Even if it had meant giving up something she had really been looking forward to…or at least modifying it beyond recognition.

She walked to her front windows and looked out, just in time to see Will's car pull into her driveway. Right on time. He got out, dressed impeccably as ever, with an open-collared pale blue shirt under a perfectly fitted blazer, and khakis. She was glad she had chosen her blue flowy pants and a cream-colored top; she and Will would coordinate, without looking matchy-matchy.

"You look wonderful," she told him, opening the door before he could knock.

"As do you." He leaned in for a sweet kiss, which was all they'd been able to share thus far. "If a little sad," he added, pulling back and gazing at her.

"I…well, yeah. I still wish we were going with Plan A."

He smiled warmly. "We will just have to roll with the punches and enjoy Plan B."

She smiled back at him. "And reschedule Plan A for next weekend."

"Indeed. I'm counting on it."

His hands were empty. "Did you bring your toothbrush?" she asked.

He kissed her again. "That, and more. My bag is in the car, along with a bottle of wine to take next door."

"Oh good." She stepped back from the doorway and gestured. "Come on in—I'm almost ready, then we can walk over."

He looked around her small living room as she stepped into the bathroom for a moment. When she emerged, he was admiring one of her older, smaller tapestries on the wall. "I remain in complete awe of your work," he said.

Lynne fought the knee-jerk urge to downplay the piece—it was rough, the colors had faded over time, it hadn't come out quite the way she'd hoped it would—and simply said, "Thank you." She took his hand. "Shall we go?"

"Of course."

At Steph's house, Lynne could see that she had rallied from her disappointment. Which was only one of many things Lynne loved and admired about Steph: her resiliency. The long tables in the back yard were gorgeously set, with bright dishes and coordinating linens; the yard itself was festooned with Italian party lights and colorful decorations. Quiet music played from artfully hidden speakers. Many of the guests had already arrived and were clustered in lively conversation groups, glasses of bubbly in their hands. Several platters of delicious munchies sat on a serving table just inside the open doorway of one of the greenhouses, and a drink station was set up in the opposite greenhouse. At the far edge of the patio, a portable fire pit blazed with a cheery fire, its wood crackling and popping.

"I see this is superfluous," Will said, holding up his bottle of Syrah after Lynne made introductions.

"Not at all, I'll just set it on the table," Steph said with a smile. "Oh, this is one of my favorites—maybe I'll sneak it away for myself when no one's looking."

"No need," Will said. "I have a case of it at home; I can set you up anytime."

When they'd gotten their drinks and Steph moved to greet more new arrivals, Lynne spotted her and Will's place cards on the table nearer to the house. "Shall we sit?" she asked him. "Or would you rather mingle and meet folks?"

"I am entirely in your hands, lovely lady." He gave Lynne such a smoldering gaze that she *knew* what she wanted to do with her hands, and it had nothing to do with this party.

IT WAS A great dinner, of course—Lynne had never had an unpleasant bite at Steph's house. And the weather had been achingly perfect.

As the two young women Steph had hired to help cleared their dishes, Will leaned over and murmured to Lynne, "I suppose we cannot just sneak away now..."

She gave a soft snort. "And skip dessert? Unforgiveable."

He grinned. "Steph is a dear friend of yours. I know she would forgive you."

"That's not what I meant. I would never forgive myself for missing a Steph dessert—and once you taste it, you wouldn't either."

Whatever he might have said in reply was forestalled by the arrival of the dessert itself, carried by Steph, David, and the helpers: a small dish for each guest. "Don't wait to start," Steph said as they set the first round of dishes down. "You don't want it melting."

"Oh my god, is this homemade profiteroles?" Lynne asked, picking up her spoon as she admired the luscious pile of fresh pastry, ice cream, and chocolate syrup before her.

"More or less!" Steph called back over her shoulder as she returned to the kitchen for more.

Will had already taken a bite; the sound of appreciation that escaped him made Lynne even more eager to get this man home… as soon as she finished her own dessert.

Conversation at both tables ceased once everyone was served, leaving only the sound of spoons on dishes, scraping for every last morsel and drop. "I was wrong," said their neighbor Ernest, as the guests finished up.

"Oh?" Steph asked him.

"Yeah. You shouldn't open a restaurant. You should open a dessert parlor."

Laughter and general agreement passed through both tables.

"Tell me there's seconds," Alicia said, holding up her empty bowl in both hands like Oliver Twist.

Steph smiled at her, and at the rest of the party. "Well, since I made the perfect amount for twenty-five—plus a little extra in case of emergencies—then yes, there's definitely enough for most of the eighteen of us to have a second helping. Who's ready for more?"

Clamor ensued.

"You don't want more?" Will asked Lynne softly, when she didn't lift her own bowl.

"I'm afraid if I eat another bite of anything, I'll regret it later," she said, trying to put even a tenth of the suggestive heat in her phrasing as he had earlier. Trying and probably failing: Lynne had been many things over the course of her long life, but a flirt wasn't one of them.

But Will had enough flirtatiousness in him for them both. He gave her that wicked smile and an actual, genuine, no-kidding wink. "I had the same thought myself," he said, laying his spoon in his own bowl as Steph's helpers brought out seconds for those who wanted them. "*Now* can we sneak out of here?"

She was about to say *Yes, oh yes* when Steph tapped her spoon on her wine glass. Lynne stifled a groan of frustration as Steph launched into an interminably long speech of gratitude to all her friends for helping her turn a huge disappointment into a grand party.

Or at least the speech *seemed* interminable. It might have been four or five minutes—underscored by the sounds of spoons scraping empty bowls once more—before the whole party was raising their glasses and calling out thanks to Steph herself for so generously sharing her bounty and culinary magic with them.

And then, at last, everyone was rising, hugging Steph and David and each other, helping to carry dishes into the kitchen, and finding their largely unnecessary wraps.

At least Lynne and Will didn't have to wait while guests jockeyed their cars out of the too-small driveway and narrow road. She led him by the hand along the pathway to her house, and then inside.

All evening, she'd been imagining—anticipating—this moment. She'd had visions of leaping into his arms the moment the door closed behind them, tumbling down onto the sofa together, not even making it into the bedroom for…for all the delights that would surely come next. She'd had to keep turning her mind away from the thoughts so that she could even focus on the wonderful dinner and the company of her friends. But now that the moment had at last arrived? Lynne became suddenly, absurdly, shy.

Trying to cover her discomfort, she moved around the living room turning on a few lamps and unnecessarily rearranging throw pillows. "That was a nice evening," she said, after clearing her throat.

"It was," Will said softly.

She stood up from straightening a pile of magazines on the side table. "I, um…"

"I understand." He stood at the other end of the couch from

her, holding his blazer, just gazing at her with that relaxed, attentive look he had. "I feel a bit of the same thing myself."

Lynne laughed, and relaxed a notch. He did understand; she hadn't even had to name it, and he knew. "I'm out of practice, you know."

"I know." He laid his jacket down on the arm of the sofa and took a single step toward her, slowly, his hands at his sides. "Should we sit down for a minute?"

"That sounds nice." She took a seat on the couch and turned to him as he did the same. They were not quite close enough to touch knees; she reached out and took his hand. "I don't know what's the matter with me."

"Nothing is the matter with you," he said calmly. "As you just said, you're out of practice." His smile radiated kindness. "And, again, I do understand that."

"Thank you." She felt herself relax a bit more. "This isn't quite what I imagined, when I finally got you alone here."

He chuckled. "We have plenty of time—tonight, and in other nights to come." His voice was soothing, and his hand in hers was gentle.

She felt her desire for him rise slowly, beginning to overtake her attack of nerves. "Can we cuddle for a minute?"

"I would like nothing more than to cuddle with you, dear Lynne."

She couldn't even disbelieve him. So she didn't. She turned and scooted closer to him; he put an arm around her shoulders, and she snuggled into his side. He was warm and his shirt was crisp but soft, and smelled like the best kind of fresh laundry, and underneath that was the best kind of clean-man scent. Lynne drank in both scents, letting them settle her further as he held her close.

They sat quietly for a few minutes. Then Will slowly turned his head, leaned in, and brushed her temple with a soft, tender kiss.

The banked flames within Lynne flared to roaring life. She turned in his arms and kissed him eagerly, suddenly hungry for this man anew. He met her perfectly, displaying his own eager-ness while never pushing, letting her lead.

It was just what she needed. After a dreamy, timeless span on the couch, Lynne slowly came to realize that they would be much more comfortable in her bed. She pulled away from his kiss while holding tight to his hand, coaxing him up to standing. "This way," she whispered, and led him into her bedroom.

SHE WOKE EARLY, turning to look at Will sleeping beside her. Even unconscious and sex-mussed, he was somehow impeccably put together. His rumpled hair looked adorable, and the laugh lines around his eyes were relaxed nearly into invisibility. He had been a delightful bed mate: he didn't drool or snore or hog the covers, or even roll around much.

He had been a skilled and sensitive lover as well, unsurprising-ly: attentive to her needs, careful not to crush her underneath him, or to rush ahead to his own pleasure before ensuring that she had been entirely satisfied. And when they were both sated, he had offered to give her the space of her own bed if she wanted; she had assured him that she wanted him to stay.

She had awakened once during the night, as she generally did, and wondered if he would wake as well and they would attempt a second round, but he'd slept on. So she'd used the bathroom quietly and returned to bed, simultaneously disappointed and grateful for the sleep. *We're not in our twenties*, she thought now; the nights of making mad passionate love till the sun rose were decades behind her.

And yet…passion itself was not behind her, as it turned out.

Smiling to herself, Lynne slipped out of bed and pulled on a silk robe before heading to the bathroom again. She took a quick shower, then contemplated whether to get dressed or put the robe back on. She peered out into the bedroom and saw Will sitting up in bed, looking at his phone.

He heard the bathroom door open and turned to smile at her.

"There you are."

"Here I am." Okay, robe it was: she put it on and came back into the bedroom, slipping into bed beside him.

"That's gorgeous," he said, looking at the embroidery along the robe's front. "And obviously your work."

"Thank you. Yes, sometimes I practice on my clothes when I'm trying to work out a design."

He leaned closer, peering at the stitching. "May I?" He held up a hand.

"Of course."

He ran his fingers down the design, beginning at her collarbone and brushing gently down her left breast, then back up the other side. Lynne sighed with pleasure as his fingers slipped under the fabric, nudging the robe open just an inch, caressing her nipple as they passed by. "It's lovely, but this is lovelier," he said, pushing the robe open further and cupping her breast.

She moaned outright and leaned into his touch. He chuckled softly and brought his clever mouth to her nipple.

Then he pushed the robe off her altogether, and they gave no further thought to fabric.

"THANK YOU FOR such an amazing night," she said to him an hour later at her kitchen table. Fresh mugs of coffee sat before them; toast crumbs and melon rinds littered their plates, over a smear of egg yolk. "I'm still sorry I didn't get to see your place, but this made a nice pivot."

He sipped his coffee and grinned at her. "'Nice' is an understatement, I'd say."

"Well, I don't like to presume…" She was smiling back at him, but he suddenly grew more serious.

"Come home with me today, then." When she didn't immediately answer, he went on. "I mean it: I'll cook the dinner I was going to make for lunch, instead. I know you can't spend the night, but why not spend the day?"

"I…actually, I can't think of any reason why not. That's a great idea."

"We can eat on my deck, or picnic down by the lake." He was growing more excited. "It might have been too cool—or too buggy—to eat dinner outside, but lunch? Ideal."

"Let's do it!"

His grin was so adorable. "How long will it take you to get ready?"

She glanced down at her robe, rescued from the tangled bedsheets. "Assuming I put real clothes on, I don't know—ten minutes?"

"What are you waiting for?"

THIS IS ABOUT *as far apart as two people can live and still inhabit the same island,* Lynne thought as she followed him out of Deer Harbor, up the entire left side of the island to Eastsound, and then around and down the right side to Olga…and then past Olga to Doe Bay…and past Doe Bay and, finally, on to the Eagle Lake community. She was pretty sure this was the very end of the road. The whole drive had taken nearly an hour. She wasn't used to driving more than about twenty minutes to get anywhere on Orcas.

He drove under an attractive sign that read "Eagle Lake," with a smaller sign next to it that sternly warned against trespassing. "You won't need to worry about that," he'd told her before they set out; "you're invited." Then he drove slowly enough that she could follow him through a confusing series of seven or eight turns until he finally pulled into the driveway of a large two-story house. She only caught a glimpse of its stature before they both parked in front of the double garage doors. The house looked smaller from this angle; it must step down the hill, and if she didn't miss her guess, it would have quite a view.

"This is your 'cabin'?" she said with a laugh as they both got out of their cars. She'd suspected as much, but wow.

"Well, you know," he said, unembarrassed. "It was smaller than our Arizona house, and meant only as a vacation home."

"It's really nice," she said, as he was unlocking the door.

He stood aside and gestured for her to enter. She did, and took a breath. Oh, indeed, this was quite a view: the Salish Sea, land masses, mountains in the distance. "Is that the mainland?" she asked, walking all the way through the large entryway and the living room to the giant picture windows framing a set of glass doors that made up the entire far wall.

"Not quite; that's Lummi Island, with Bellingham beyond it."

"Oh, I didn't realize Lummi was so big!"

"Yes."

"What are those over there?" She pointed to a cluster of islands off to the left, as he joined her at the window.

"It's easier to see from the deck." He opened one of the glass doors and led her out onto a spacious deck which did indeed cantilever out over the steep landscape below. She couldn't even see the ground underneath them, beyond the rail; it looked as though stepping over the edge would drop you straight into the water. *Good thing I don't have a fear of heights*, she thought, walking with him to the rail.

"Clark is the biggest," he said, pointing, "with Barnes next to it, though Barnes is a bit hard to see. Probably time to trim up that tree... Then the smaller specks are The Sisters, Little Sister, and Lone Tree."

"Wow." She just stared out, taking it all in. "Do you ever get out there, to those little islands?"

He shook his head. "I don't keep a boat anymore—I wasn't using it enough to justify the moorage and maintenance. Do you like boating?"

She laughed. "I was just thinking of kayaking, but yes, I do—I love being on the water any way I can. And I don't do it nearly enough."

He looked thoughtful. "Well, perhaps I'll see what I can do

about that."

She turned to him, surprised. "You'd buy another boat just because I like to be out on the water?"

"Perhaps." He shrugged. "Or at least hit up a friend with one—I know several fellows who keep a vessel on the island. One guy asked me if I wanted to go in with him on a Palmer Johnson sailing schooner a few years ago. I told him no at the time, but he went ahead with the purchase. I'm not sure if he ever did find a partner or just bought it alone, but either way, I know he'd be happy to take us out."

"You travel in a rather different social circle than I do." She looked out over the water again, unable to tear her gaze from the view for more than a minute. Even if the alternate view was her handsome new lover...and his truly very nice house.

"And yet you're a doctor!" He said it teasingly, but Lynne felt something sink inside her. She had not gone into medicine for the money; it had never been important to her. But so many people seemed to think all doctors were millionaires.

"I'm a country doc, remember, working for a podunk little clinic," she said. "Not a big-city surgeon in a fancy practice." She spoke perhaps too sharply, for his face fell.

He put a gentle hand on her arm. "Lynne, Lynne, lovely Lynne. I did not mean to offend: please forgive me."

She put her hand on his and smiled at him. He hadn't meant it—he couldn't have known how a harmless throwaway comment like that would land. "Nothing to forgive. I'm...maybe a little too sensitive about that. People make assumptions."

"They do, and that was careless of me. I know better. I know you, and I've met your charming friends, and now have spent time in your comfortable, perfect home. I truly did not mean to touch any sensitive spots."

She stepped into his arms and kissed him, catching him by surprise, though he recovered quickly. "And yet you're so *good* at touching my sensitive spots," she murmured against his lips.

He gave a hearty chuckle and kissed her back, tugging her tight against him.

After a few minutes, he pulled back slightly and said, "I hate to interrupt this most compelling line of discourse, but I did offer to make you lunch…"

She gave a low growl and did not let go of him. "Lunch can wait. Show me the rest of the house…most particularly your bedroom."

ULTIMATELY, THEY COOKED together in his astonishing kitchen. Lynne kept finding herself thinking *Steph should see this.* Such a well-designed, well-equipped space—for a second home!

Just how rich *was* Will?

When the fresh ravioli stuffed with porcini mushrooms in a creamy truffle sauce was ready, Will dished it out of the pan and onto a serving platter, then shaved curls of parmesan cheese over it. He finished with a generous grinding of black pepper. Lynne gave the green salad one final toss in its dressing.

"As I'd hoped," Will said, "it's a perfect day for the deck."

"Sounds good to me."

She helped him carry out place mats, plates, and silverware; he returned inside for the food, several different kinds of glasses, and, on his next trip, a bottle of white wine.

"I don't normally like Chardonnay with this pasta," he said, as he worked the corkscrew in, "but this winery does an amazing job. It's not buttery, or oaky; it stands up to the truffles and the cream." He poured a small measure into her glass. "See what you think."

She picked up the glass, swirled it around to enjoy how the light caught the pale yellow of the wine, and took a sip. "Wow. That's very nice. I would have had no idea it was a Chardonnay."

"Napa Valley has a lot to answer for. Chardonnay used to be known as a perfectly acceptable Burgundy grape, and then…" He shook his head and topped up her glass, then poured his own.

Sitting down, he lifted his glass. "To you, lovely lady."

"To us," she said, and clinked her glass to his as she spared a thought for poor Ron. If he'd been able to keep his act together, he and Will could be wine-buddies. "What's the winery?" she asked, after taking another sip. "I don't recognize that label."

"You likely wouldn't." He set the bottle in front of her, and now she could see it was all in French. "It's a small outfit, with only a few acres of grapes. I was able to arrange a visit to their cellar on my last trip over there, though they are generally not open to the public."

"Ah." She glanced over the label, but didn't learn anything.

He looked at her with a question in his eyes. All he said, however, was, "Bon appétit."

"Yes, same to you." She smiled at him and took a bite of her pasta. "Oh, my goodness, this is even better than I imagined it would be."

He took a bite as well, chewing thoughtfully. "It came out well."

They ate in silence for a few minutes. Lynne felt a little off, though she couldn't articulate just why. And it was hard to focus on, anyway, between the delicious meal, the lovely wine, and the spectacular view.

Finally, Will cleared his throat and said, "Money is merely a tool, Lynne. A useful tool, to be sure, but nothing more."

She looked up at him. "I'm sorry?"

"It cannot have escaped your notice that I have done well for myself in life. I have made no effort to hide it, because I am not ashamed of it. I worked hard, particularly when I was younger; I got lucky a few crucial times; and I have invested wisely. But none of that means anything more to me than how it can ease and enhance my life—*and* the lives of those I care about." He leaned forward, holding her gaze. "I do not earn money for the sake of piling it up in some bank account somewhere, or even a fat investment portfolio. I earn money so that I can live in places that appeal to me, drive a safe and comfortable car, and travel the world—including to hard-to-find private wineries in Burgundy." His gaze sharpened. "It would give me untold pleasure to take *you* to Burgundy, lovely lady." Then he chuckled. "As soon as you can get free of your sudden, inconvenient full-time job, that is."

She laughed as well, the tension broken. "You know what? I would absolutely let you take me to Burgundy." She took another bite of her pasta. "Though I didn't mean to imply that I'm impoverished. I *could* take myself to France."

He raised an eyebrow. "First class?"

Lynne only shook her head, smiling. *Is he for real?*

Chapter 6

JULIE

Julie stared at the text that had just come in.

It was from Ron Alderson. *It's been over two months, and, as you inform me, Alicia is doing well. I see from the group calendar that tonight is a soup group evening at your house. How long must I be barred from the convivial company of my closest friends? I would like to attend tonight's gathering. I will, of course, bring sufficient wine, if you let me know what soup you are preparing.*

"Are you kidding me?" she said aloud.

"What is it?" Gavin asked, from the living room.

She shook her head and carried the phone out to show him.

"Wow," he said after he'd read it. "There's some gall."

"That's our Ron." She started typing out an answer.

"Are you just going to tell him no?"

She stopped, and looked at Gavin. "I thought so? Do you think I should ask the group?"

He shrugged. "Maybe just ask Alicia?"

"Good idea." She deleted her words to Ron and opened her text string with Alicia.

Hey, you'll never guess who's trying to RSVP to tonight's dinner.

Robin? came the response a minute later. *I haven't talked to her about it yet, did you invite her?*

No. Ron.

A pause. Three dots bounced, then stopped, then bounced again. *Are you kidding me?*

Julie laughed and showed Gavin the phone.

"There's our answer."

"Yep."

I'll tell him no, Julie wrote her.

A longer pause this time, but with more bouncing dots. Then: *If you want him to come, that's okay with me, but I'll bow out.*

You're the member, not him, Julie wrote, typing as fast as she could. *We only tolerated him because he came with you.*

Ha! Alicia wrote back. *And because he brought good wine.*

Well, there's that, Julie wrote. *But we're just doing fine providing our own damn wine. I'm telling him no. See you at six.*

Are you sure?

ONE HUNDRED PERCENT. I choose you.

Aww thanks!

Julie switched back to the message from Ron. *Sorry, it's still way too soon. Maybe in the fall. I'll let the others know you say hi, though.*

She held up the unsent text for Gavin to read. "Too blunt?" she asked.

"Is it possible to be too blunt with Ron?"

Julie chuckled. "No, probably not. Steph told me how many times she tried to fend him off before he actually straight-up made a pass at her."

"Poor Steph."

"Oh, she's fine—I mean, yeah, that was creepy, but she wasn't threatened or weirded out or anything by him. She just said it made her sad."

Gavin said, "That's still a bummer. And then her new business crashing before it gets off the ground on top of that."

Julie felt her righteous indignation rise again. "I still think that worm McLeod is behind that."

"How do you figure? He's not with the county."

"Yeah, but he's got pull everywhere, obviously. He's clearly got it out for me, and he knows Steph and I are friends…"

Gavin was shaking his head. "Maybe," he said dubiously. "It seems like a stretch."

She took a breath. "I don't want to get into this now—I've got to get back to the soup."

"Are you sure there's nothing I can do to help?" He put a hand on her knee and gave it a gentle squeeze.

Julie smiled at him. "No, it's nearly done. I just need to stir it."

"And send that text to Ron."

"Right." She rolled her eyes. "That too."

"OH, I KEEP meaning to tell you," Gavin said, as he helped her with the dishes after the group had left. "There's nine people signed up for the book group."

"Nine! Wow, that's great!" She plucked another soup bowl out of the dish drain and dried it, setting it on the table. "How many of them are the flakes from our first attempt?"

He laughed. "None, you'll be happy to know. I think they were all too embarrassed."

"Or maybe they decided they didn't want to read Libby Perrine after all."

Gavin turned back toward the sink. "Ah, yeah, that's the other thing." She looked at him, but he wasn't facing her; were his shoulders hunched up a little? "They, ah, would rather start with a different book."

"Oh, well, that's okay, I guess. I'm flexible."

He washed two more bowls and put them in the dish drain.

"Have they actually chosen a book?" she asked, when he didn't say anything more. And when had they all made this decision anyway? How did a bunch of random library patrons get together and choose a book for a book club that hadn't even had its first meeting?

"It's a younger group of people," Gavin finally said, turning back to her with a *forgive me* smile. "I asked Amy, who does the young adult collection, to let some of her teen groups know, and, well, they were very into the idea. And, um, they want to read a…" Gavin mumbled something that Julie couldn't make out. Harpy something?

"What?" she asked, stepping closer to the sink and turning off the water. "What was that last word?"

Gavin was red in the cheeks. "They unanimously chose *The Crimson Knife of Al'th'ara*."

Julie stared at him. "What in the world is that?"

"It's the novelization of an RPG."

"Do I want to know what an RPG is?" She wasn't even going to touch *novelization*—what was that even? A novel was a novel was a novel.

"Role playing game." He turned the water back on and washed another bowl.

Julie put her towel down and sat in one of the dining chairs. "Role playing game. Like Dungeons and Dragons?"

"Like that. But this is a newer one—very popular these days." He glanced over his shoulder at her before turning back to the sink.

"Does it have dragons in it?"

"Ah, I think, er, chupacabras. And animated gargoyles. And selkies."

"Selkies?"

"Seal people."

She shook her head. "Are those things all even from the same mythology? That sounds awfully random."

He turned back to her. "I'm sorry, I know this isn't what you had in mind—"

Julie laughed, but without any humor in it. "Not hardly! Oh, Gavin. Seriously?"

"Seriously, that's the book they want to read."

She put her face in her hands for a moment, then looked back up at him. "Well, then that's what they should read, and I wish them all the joy of it. I will be continuing to try to form a book group for grown-ups, where we will read grown-up books."

He turned back to her. "Don't you want to give it a try? They're so enthusiastic! They're such good kids—Amy loves them. We might be able to persuade her to join the group as well, and then after we read the first book, maybe—"

"No," Julie said, and it came out rather more harshly than she intended. She got up and put her arms around Gavin. "I'm sorry, but no. I've raised kids, and I loved doing it, and I'm done now. If I'm going to read young adult literature, I'm going to be reading it to my own grandchildren."

Eyes wide, he stared at her. "Is there something you're not telling me?"

"No! And that's the point. I'm *not* a grandmother, I *don't* have grandchildren, and I want to read mature literature written by mature adults and discuss it with other adults! Is this so much to ask?"

He wrapped his arms tightly around her and held her for a long moment. "I'm sorry. I thought...I thought it might work. That it might grow into the group you're looking for—kids grow up, after all. You could introduce them..." He trailed off and looked down at her. "I guess not."

"Amy can run the group," Julie said. "We'll just keep on trying for our own."

He shook his head. "She's already stretched way too thin. She can't take on anything else. So I offered..."

Julie pulled back and stared at him. "You didn't."

Gavin blushed again. "I told her...well, I thought you might want to lead it with me..."

"Gavin Jones, I am not going to read *The Bloody Knives of Algernon* with a bunch of teenagers!"

He barked out a laugh, then quickly sobered. "It's *The Crimson Knife of Al'th'ara*, and according to all the reviews, it actually has a really good story line—"

"Great," she snapped. "Then you read it with them, and discuss it with them, and trade the action figures or whatever, and have a blast. I would not dream of standing in your way."

He put his hands on his hips and glared back at her. "Who's the literary snob now?"

Julie took in a breath. "Excuse me, what?"

"You gave me such a schooling when we had our little, you know, misunderstanding—all about keeping an open mind and not being all judgmental about what kind of creative output matters. And now you won't even consider a hugely popular story that is resonating with all kinds of young folks!"

She just stared at him, at a loss for words. Suddenly, infuriatingly, she found tears coming to her eyes. Tears of frustration, obviously: she was not going to cry over something this stupid.

And then the air went out of all her anger as she breathed a heavy sigh. "Why is it so hard to put together one simple book group?"

Gavin's gaze softened too. "Do you want a real answer, or was that a rhetorical question?"

"Why? Do you *have* a real answer?"

He shrugged. "I have a thought, anyway."

"Okay. Let me hear it."

He reached over to turn off the water, which had been running this whole time, in a slow stream over the dishes piled in the sink. "Shall we sit?"

Julie took her chair at the table again, and Gavin sat next to her. Her last half-glass of wine was still here, forgotten in the cleanup; she took a sip. "Okay."

"Okay." He took a deep breath. "My thought is…maybe you've got too specific an idea of what a book group might look like? I mean, grown-ups and mature books, sure, I get that; but you seem to have your heart set on starting with this one specific book by this one specific author. I'm not sure everyone loves Libby Perrine as much as you do."

Julie's mouth fell open; she grabbed her glass and took another sip of wine to cover her shock. "Sweetie, starting with *The Glory*—with Libby Perrine at all—was *your* idea, not mine. I would be happy to read any…not-bloody-knives-and-gargoyles book."

"But I thought—"

"Yes, she's my favorite author, and yes, that's her best book—but that was all you! Or do you not remember the day you turned up here with an armload of her books and a heartfelt apology?"

He looked like he was about to argue further, but then he just nodded and looked down at the table. "Okay. You're right. That was me."

"And that was the sweetest, most thoughtful, most *knowing-me* thing anyone had ever done. I still think you know me better than anyone else ever has. I hope I'm not wrong."

"Julie, I am sorry." He looked devastated. "I just…I mean, they're such enthusiastic kids, and they're *reading*! It's kind of the whole joy of working in a library, is seeing people discover the love of reading. I thought…I thought you might be on board with it."

"I'm sorry too," she said, and she meant it. She had loved reading to Megan and Lori, and watching them discover at least a little bit of her love for literature. "But I really do feel like I've put in my time in that department. You know?"

"Yeah. I get it."

"You should definitely lead that group, though. You'll be great at it, and they'll love you." She chuckled. "And maybe eventually, they'll grow up and you can steer them to more, um, interesting books."

"Oh, I'm sure *The Crimson Knife of Al'th'ara* will be downright fascinating," he said dryly, but he was smiling as well. "I'll be sure to let you know if your snap judgment was too hasty."

"You do that," she said, equally dry.

They sat looking at each other fondly for another long moment. Then Gavin sighed and said, "Well, those dishes are not going to finish themselves."

"Sure they will," she said. "You've done quite enough for tonight, mister; the rest can wait till morning. I'm tired of drying anyway. Should we get on to the making-up part of this evening's quarrel?"

His smile turned delighted. "Oh, that's the best idea I've heard all day."

ALICIA

THINGS WERE, FOR the most part, improving. She still loved her tiny cottage, her work was keeping her nice and busy, and the pickleball tournament fundraiser was garnering lots of signups and pledges.

She still believed that leaving Ron had been the right decision...and yet, she also still grieved. Mostly for what they'd once had, and for the life she'd thought she had signed up for "forever," but even little things from more recent times could catch her by surprise. Waking up in the morning all alone in her bed...for that matter, going to sleep at night alone between cold sheets. Catching the scent of Ron's aftershave in the grocery store and turning to say something to him—but it wasn't him, it was some random old man.

And, well, she had to admit that the wines she chose for herself were never quite as amazing as the ones he served.

Well, too bad, she thought, yet again, as she closed her laptop on her work for the day and began contemplating what she should prepare for dinner.

Which reminded Alicia that it was her turn to host the next soup group (how time flew!). On her last turn, she'd still been staying at Steph's, so they'd had it there. But where to hold it now?

Her old house was out of the question. This cabin was far too small to have more than one other person over. *Time to talk to Robin, then,* Alicia told herself.

She pulled on her shoes and went to knock on Robin and Greg's back door.

"Hey!" Robin said, with a welcoming smile. "What's up?"

"I have a question for you."

"Come on in." Robin opened the door more widely.

"Thanks." Alicia followed her into the kitchen. "Wow, it smells good in here."

"Pizza night—want to stay for dinner? We've got plenty."

I shouldn't, I don't want to be a pest, Alicia thought, even as her mouth said, "Sure."

Robin poured her a glass of wine. "Greg's still in town—he'll be back anytime. Grab another plate and add it to the table."

Alicia headed for the dish cabinet. "Do you need any other help?"

"Nope, I've got it all under control. Salad's already done, and as you can see, I made too much of that as well. It's like I knew you'd be coming!" Robin laughed as she opened the oven door and peered inside. "Five more minutes, I think." She closed the oven and turned to Alicia. "What did you want to ask me?"

Alicia sipped her wine. It was good, rich and dark and red; she should ask Robin where she got it. "You know that soup group I belong to?"

Robin nodded. "You want to host it here?"

Alicia blinked in surprise. *Am I that transparent?* "I, um. Well, not exactly—but, actually, yes. Oh, this is all backwards." She laughed and took a breath. "The group talked about it, and we all agreed that we would like to invite you to join us—and Greg too, if he's interested. But definitely you. I know you love to cook, and to host, and you know most of the people in the group and you all like each other, and this house is plenty big enough—"

"Oh honey," Robin interrupted, laughing. "You don't have to invite me into your little club just to be able to use my house. You couldn't hurt my feelings if you tried."

Alicia flushed, feeling just completely sideways through this whole conversation. "No! It's not like that. Everyone likes you, like I said; and we're down a few members, so—you can think about it if you want. But it's my turn to host next time, a week from Sunday, so, what do you think?"

Robin took a generous sip of her own wine and then set her glass on the table. "Sure, let's give it a try. We'll have it here. What kind of soup do you want to make?"

Alicia laughed again, relieved and still a bit embarrassed. "I don't know! I've only just started thinking about it. Do you have a favorite?"

It had been such a fun evening. When Greg had gotten home, he'd been just the precise degree of politely noncommittal to the soup-group invitation that it was clear that he would welcome an occasional night out with his friends—or home alone while Robin went out. And that was fine. Then the three of them had talked and laughed and eaten altogether too much pizza and perhaps even drank a bit too much wine.

Now Alicia was making her way back through the darkened yard to her cottage, wishing she'd thought to turn on a porch light before she'd left. In her defense, she'd thought she was just running over to ask Robin a question, not inviting herself to dinner.

I should invite them over, she thought now. She did want to be careful about imposing on their privacy. Just because they were renting her a little house didn't mean they wanted to spend every evening with her. But the occasional social event would be nice, and her cabin would certainly fit three people for drinks and munchies...

An odd sound in the darkness stopped her. Like someone crying? But not exactly. She stood, holding very still, trying to figure out where the noise had come from. Now, however, she heard only the usual night noises.

"Hello?" she called out softly. "Is someone there?"

She was just about to start toward her door once more when she heard it again—louder, and near her feet.

"Oh!" She leaned down, looking around, but it was way too dark to see anything. She pulled out her phone and turned on its flashlight. "Oh, poor thing! Are you hurt?"

A calico cat lay by the path between Robin and Greg's house and Alicia's cabin. She looked away, blinking, as the light hit her eyes, so Alicia aimed the beam off to the side and bent over. The cat mewed again, sounding pained. And was she panting?

"Poor baby!" Alicia crooned, putting a gentle hand out toward the cat, hesitating before touching her. The cat sniffed at her hand and then nudged it with the top of her head; Alicia took that as permission and petted her gently down her back, even as she was trying to assess what was wrong. The cat was trembling, and didn't get to her feet, but she didn't seem scared; she seemed grateful that Alicia had stopped.

"Where did you come from?" She rubbed up closer to the cat's neck, confirming that she wore no collar. Alicia couldn't remember seeing this cat at any of the neighbors' houses, though of course cats did roam. "Will you let me see if you're hurt anywhere?" She continued petting her, eventually encouraging her to shift to her other side, but she saw no wounds, and felt no blood. "It's so dark out here, sweet thing. And there might be nasty old raccoons nearby. Will you let me bring you into my house?"

The cat mewed again, slightly less pathetically than before, Alicia thought. Or was she just projecting what she wanted to hear? In any event, she couldn't do the creature much good out here in the dark, on the dirt path. "Okay, I'm picking you up now." She began easing her hands under the cat, alert for any unseen injuries or resistance on the cat's part, but the calico let her take her in her arms.

Alicia slipped her phone back into her pocket and brought the cat into her house.

In the main room, she set the cat on the comfy chair and then turned on every light in the place. "You're a pretty one, all right," Alicia told her. Her black, orange, and white fur was lush and clean, though a little dusty; she seemed to be a healthy weight, maybe even a little thick in the belly. "I don't guess you're a stray, though you don't have a collar. So where did you come from, and why are you here?"

The cat meowed, sounding pathetic and pained.

"Hungry? Thirsty? I don't have any cat food, but I can get you some water." She brought a small bowl of water to the chair and set it down. The cat was very thirsty; she leaned up immediately, though she didn't seem to move comfortably, and started lapping up the water.

Alicia watched her, frowning. What could she feed her? A can of tuna would be ideal, but of course she didn't have tuna. Did she have any meat at all? She went back to her fridge and poked around. Not even lunch meat.

"Do you like cheese?" She pulled out a half-finished block of sharp cheddar and cut off a small slice. When she brought it to the cat, the dish of water was empty. She handed her the cheese; the cat sniffed at it, then looked at the water bowl again.

"All right." Alicia refilled the water; the cat lapped up half of it this time, then lay back on her side. Was she breathing heavily? She had seemed to be panting earlier, outside; she wasn't now, but she didn't seem to be breathing normally. "I suppose you need a vet," Alicia mused, "but I don't know if any are open at night." She'd never had a cat; her parents hadn't approved of pets, and then as a young adult in rental apartments in the city, it had never been possible. And of course Ron would never countenance an animal in the house. "A vet might be able to tell if you're chipped, too."

The cat looked at her and gave a louder wail, and began awkwardly trying to get to her feet.

"Oh, wait, whoa! Let me help you." Alicia bent down and lifted the cat to the floor, making sure she was steady on her feet before letting go. Yes, that was a plump little belly, wasn't it? The cat didn't seem to like her touching it. "Sorry, kitty," Alicia said, petting her on her back again.

The cat made a wobbly beeline for the corner of the room where Alicia's bed nook was. She wailed one more time, then sank to the floor at the foot of the bed and began licking herself...down...there.

"Oh my god," Alicia whispered. "Are you...is that...are you having *kittens?*"

Things happened quickly after that. The first tiny dark baby had already slid out and was being licked clean by its mother before Alicia thought to grab a towel for the cat to lie on. Then it was some work getting her onto the towel and at least potentially comfortable when—oops—here came another one. The first baby was tucked against mama's belly; could it be nursing yet, not even two minutes old? The cat was long-haired, and the kitten was miniscule; it was a little hard to tell what was going on down there.

Before fifteen minutes had passed, the calico had given birth to four kittens, licked them all clean, and cradled them to her belly. Now she was making a different, strange sound. Not quite growling...

Alicia leaned in to hear better. "Are you purring?" Of course she'd heard cats purr before, but never this loud.

The cat looked up at her, and Alicia could swear she had a smug, relieved expression on her face. Her purr somehow grew even louder.

"Oh, mama cat, that's a fine little brood of babies you have there!" Alicia giggled, looking at them. They hardly looked like cats: they were little beans, little worms. She'd thought they were all dark-furred, but as they dried off, she could see that one was a calico like her mother, one was maybe some kind of tabby, and one might almost be an off-white. The fourth one was entirely black…no, did it have white paws? "Aww," Alicia whispered, and fell hopelessly in love.

Chapter 7

RON

When his phone rang, he thought, as he did every time, that it would be Alicia.

It wasn't.

"Matt," Ron said, after pushing the button to answer the call.

"Hey Ron," said Matt, sounding a little too casual. "I was just, you know, thinking about you and thought I'd give you a call."

Well I wasn't thinking about you, Ron thought. But he was trying hard to be less curmudgeonly, so he said, "It's good to hear from you. What's new?"

"Oh, you know, the usual, and plenty of it." Matt chuckled. "Say, would you be interested in getting together to catch up? Grabbing a beer or something?"

"A *beer*?" Ron asked.

"Right! Duh. I mean a glass of wine—or, what I really mean is just, well, what I said: getting together to catch up."

Why in the world do I want to catch up with Matt Richards? Ron thought, but, again: less curmudgeonly. The man was reaching out. This was a *nice* thing. Right? "You should come over here," Ron said. "Anything I have in my cellar is going to be better than whatever we could get anywhere in town." Oops. That was kind of curmudgeonly. But honestly.

Matt hesitated a moment, then said, "All right, but can I bring dinner at least? And when would be good?"

Ron glanced at his calendar, lying on his desk. Every square was blank. Behind the calendar sat the ever-increasing manuscript pile. Was any of it any good? He had no idea. But Matt had asked a question. "I don't have any plans."

"You don't...?"

"Ever. I don't have any plans, ever. I'm free—today, tomorrow, the weekend, next week, until the end of time." Ron caught himself, clearing his throat. *So I've achieved "not curmudgeonly" only to vault straight into "pathetic".* "Would you like to come over tonight, or do you need more time to arrange for that woman to come babysit your father?"

Matt made a sort of strangled sound, then said, "Tonight works. Shall I come at six?"

"Let me check my calendar. Oh wait, I just did, and it's empty. Six works fine." Ron chuckled to indicate that he was joking, but he wasn't sure if Matt got it.

"Great. See you then!"

Ron set the phone down and stared at the pad of paper in front of him. Today's writing had been logy, slow, pathetic. He'd crossed out as many sentences as he'd written.

But that was fine: now he could stop for the day. Matt Richards was coming to the house! Which was...well, Ron had been trying to keep the place reasonably non-disgusting, in case Alicia ever wanted to come over and...get more of her stuff, talk things through, return to their marriage, whatever. So far, she had only come the once, after making sure he wouldn't be there. But a man could hope.

A man *did* hope. For all the good it did.

Ron got up and started getting the house ready for company.

MATT[*]

HE'D BEEN DITHERING about this for weeks, and finally decided that he couldn't call himself any kind of friend to Ron if he didn't reach out.

So he did, but, whew. *Awkward.*

Hoping this was all not the world's worst idea, Matt began trying to figure out what to make for dinner. He hadn't expected this—he'd imagined they'd meet at the Lower Tavern or maybe Madrona, chat for a while, then go their separate ways. But duh indeed, what had he been thinking? Ron Alderson was never going to set foot in the Lower Tavern.

"What am I going to make?" Matt asked aloud, alone in his kitchen—Gordon was napping in his easy chair in front of a game show. "Not soup." Unfortunately, soup was more portable and reheatable than most anything Matt knew how to cook.

Maybe he could pick something up in town? Yeah, that was the safest option. Because Ron surely didn't want to eat a dinner consisting of fine and fancy wine with cheese straws and tarted-up Chex mix.

He pulled out his phone and began googling. Score! The Lone Pine Larder closed at five thirty. He immediately pulled up their online menu and placed an order to pick up right at their closing time. They were sold out of his first choice—the roasted dark-meat chicken—but they had two servings of white meat, and the Tortilla Espanola, and the mac & cheese side.

Should he add the Basque cheesecake?

Silly question. He ordered two pieces.

Then all he had to do was get Gordon ready for Ramona's arrival.

MATT SPENT A few extra minutes talking to Ramona before he left—she was still waiting to hear the results of her scan, even though it had been weeks and weeks. "If it was bad news, they'd have called you right away," Matt assured her, and hoped he was right.

"Your lips to God's ears."

He got to the Lone Pine Larder shortly after they closed, rushing in full of apologies. "That's just fine," said the cheerful young woman behind the counter. "We're here another hour or so—we wouldn't eat your dinner."

"Not right away, at least," called the chef from the kitchen, laughing.

"Thank you!" Matt said, clutching the warm, yummy-smelling bag.

Then he had to sort of dawdle on his way to Ron's house, only about a ten-minute drive from town. Why had Matt suggested six o'clock? That had been dumb.

Should he call Ron and ask if he could arrive early? No, it was already awkward enough, even though Alicia had told him she thought his reaching out was a great idea. He just drove on past the turnoff to Rosario, through the park and on to Olga, then slowly turned around in front of the old Olga store and made his way back, pulling into Ron's driveway just as his car clock turned to 6:00.

"Come on in," Ron said, giving him a genuine smile. "Wine's already breathing, though I wasn't sure what you were bringing, so I chose something versatile."

"Chicken, potato-egg tortilla, and mac and cheese," Matt said, holding up the bag.

Ron stared at the bag a moment, seemingly baffled, then gave a gruff laugh. "You *bought* dinner. That's probably for the best."

"I thought so too." He followed Ron inside and set the bag on the big kitchen island/bar, next to two open bottles of red wine. Something smelled odd in here...was it ammonia, cleaning fluid? Had Ron done an emergency house-cleaning? Aww.

"Chicken," Ron said. "White or dark meat?"

"White."

Ron nodded and picked up the nearer bottle. "We'll start with this one then," he said, pouring two generous glasses. He handed Matt one. "And should we eat while the food is hot?"

"Sure, good idea."

Matt had been to enough soup groups here that he knew where all the dishes were kept. He got out two plates, and turned to carry them to the big dining table…but the table was piled high with Amazon boxes, unopened mail, an empty grocery bag, a few used dishes and a lot of empty wine bottles, and a dead house-plant. And that was just what Matt could see from over here.

"Oh," Ron said, following his gaze. "Right. Let's eat here." He pulled out a barstool and nodded at the one next to it. "I didn't get to the table yet. I've been busy…with my book."

"Great," Matt said, setting the plates at their places and taking a seat. "The book is coming along well, then?"

"Well enough." Having brought it up, Ron seemed uneager to talk about whatever he was writing. He lifted his glass. "Cheers."

"Cheers."

The wine was delicious, of course. Matt took a second sip before setting it down and reaching for the bag of food, pulling it closer.

Ron snorted as Matt unpacked the bounty. "How many people are we expecting for dinner? You're not going to surprise me by having the whole group show up, are you?"

Matt stifled a grimace and shook his head. "I'll leave anything we don't eat tonight. I thought you might…appreciate leftovers."

"Hmm." Ron focused on opening the two boxes with chicken, and served a small measure of breast meat onto his own plate. "Yes, cooking for one is a pain in the ass."

"I imagine." Matt opened the box with mac & cheese in it and spooned a generous portion onto his plate. "So…how are things, speaking of that?"

"Oh just fine," Ron said immediately. He sawed into his chicken and took a bite, then a sip of wine. Then he grumbled something under his breath and added, "Well, not entirely fine."

"Do you want to talk about it?"

"I suppose that is the usual way of things, isn't it?"

Matt glanced over at Ron, trying to gauge him. His voice was gruff, and he was frowning, but...was this his usual defense mechanism, bristling at anyone trying to reach out? Was he actually lonely underneath it all, wanting someone to confide in?

The Ron that Matt knew, at least, would not have agreed to this evening if he hadn't wanted to. Ron was never shy about making his desires known. So Matt had to assume that his presence was welcome here—if grudgingly—and that a little bit of prying might also be warranted. Or at least some softening of the ground.

"I was blindsided when Heather left me," Matt said. "I'd had no idea she was so unhappy."

Ron sliced another bite of chicken and ate it.

"I mean," Matt went on, "we had our issues, and I knew she didn't love having my dad living with us, but I thought we were talking those things through. I always did the lion's share of Dad-care even when Heather did live there; I didn't want to burden her with him. So when she just announced out of the blue that she was leaving...it took me a while to even really believe it."

Ron picked up his wine glass and took a larger sip, then set the glass carefully down beside his plate. "Did Alicia seem unhappy to you?"

Matt took a moment to compose his answer. "She's a pretty upbeat person, I think; so no, she didn't seem *unhappy*. But you guys...I can't say you've seemed happy *together* for a while." *Even before you made a pass at Steph.*

"Hmph." Ron picked up the mac & cheese box and plopped some on his plate. It glistened next to the chicken. Ron didn't touch it, instead taking another bite of chicken.

"Were you happy with her?" Matt ventured.

"Of course I was!" Ron said, shaking his head. "I mean, she's my wife."

"I know that. But, and don't take this the wrong way, you often seemed frustrated with her."

Ron exhaled heavily and finished his wine. He reached for the bottle and refilled his glass, and topped off Matt's, even though it was still more than half full. "Well, any marriage has its frustrations."

"True—any relationship does, marriage or not." Matt took a bite of mac & cheese. God, it was good. Now he was kind of sorry he'd offered to leave all the leftovers here. "But if there isn't sufficient joy and connection to balance those frustrations, then…" He waved his hand to indicate *Then she leaves you.*

"Hmph," Ron said again.

Well, this is going great, Matt thought glumly.

Ron opened the box with the Tortilla Espanola in it. "What's this?"

"It's the potato-and-egg thing. A Spanish dish. Try it: it's really good."

Ron sliced off a tiny sliver and took a bite. "Oh. That is good. But it wants the other wine." He hopped down off his barstool and went to the cabinet beside the fridge, returning with two clean wine glasses, which he filled from the second bottle. He drank from his own and nodded. "There we go." He was almost smiling.

Matt served himself some tortilla and followed suit. "Wow. You're right: that's amazing with this."

Now Ron really did smile. "I'm not completely worthless."

WELL, THAT WASN'T *so bad after all*, Matt thought as he drove home. Everything had gotten a little less awkward after the second bottle of wine was well underway, and the meals—and cheesecake— were resting happily in their bellies. Ron hadn't exactly opened up about his feelings or anything, but he had allowed as how it was kind of hard, living in that big house all alone; and that he really did appreciate Matt reaching out and bringing dinner.

"We should do this again sometime," Ron had even said, when he showed Matt out at the end of the evening.

Not only that, but he'd sent Matt home with the leftover mac & cheese. "Too creamy for me," he'd said, but only after he'd clearly noticed how much Matt was enjoying it.

Maybe there's a decent human being somewhere in there after all, Matt thought, as he turned left on Crescent Beach Road. *Though he sure works hard to hide it.*

LYNNE

JULIE AND GAVIN had challenged her and Will to pickleball. "We need to get our practice in," Julie had said, "and I bet you guys do too."

"True," Lynne had told her. "I don't get out on the courts nearly as often now that I'm working full-time."

"Tell me about it!" Julie had suggested they get together at six fifteen, after their long days at her shop and the medical clinic were finished. "It's still light for an hour anyway then, and the courts should be empty." Then they'd all go out to dinner afterwards, and be home and tucked into bed in time to get up and do it all over again early the next morning.

Lynne pulled in and parked at the courts. Well, they weren't completely empty; a half-dozen or so teenagers were noodling around on one of them. They were laughing and flirting and goofing off more than actually playing, but they left three courts free, so that was fine.

She got her bag out of the trunk, then made her way to the vacant court farthest from the kids. By the time she'd gotten her paddle out, pulled on a glove, and found a decent ball, Julie drove up, with Gavin in the passenger seat.

"Are we late?" Julie asked, joining Lynne on the court.

Lynne dinked the ball to her; Julie dinked it back. "No, I was early, and I don't know where Will—oh, there he is."

The men took a few minutes getting geared up, and soon they had a game underway.

And a good game at that. Lynne found herself feeling smugly happy in her choice of partner—on the court as well as off. Will had a killer serve, with a deceptive spin on it, and he was quite good at returning anything that Julie or Gavin sent his way. Neither Will nor Lynne moved around as nimbly as the younger couple, but they more than made up for this shortcoming with their control and accuracy. And he was really fun to play with, never poaching her shots, but backing her up when needed; always complimenting anyone on a good hit.

Will and Lynne took the first game, eleven to six.

"Shall we switch sides?" Julie asked. "I'm tired of hitting into the wind."

"Sure," Lynne said, then added teasingly, "if you think that will help."

"Oh just you watch," Julie said with a grin.

After Lynne and Will took the second game eleven to four, Gavin said ruefully, "Looks like hitting *with* the wind isn't that much better."

"Shut up," Julie told him, though she was smiling as she rolled her eyes. "I just need a little more time to calibrate my shots."

"So you want to stay on that side for game three?" Will asked her.

"Sure." Julie rolled her shoulders and cracked her knuckles. "We'll get you this time."

Game three also went to Lynne and Will, though it took them fifteen points, and nearly half an hour, to win by two.

"That's enough for me," Gavin said, wiping his brow. "You guys are amazing together."

"Thanks." Lynne couldn't help beaming. "I think so too."

Will flashed her a private smile before turning to the others. "Are we ready for the reward part of our evening?"

Julie nodded vigorously. "Oh, absolutely."

They caravanned to the New Leaf, where Will had reserved a table for four—"their" table, just above the corner room. "I know we should try some of the newer restaurants that keep opening up," Will said, after the cocktails had been served, "but I have a hard time wanting to go anywhere but here."

"I know," Lynne said, as Gavin and Julie both murmured agreement. "Why fix what isn't broken?" In her purse, her phone buzzed, sending a little shiver of dread through her. "Sorry, let me see who this is." She wasn't on call tonight, but it still could be work-related—and if it was, that would be bad news.

She pulled out the phone to see a text from Kate Evintrude. Apparently she'd also missed a call, while they were on the courts. *Give me a call when you have a moment?*

Sure, Lynne typed back. *Out at dinner now; can I call when I get home?*

Of course.

Lynne put the phone back into her purse. Will met her eyes. "Everything okay?"

"Yes, it's fine—it's my gallery owner." That still felt so weird to say: *my gallery*. So weird, in fact, that Lynne had given this spring's show almost no thought since it had opened—except to think fondly back on connecting with Will that evening. She hadn't even been back to the gallery to see her work on the walls. "I'll call her when I get home."

"How is the show going?" Julie asked. "Have you sold many pieces?"

"You know, it's funny," Lynne said, "but I haven't even asked. I've been so busy!"

"When does the show close?" Gavin asked.

"Mid-July—just a few weeks," Lynne said. "That's probably why she's calling: to make arrangements to get my stuff out of there so she can set up the next show."

The appetizers arrived, to general sighs of anticipation around the table. "Pickleball doesn't seem like *that* much exercise," Julie said, putting a truffle fry in her mouth, "but it sure does make me hungry."

"Hear, hear," said Will, joining her.

WHEN LYNNE GOT home, she almost forgot to call Kate back, only noticing the missed call once more after she'd gotten ready for bed and was plugging in her phone by the nightstand.

"Hi, is this too late?" she asked, when Kate picked up.

"Not at all! I'm a night owl, or at least an evening one."

"Oh good. Sorry I missed your call earlier—I was playing pickleball."

"That's right," Kate said, "I saw a sponsorship signup sheet for the tournament. What a great idea; I'm going to get a copy to keep at the gallery."

Lynne was touched, and a bit surprised. "That's very nice! Thank you."

"My pleasure. Anything for one of my amazing artists—and for a very good cause as well."

I love this island, Lynne thought. "Well, gosh. Seriously, we appreciate it." After a small pause, she added, "So, what's up?"

"Well, I just wanted to check in, and let you know a few things. It's been a while since I've seen you."

"I know! I've been so busy. I probably didn't even tell you that I've been working full-time at the clinic, since one of the other doctors left with no notice."

Kate made a small sound of dismay. "No, I didn't know that. I'm sorry to hear it."

"Me too, she was really great. I've taken on the majority of her caseload, and it's got me scrambling. And every spare moment is spent—well, do you remember that friend of Gavin Jones's who was at the opening reception?"

"I do," Kate said, now sounding delighted. "Your pickleball partner...and more than that, I'm assuming?"

Lynne chuckled. "Yes, in fact, quite a bit more than that."

"I guess that explains where you've been! I'm glad to hear it's all good things—well, mostly good," Kate said. "I know how much you wanted to fully retire."

"And I will someday. We're actively recruiting for a new doctor, and have a few promising applicants. This won't be forever."

"Good, good." Kate paused, and cleared her throat. "Because you're going to need all your time to work on the three new commissions I have for you."

"Three!" Lynne nearly stammered. "I…from who? For what?"

"Three, yes, and one of them is quite large. A new inn is opening up out past Olga, and the owners want a tapestry for each of the guest rooms. They're having a soft opening in the fall so they want them by the end of August."

"Wow. How many rooms?"

"Fourteen."

Lynne stifled a gasp. "Fourteen," she said, wonderingly. Anything larger than a handkerchief could take her a month at least—or more, given how little time she had at the moment. "My goodness. How big do they want the pieces to be?"

"They're open to discussing it, but 'not tiny,' they said. I'm imagining something along the lines of your mid-sized landscapes. They want to put them over the heads of each bed." Kate chuckled. "They're from San Francisco, and were very careful to explain to me that when you come from earthquake country, you learn early on never to put framed pictures, or anything with glass, over a bed."

"We have earthquakes here too," Lynne said.

"Uh-huh, so I didn't argue with them, because Lynne, fourteen pieces! Well, sixteen, with the other two commissions."

"I…this is crazy, Kate. I don't have time to make sixteen new pieces. I barely have time to sleep at night. Can't you persuade them to buy works from the show?"

"Well, I can't do that."

"Why not?"

"Because the show is almost entirely sold out as well."

Lynne, stunned into silence, sat on her bed staring at her phone. "Lynne? You still there?"

She gulped, and brought the phone back up to her ear. "Yes, I'm here. Sorry. This is just…I don't know what to say."

"Say 'Wow, Kate, this is great! I'll get my needles and thread out right now!'"

Lynne laughed weakly; she felt her dinner curdle in her belly. "Oh Kate. This is crazy! I can't possibly make fourteen—sixteen—new pieces between now and the end of August."

"Well, the other two commissions don't have as big of a time crunch, although I'm sure they'd be happy getting them sooner rather than later. But the inn…"

"Wait, I have other pieces here—things I didn't choose to put in the show," Lynne suddenly remembered. "Lots of stuff! Do you want to come and see what I've got?"

"Sure, I can take a look," Kate said dubiously, "but they really do want all new pieces—and to have them go together thematically. They didn't say this, but I got the impression that this could lead to an even bigger commission—something huge for the common area, and maybe for the dining room. If the guest room pieces work out like they hope."

This was crazy. Who *were* these people? "Do you think you could explain that I just can't work that fast? I don't know any fiber artist who could do that much work in that short a time, honestly."

Kate *hmm*'d. "I suppose I could broach that with them. Explain the difference between real art and something they order in bulk from an overseas sweatshop." She paused, thinking. "So: I'll come look at what you have in your storeroom, and maybe we can get them something for their walls so they aren't bare for their opening, while you work on what they actually want."

"That would be great. I ought to—"

Her phone beeped: another call was coming in. It would be Will, to say goodnight.

"Kate, I'm getting another call. Can you come over this week-end sometime? Just text me when you can make it and we'll fig-ure it out."

"Will do. And Lynne: this is *good* news. You're on your way!"

"I know! But also, yikes!" Her phone beeped again. "Talk soon!"

"Bye!"

She'd already taken out her contacts, so she just clicked over to the incoming call by muscle memory, unable to see who it was. "Hey handsome," she purred, her voice soft and sexy. "You'll nev-er believe what Kate Evintrude had to say."

"Mom?" came Ethan's shaky voice.

Lynne blinked and sat up straighter. "Ethan! I thought you were Will."

"I, uh, gathered that."

"What's the matter? You sound—odd."

He gave an even more uncomfortable laugh than the one she'd given Kate a minute ago. "I am odd. No, I'm awful. Oh, Mom…I…can I stay with you for a little while?"

"What? Why? What's happened?"

"Marie…found some things, and she locked me out. She says we're through. I don't have anyplace else to go."

"Oh honey. Of course you can come home." She glanced at the bedside clock; it was nearly ten. "Where are you now? Do you need money for a hotel room? I can call with a credit card…"

He laughed weakly again. "I'm on the ferry. I just got in the car and drove…and, yeah. We're landing at Orcas in about, uh, ten minutes I think."

Good god. Lynne got up and started pacing around the bed-room, unable to sit still. "Okay. Wow." Poor kid. But also, more yikes! "So just come on home. We'll talk when you get here." It would have been great to have a little warning for this! Though of course, what difference would it have made if he'd told her earlier? She wasn't ever going to turn her only child away.

"Thanks, Mom. I'll see you soon."

And now her phone beeped with what had to be Will's goodnight call.

Chapter 8

LYNNE

She was up, and dressed, and sitting at the kitchen table, a pot of hot chocolate steaming on the stove, when she saw headlights in the driveway. She turned off the burner and began preparing two cups as Ethan let himself in.

"Aww," he said, seeing what she was doing.

"Come here," she said. He looked terrible: red-rimmed eyes, pale cheeks, a slight tremble.

He dropped a duffel bag on the floor and crossed the kitchen to his mother's waiting arms.

She held him for a long time, until he pulled away. "That cocoa smells good."

"It doesn't cure everything, but it's a good start."

They sat at the table together, sipping in silence. Lynne was dying to ask questions, follow up on what he'd told her. But she knew he would tell her everything he was going to in his own good time—probably sooner, if she didn't pry. So she bided her time, and looked at her sad, beloved son.

He finished his cocoa and cleared his throat, staring down into his empty cup. When he didn't say anything, Lynne finally asked, "Do you want to talk about it?"

"Yeah, but...maybe not right now. I'm pretty wiped."

"Your bed is made up, though it might be a little dusty in there."

He gave her a crooked smile. "I don't mind dust."

"And Kate Evintrude, from the gallery, is coming over this weekend sometime to look at the rest of my pieces. Other than that, your room is yours."

"Oh, right," he said. "I was wondering why that name sounded familiar." He picked up his cup and carried it to the sink. "She wants more of your work? That sounds like good news."

"It is, and it isn't." She shrugged. "I mean, it mostly is. We can talk about that too tomorrow."

He nodded sadly and grabbed his duffel bag on his way out of the kitchen.

She cleaned up the cocoa, stalling till she'd heard him finish in the bathroom and close himself into his room.

ETHAN'S DOOR WAS still closed when Lynne was ready to head to the clinic the next morning. Even when things were fine, he was not an early-to-bed, early-to-rise fellow. She left a note on the kitchen table telling him when she expected to be home, and that he should eat anything he wanted.

Work was extra busy today, and it wasn't entirely clear why. Every patient seemed to have an unusually long list of questions and concerns—and not just Lynne's patients, but the other docs' too. *I don't want to stay late, tonight of all nights,* Lynne thought, standing outside the door reading the chart for her three-fifteen patient, a young woman who had made an appointment to have a persistent rash on her elbow looked at. She was also pregnant with her fifth child.

Five kids? Did I read that right? Lynne thought, going back over the chart again. Yes, and the woman wasn't even twenty-five.

She put a professional smile on her face, knocked on the door, and went in.

The young woman was alone in the room, which wasn't unusual for a routine visit. "Hi, I'm Dr. Daniels," Lynne said, putting out her hand to shake.

"Hi." The patient was sitting on the edge of the examining table, wearing the usual gown snapped in the back. Her hand was a little clammy. "I'm Sara."

Lynne set the chart and her laptop down on the table and pulled up the stool, sitting to face Sara. "So, you're here about a rash?"

"No."

Lynne blinked; she'd been about to ask which elbow she should be looking at. "No?"

Sara gazed back at her. "There's no rash, but I couldn't make an appointment for a pregnancy checkup here, so I just put that."

"That's...because we don't do prenatal visits here. I'm not an OB/GYN; none of the providers here are."

"I couldn't take a whole day off to go off-island," Sara said, almost tonelessly. "I just need a regular checkup, okay? Everything's fine."

Lynne looked more carefully at the chart. "I do see that you're scheduled to deliver off-island, at Island Hospital in Anacortes. Is that correct?"

"Yeah."

"Does your regular obstetrician know that you're seeking care here?"

Sara shook her head. "You can just tell her, right? You put it in the computer thing and she can see it." Now she looked up at Lynne almost pleadingly; it was the first emotion she'd shown. "You're a real doctor though, right? You can just look at me and ask me questions about the baby and stuff, like the Anacortes doctor does."

Lynne stifled a sigh. She should send the woman out of here and to her regular OB. But would she go? Or would she just skip the prenatal checkup altogether? She was here now; she'd undoubtedly already coughed up her co-pay. And Lynne was, indeed, a real doctor. "I'll examine you, and put notes in your file, but I really do think your obstetrician should see you as well."

"I'll go to her for the next one," Sara said, a bit sullenly.

"Good." Lynne checked the dates in the file. "I see you're six months along. How is everything going?"

Sara shrugged. "Okay, I guess. Everything's fine, like I said."

Lynne studied her briefly. She'd do a more thorough physical examination in a minute, but even under the loose gown, she could see that Sara had gained very little weight. "Is your appetite okay?"

"Sure." She shrugged again; her bony shoulders poked the top of the gown. "I barfed a lot for the first three months, but I'm good now."

"And it's not your first rodeo."

Sarah looked confused. "Huh?"

Oh, very professional, Lynne thought. She was still off-balance. "I mean, I see in your chart that this is your fifth pregnancy. You know what to expect by now."

"Yeah."

Lynne turned around and made a note on her pad: *Previous children ok?* Then she turned back to Sara. "Have you lived on Orcas Island long?" Maybe she was new to the whole *this is only a rural clinic with limited resources* thing.

"All my life. I was born here."

"Ah. Did you deliver your other babies at the hospital in Ana-cortes?" *Please tell me you're not going to try a midwife...* Midwives were great—in places where there was a well-equipped hospital nearby, in case something went sideways.

"Yeah."

"What do you do for a living?"

"I do caregiving. Old folks, mostly. And I don't get sick leave or anything. If I don't work, I don't get paid. So I couldn't just keep going to the hospital for, like, a ten-minute appointment."

Caregiving—that's hard work, with four small children at home, and another on the way, Lynne thought. "I understand," she said. "And what does your partner do?"

"My partner?"

"Your…husband or boyfriend?"

"Oh, Henry. Construction, mostly; some car repair stuff in the winter."

"All right." Lynne made another note: *Henry?* "Do you have any specific questions or concerns you'd like to talk about before we start the physical examination?"

"No."

"Then if I could get you to lie back on the table here, and put your feet in the stirrups…"

LYNNE SAT IN the clinic's tiny breakroom after Sara's appointment, trying to shake the sense of—what was it, even? Sadness, concern, despair, imminent doom?

The woman was healthy enough, if a bit thin; the fetus appeared to be entirely healthy as well, and developing normally, from what Lynne—entirely not an obstetrician—could tell. Sara and her partner were both employed, in reasonably well-paying jobs (though a stretch for a high-cost-of-living place like Orcas). At least she was not completely blowing off her regular prenatal checkups, and she had a birthing plan in place at Island Hospital.

But…she was so young, and so…listless. And had already had so many children.

She gave no indication she didn't want another child, Lynne lectured herself. *Your choice is not everyone's choice; perhaps she has religious or familial reasons for wanting a large family.* She knew she should let it go, should get up out of this chair and in to see her next patient, already waiting in the exam room.

I need to contact her OB directly, not just send notes through the system, Lynne thought. Would that help, though? Maybe? A doctor could only do so much.

Lynne took a deep breath, ran through some exaggerated-smile exercises to shake the tension out of her face, and went to see her next patient.

SHE WORKED AS efficiently as she could and still managed to be the last one out of the clinic, though at least it was before six this time. *Heading home now*, she texted Ethan.

Cool, he wrote back, as she was getting into her car.

The smell of something cooking greeted her when she opened the front door. "It's me!" she called out, dropping her purse on the catch-all table just inside the door.

"I'm in here," he answered, from the kitchen.

Billows of steam wafted out the kitchen door. Lynne crossed the small living room and peered in. "You're cooking, wow! What are you making?"

Ethan turned and gave her a sheepish grin. "Nothing very exciting—I just felt like noodles and butter, so I'm making a lot. You can add some real food if you want."

Lynne laughed. "Noodles and butter sounds like real food to me." *Just don't let Steph—or Will!—drop in*, she thought. "I'll set the table."

Within a few minutes, Lynne and her son were stuffing their faces with classic comfort food. She'd poured them each a glass of white wine; when she'd done so, Ethan had joked that they should have vanilla ice cream for dessert, to keep in theme. She had laughed a bit too heartily at that, relieved that he wasn't in last night's gloomy funk.

"How was work?" he asked, around a mouthful.

"Good," she said. "Long, and sometimes a little challenging, but good." She took another bite of buttery salty noodles. "I really do need to retire for real, sooner or later."

"Yeah, you keep saying that."

They ate in silence for another few minutes. "How was your day?" she finally asked.

"Okay, I guess. I called Levon, but he's off-island on a job till the end of July."

Ah, so I'm your second choice for dinner, she thought. "That's good news, though, isn't it?" she asked. "Last time you saw him, you said he was basically stuck."

Ethan shrugged; the gesture reminded her painfully of pregnant Sara. "Yeah. I don't know, though; this might be more of the same."

"I guess time will tell."

"Yeah."

Silence fell again. Ethan finished his noodles, scraping his plate with the side of his fork. "Want some more?" he asked.

"No, this is plenty for me," she said.

He got up and dished himself another heaping pile of noodles and brought it back to the table. "So," he said, when he sat down again. "I know you want to hear about me and Marie."

"If you don't want to tell—"

"I do, though," he said quickly. "I mean, I just need to get it out. The longer I don't talk about it…the worse it gets."

"All right," she said, setting her fork down. "I am very curious. You guys seemed fine to me, just last month."

Ethan took a deep breath, looked her in the eye, and then dropped his gaze to his plate as he said, "I told you she found some things?"

"Yes, you said. What things?"

Another sigh. "Texts, and…panties."

Lynne blinked. "Panties?"

"Another woman's panties."

"In your apartment?"

"Yeah."

Her brain was moving slowly, because it took her altogether too long to parse what he was telling her. "Ethan, have you been cheating on Marie?"

He seemed to close in on himself even further. "God. When you put it that way…"

"Well?" she asked softly. "Is it true?"

"I didn't—I hadn't—" He shook his head, still staring at his plate. "Yes." Then he looked up at her at last. "I shouldn't have. I didn't mean to. I'd been feeling…shitty, and she'd been out so much, working and—and I don't know what."

"She does have a very demanding job," Lynne pointed out, though of course Ethan knew that better than she did.

"That's not an excuse though."

Lynne didn't bother agreeing with him. She just kept listening.

"I shouldn't have did what I did. Lena had been flirting with me at work—I've been training her, she's one of the newer artists—and she's just real easy to talk to. We worked at my place a lot—it's hard to train someone at the studio, it bothers the other artists. So one day…Marie was out, like always, and we were working at the apartment, and I was showing Lena something, and, and…" He shook his head again. "Like I said. I shouldn't have. I knew I shouldn't but I did."

"When was this?" Lynne asked.

"A few months ago. Maybe a little more."

So it had already happened when they'd been up here for her gallery opening. "And Marie just found the texts and, uh, panties now?"

Ethan looked away again. "Well, um, it kinda wasn't just the once. We kinda fell into a…thing."

"A thing." Mother and son sat looking at each other with nearly equal dismay. "Do you love this Lena? Do you love Marie?"

"I don't know, Mom!" he burst out. "I'm all mixed up. Lena is cool—she's low-key, she's easy to talk to…she's a bit younger than me though."

"How much younger?"

He shrugged. "I don't know exactly. Not a lot. In her twenties? Maybe?"

"So, maybe as much as ten years younger than you?"

"Maybe?" he said again. "I told you, I don't know. It hasn't come up."

What has *come up?* she wanted to ask, but also didn't want to ask. Since the answer obviously involved some version of *Things that involved her leaving a pair of panties behind,* Lynne didn't really want to hear the details. "Well, I know you didn't want to get kicked out of your home, but it's probably good that you're getting away from the whole mess for a little while. But what about your job? Can you work remotely from here?"

Ethan, who had just begun opening up, shrunk down into himself again. "I...don't have my job anymore." Before she could follow up, he went on. "I told you, Lena works there too. When Frank, our team lead, found out, he fired me."

"Just you?"

He nodded.

"Why you, and not her?"

"Because, um, I was her supervisor."

"Ethan!" Not just training her, but actually officially supervising her... Lynne bit her lip, forcing herself not to chastise him further. He knew he'd screwed up.

"And now I can't get unemployment, even," he said. "Because I was fired 'for cause.' And good luck getting a job anywhere else, especially in this economy. I'm not even gonna bother asking for references." He hunched his shoulders. "It's all my fault, I know, you don't have to tell me."

"I...am trying not to." She put a gentle hand on his shoulder. "I'm sorry. This is awful, all of it. I know you didn't want to... mess up like this. But—" She bit her lip again.

"But what?" he asked, when she didn't go on.

"But nothing. You're right: anything I'd say, you already know yourself."

"Yeah—me, and Marie, and Frank. And Lena, for that matter." He leaned back in his chair and blinked up at the ceiling. "I didn't mean to do this."

And yet you apparently did it again and again, she thought, struggling with her own judgmentalism. Where was her empathy? Had she never screwed up in the past? *Not like this*, she told herself. She had made mistakes, she had hurt people, she had disappointed friends and left jobs and even broken a few hearts when she was much younger, before she'd met Charles, but…she had never so thoroughly blown up her life like Ethan just had.

She looked into his face, saw the suffering there, and her heart broke for him. Ah, here came the empathy. Her own son, her poor little boy, who had lost his father before he could fully learn from him how a decent, honorable man conducted himself—her Ethan had brought an enormous amount of pain and woe into his own life, because he hadn't had the courage to confront what wasn't working. He had, as so many people seemed to do, taken the easy way out, finding comfort in another woman's arms instead of working things through with the woman he shared his life with. Lynne now felt nothing but sorrow and love for him, and a little twinge of shame: she was his mother; it had been up to her to teach him everything his father had been unable to be here for. "You can stay here as long as you need to," she told Ethan now. "I am so sorry this has happened, and I know it all feels hopeless now, but you will be able to rebuild." She gave him a small smile. "You'll probably even be able to get another job someday."

He looked back at her, a little puzzled. "You don't think I'm a complete asshole?"

"To be honest? A bit, I won't deny it. I don't entirely understand why you did what you did." She held his gaze. "But, as you said, you know you made some wrong choices here—and not just in the heat of the moment, but it sounds like more than once." He nodded glumly. "I am going to go out on a limb here, though, and say that I expect you won't make these particular wrong choices again in the future."

"Oh god no!" he blurted. "I'm…this is awful. The look on Marie's face…" He looked away. "I couldn't tell if she was going to cry or murder me. Or both." Then he added in a low voice, "I would have murdered me."

"So…" Lynne tried to parse everything he'd just told her. "Walk me through the timeline? Marie found out last night and kicked you out—so when did you get fired?"

"Well." He looked down at his plate again. "It wasn't exactly like that. She found out…well, I don't know, I think she suspected something was weird a week or so ago. She asked some questions. I don't know exactly when she took my phone and looked at the texts…but they were pretty, um, revealing."

"Ah."

"She confronted me, and I did tell her the truth. I fessed up, and I promised not to do it again, said that me and Lena were through. Marie was pissed, but also she was understanding. Sort of." He looked so hangdog, Lynne thought; Marie probably felt sorry for him. "She said we had to work this out, that it would take some time, but that we could do it."

"I see. And then what happened?"

"She, um, also told me I needed to stop working at the studio. Well, either I did or Lena did. I told her that wasn't fair to either of us, but she said she wasn't ever going to feel comfortable with me going to work there if she knew we'd see each other."

"That seems fair to me," Lynne observed. "I don't know if I'd ever be able to countenance your father continuing to work with someone he'd betrayed me with."

Ethan's face reddened. "I, jeez, I don't know. We'd actually talked about maybe being poly, sometime, in the future! Just theoretically, but, it's different these days, Mom. 'Betrayed' is…kind of an old-fashioned way of thinking about it."

Is it? she thought, but only nodded. "Whose idea was the polyamory?"

"I don't know," he said, then looked up at her. "Honest! I don't remember who brought it up first. We have these friends, Jordan and Petra, and they're poly, and they're always talking about how it's the best thing. We've had a bunch of conversations about maybe trying it out, how it might work, who we might want to hook up with, that kind of thing."

Lynne snorted softly. "There's nothing new under the sun."

"What?"

"Oh, only that back in my day, it was called swinging, and before that it was free love. It never worked out then either."

"But it is! For them, anyway; they've been together for years and years, poly the whole time, and they're so happy. Jordan has two other sweeties—one of them he's been with for, like, three years—and Petra has another serious partner. And everybody totally gets along! They all say it's the best thing ever for their communication and all."

Lynne shook her head. "That may be, but we're getting off-topic. Clearly, you and Marie are not currently polyamorous, and you broke her trust in you. So what happened about the job?"

"Yeah, well. We, uh, talked about it a while, her wanting either me or Lena to quit; and I told her that wasn't fair, it's hard to find such a good job these days, and that maybe we could be adults about this and talk it through. I offered to have Lena and Marie meet, maybe even without me, and work stuff out."

"I take it Marie didn't like that idea?"

He shook his head. "Nah. She just said she'd made her position clear, and I could take it or leave it. So I asked Lena if we could talk about this...maybe figure out who would be the one to quit. And obviously, we had to stop fooling around."

Oh, no, thought Lynne. "You invited her to your apartment to have this talk?"

He blushed even more furiously. "Yeah. Well, we needed privacy—and we'd been working together there, before, obviously. And, yeah, well, things got a little heated. And then Marie texted saying she was on her way home, and Lena had to sort of scramble out of there, and she didn't manage to grab all her clothes... When Marie found the panties, she grabbed them and ran out of there and, like, drove straight to the studio. She talked to Frank and told him everything. I followed her there, trying to get her to not do this—so Frank asked me if this was true, and I had to tell him yes. That's when he fired me.

"I was kinda pissed," he went on, mumbling to his plate. "So I stormed out of there and, I dunno, just drove around a lot till I felt like I could talk to Marie without screaming. But when I came home, she'd deadbolted the door and wouldn't let me in. She'd left my laptop and my duffel bag in the hall. Just right out there in the apartment building hallway, where anyone could have grabbed them…" He blinked, clearly seeing the scene again. "That was yesterday, around four. I took my stuff and I got in the car and I just drove to Anacortes. I couldn't get on the six-what-ever boat, so they put me in line for the later one. And, well, here I am."

He must have sat in his car at the ferry terminal for hours. Again Lynne wondered why he hadn't called her sooner, but at some level, she thought she understood. Calling her would have made it more real. Perhaps he had been sitting there waiting to wake up from the nightmare his life had become. Or trying to decide whether to turn around and drive back to Seattle. "Here you are," she said gently. "And again, you're welcome to stay here as long as you need."

"Thanks, Mom. I know this is awkward, with your new boy-friend and all…"

She smiled. "Not an issue. I only really see him on weekends anyway, since I'm so busy with work; and I'm happy to go to his place. But Kate is coming over sometime, remember."

"Right. That's no problem."

"And Sunday is soup group."

"Here?" Ethan asked. "Are you hosting?"

"No, we're having it at a new person's house: Robin, who rents Alicia the cabin she's living in now, just outside of Eastsound."

"Oh, that's cool."

"Yes. I like Robin—we play pickleball together—but I don't know her that well."

"Pickleball." Ethan grinned sadly. "The old-people sport."

"Not at all," Lynne said, serious as could be. "Talks are underway to add it as an Olympic sport, you know."

"No! You're kidding!"

She shrugged. "Just talks. But it's a very popular game, and fun too. You should come out with us sometime."

"Never, not ever, not in a million years." He was gamely holding onto that grin, though, trying to lighten the conversation by sheer force of will. "Not even if you make it a condition of my staying here."

"I would never do that."

"You better not." His grin finally gave up. With a sigh, he got up and cleared their empty plates, putting them in the sink and running water on them. "So. I didn't really do anything today, but I'm kinda beat. Is it okay if I turn in?"

"Of course. I'll get the dishes from here—such as they are."

"Thanks, Mom." He came over and gave her a hug. "I'm sorry about everything."

"I'm sorry too. You sleep well."

"You too."

After she'd put the plates, silverware, and noodle pot in the dishwasher, she refilled her wine glass and carried it into the living room, setting it on the table beside her chair but not sitting down. She went into the hallway; she could see light under Ethan's door, so he wasn't asleep yet.

Normally, now was when she'd watch TV or listen to a podcast while she worked on some stitchery, but she felt exhausted, wrung out—and, weirdly, with the request for her to produce more art, she also felt a little stymied. Blocked, even.

What she really wanted to do, she realized, was call Will.

She carried her wine back into the kitchen, wishing this room had a door that closed. Well, Ethan probably wouldn't hear her conversation, across the living room and behind his own door. Probably he'd put his earbuds in. She hoped so, anyway.

"Dr. Daniels!" Will said when he picked up. "Going to bed so soon?"

"Are we already that predictable?" Lynne asked with a laugh.

He laughed as well, easing a bit of the tension in her breast. "I like to think of it as a treasured tradition, an end-of-the-evening treat. So tell me, why the mid-evening treat?"

With a sigh, Lynne told him everything that Ethan had relayed to her. "So he'll be here for the foreseeable future," she concluded. "Which is fine with me, but I also have all this new embroidery to do—not to mention working full-time. I'm just feeling a little overwhelmed."

"I can imagine," he said, his voice warm and kind. "I'm a bit overwhelmed just hearing about it all. I wish I knew my way around a needle and thread; I'd offer to help you."

She chuckled again at this. "I would absolutely take you up on that."

"I can't do your doctoring either."

"Nope." She sipped her wine. "But you can listen to me, and sympathize, and that helps more than you know."

"I can do more than that, I hope," he said, in that low, suggestive way he had that always warmed her all the way to her toes.

She smiled. "Speaking of my doctoring, I had a patient today that I'm a bit worried about."

"Oh? Are you allowed to tell me about him or her?"

"Her," she said, "and yes, because I'm not telling you her name, or any identifying details. But I could use a bit of a sounding board, if you're willing."

"Of course."

She told him about Sara, concluding with, "I sent a note to her OB asking to talk to her on the phone, but I'm wondering if I should reach out to her former doc here as well."

Will thought a moment. "There was nothing in her chart about difficulties in her home life or anything like that?"

"No, but that doesn't mean there aren't any. Just that Kathy didn't put that info in writing." She gave a rueful chuckle. "Chart notes go straight into the patient portal these days, you know—for the patients to read. It's taught us all to become a little more circumspect."

"Hmm." After another brief pause, he added, "I'd still wait till you've talked to her OB before calling her old doc. This is the woman who left without notice, right?"

"Yeah, that's her. But she's a good person. She didn't intend to leave us in the lurch...it's just how it worked out."

Will made a dubious sound. "She should have given notice."

"Oh well." Lynne sighed. "It is what it is."

"How *are* you doing, Dr. Daniels?" Will asked, a sweet note of concern in his voice. "You sound more than just overwhelmed."

"I'm..." she started, then stopped herself before she could automatically say *I'm fine.* "I guess I feel kinda crappy about—well, all of it. I don't feel good about my doctoring today, and I really don't feel good about myself as a mother."

"What?" Will asked, clearly surprised. "You've just taken your son in when he's run into trouble. What better kind of mother can there be?"

"The kind of mother who would raise a son who wouldn't cheat on his very lovely girlfriend, for one thing." Lynne could almost taste the bitterness in her voice. "I'd like to think I taught him better than that, but evidence suggests otherwise."

"Lynne, Lynne, Lynne." Will's tone was gentle but insistent. "You did nothing wrong. You did not cheat on that girl: he did. Ethan is a grown man, and his choices were entirely his own."

"I know that, logically," she said with another sigh. "But it just feels like...I don't know. Why would he do this?"

"Only he can answer that. It does sound like he's pretty miserable. No doubt he's learned his lesson."

"I hope so."

"Come over tonight," Will said, suddenly. "Pack a bag and come stay here. Eagle Lake isn't *that* much farther from town than Deer Harbor is."

"Oh, I don't know," she said. "It's tempting..."

"I even promise I'll behave in the morning. I know you need to get in early."

She smiled even as she was shaking her head. "Ethan's pretty fragile tonight. I would feel better if I were here."

"I understand," Will said. "So when will I see you next? I know you have a busy weekend."

Should she invite him to soup group? Was it too soon? She'd been wanting to. Everyone had already met him, at Steph's dinner and a number of them at pickleball as well, but there'd been so many changes to the group already... Maybe the next time, after she saw how it went with adding Robin. "What about Friday night?" she said.

"If you can manage it, I would be delighted to see you. Shall I cook here, or do you want to go out?"

"Dinner out twice in one week?" She patted her belly, though he couldn't see it. Not that his cooking was low-calorie either. "I am always delighted to have you cook for me—and to help, if you like."

"It's actually looking like it might be barbecue weather," he said. "How do you feel about tri-tip?"

"Love it!"

"Good. It's decided. Get here as soon as you can after work on Friday, and I'll feed you well."

"Oh yes," she purred. "I trust you will."

Chapter 9

STEPH

"Alicia is so cute with those kittens," Steph told David on Monday morning, as they enjoyed a leisurely breakfast on the back patio.

Last night's soup group at Robin's had gone well, she thought; Robin was warm and friendly, and she and Alicia together had cooked a delicious Mexican tortilla soup.

"She's not really going to keep them all, is she?" David asked, sipping his latte before breaking off the corner of a third Earl Grey cream scone. "That's like a crazy cat lady starter kit."

Steph snorted with laughter. "In that tiny cabin? There's hardly room for her and one cat, let alone five!" She smiled to remember Alicia proudly showing the group her space—and the wee kittens she shared it with. Their eyes were barely open. She'd been doing research, though, learning that handling kittens from their earliest days made them much more relaxed and trusting of humans, and therefore better, happier pets, ultimately. So she had picked them all up and passed them around, insisting that everyone hold one and stroke it gently, and croon at it. "I'm sure she'll find homes for them all when they're old enough to leave their mother."

"And nobody ever reported a missing cat?" David asked. "She

doesn't look like a stray."

"No, she doesn't; but she didn't have a collar, or a chip, and none of the neighbors knew where she'd come from. She's Alicia's cat now." Steph sighed softly, gazing down into her own coffee.

When she looked up, David was studying her. "You don't want a cat, do you?"

"Oh, no!" Steph said, too fast. "No pets. We agreed."

"We did, but that was a long time ago. We've…changed rules before, you know."

She thought about it. *Did* she want a cat? She hadn't thought she wanted a child, until she thought one was coming…and then that one wasn't coming. And would never be coming, and then she'd had to figure out how she felt all over again. "I don't know," she finally said, then laughed. "Or, rather: yes, no, I don't know."

David laughed with her. "Our mantra. We should carve it on the mantelpiece."

"Under Lynne's tapestry—when we ever get it. How long is that exhibit going to be up, anyway?"

"It comes down in two weeks, as you know very well," he said, still smiling. "So, do you want to talk about a cat, or just think about it? We have time; they won't be adoptable for another few months, I'd think."

"They are awfully cute," she allowed. "But cats…they're a lot of trouble. I'm not excited about a litter box. And it would be hard for us to travel."

"We don't really travel all that much."

She nodded. "But we could. If we wanted to. And it would be more complicated if we had pets."

"There are cat-sitters in the world."

She studied his face. "Do *you* want a cat?"

"Yes—no—I don't know as well," he said easily. "I'm with you there. But I would be happy to think about it." He broke off another piece of the scone and popped it in his mouth. "I would be more inclined to adopt a cat that had been raised from birth by somebody I know and trust, who knows what she's doing, rather than getting one from the shelter, or something."

"True. I did enjoy picking them up and snuggling them and all."

"So I think we should both think about it, and when they get closer to being adoptable, we should see how we feel." He grinned at her. "I can build a spreadsheet, and we can start collecting pros and cons."

"You and your spreadsheets!" She laughed again. "Because the last one worked out so well. What we really should be working on is trying to figure out how I can actually build this business of mine—do battle against county planning and emerge victorious."

He frowned. "You haven't heard anything new since you applied for the business license?"

"No, nothing. They said it might take up to six weeks…it's only been about four by now. So, two more weeks, maybe."

"Your license will arrive on the same day as our new tapestry, I like it," he said. "That will be cause for celebration."

She raised her latte to him in a toast. "My love, *every* day is cause for celebration."

He clinked his glass against hers, his sky-blue eyes shining with love. "Every day with you is, I agree."

Aren't we sappy! she thought, unable to stop smiling now. *I wouldn't have it any other way.*

LYNNE

LAST FRIDAY NIGHT had gone so well, Lynne had eagerly agreed to a repeat. "And this time," she said after Will greeted her at the door with a delicious kiss, "I don't have to go anywhere tomorrow. We can spend the whole day in bed if we want to."

Will kissed her again, pulling her close. "Starting now?"

She gave a delighted chuckle as she dropped her overnight bag on the floor. "Of course."

Afterwards, they lay in each other's arms; he played with a lock of her hair, which both tickled and felt wonderful. "I did promise you dinner, however," Will said. "Which will be hard to cook from bed."

"That is a valid point," she said, snuggling a little closer. "I suppose we're going to get hungry sooner or later."

"And I put a bottle of the Chardonnay you like in the wine cooler."

"Ooh," she said. "Now I'm torn."

"Shall I get us each a glass and bring it back here?"

Lynne extracted herself from his arms and sat up. "That's sweet, but let's have it on the deck." She reached down to the end of the bed for her clothes, but came up with his shirt instead. Playfully, she pulled it on, buttoning two of the front buttons.

Will growled mock-hungrily. "Only if you agree to wear that."

"This and only this?" she teased.

"If I had my druthers…"

She compromised—sort of—by also finding a clean pair of panties in her overnight bag. His shirt was long enough to serve as a short dress; she felt both silly and cute in it. If she didn't look in a mirror, she could pretend she was some sexy Hollywood actress in her twenties.

Will certainly looked at her as though she was.

They clinked glasses on the deck, and sipped. "This is such good wine," she said.

He nodded. "We'll need to plan our trip to France before too long, so we can restock," he said, with an entirely straight face. "How long again until your clinic hires another doctor?"

"Your guess is as good as mine," she said, setting her wine glass on the low table in front of them and admiring the view. Light sparkled on the water as the sun lowered behind them. "We've got interviews scheduled, but you never know whether someone's coming out here because they're actually interested in the job, or whether they want to just visit Orcas Island—and maybe pick up a job offer to use as leverage with their current job."

"I would say 'how dishonest,' but I know that's the way of every industry." Will shook his head. "But that's all right: someone will come along before too long, I am sure. We don't want to travel during the high tourist season anyway. Autumn—September, early October—is a much better time for France. Fewer people, gentler weather: spring and fall are my favorite times in much of Europe, actually."

"It all sounds amazing to me."

They sipped in companionable silence for a while. When they finished their glasses, Will went inside to fetch the bottle, returning with it and a platter of sliced cheese and rolled-up salami.

"Mmm," Lynne said, popping a piece of cheese in her mouth. "Thank you."

Will refilled their glasses and sat down beside her again. "My pleasure."

She smiled over at him. "It's amazing here. *You're* amazing."

"Why, thank you, Dr. Daniels. You are a continual delight as well."

"I really do want to be able to spend more time together," she said. "It's crazy that my life got this complicated right after I met you. I used to spend nearly every evening home alone, and I was rarely at the clinic more than one or two days a week."

"When it rains, it pours," he said. "So, speaking of home alone, Ethan is all right without you this weekend?"

"Oh, yes," she said. "He's still not happy or anything, but he's a lot better than he was last week. I think it's only now really sinking in for him, that it isn't just a blip, or a bad dream. But he's also realizing that this might be an opportunity to figure out what he really wants to do. Rather than just flowing along with what was happening, letting others make his life choices for him."

"It still seems like quite an abrupt change, though," Will observed. "You liked Marie, yes?"

"I did, a lot. I *do*," she corrected herself. "And they seemed good together. She did always strike me as maybe a little more driven than he is, but not so much that they weren't compatible. If you get two people in a relationship who are both a hundred percent career-focused, then you don't have anyone to counterbalance that. To soften it." *Then you end up with two doctors marrying each other*, Lynne thought, surprising herself a little. "But I don't blame her at all for what she's doing here. He blew it, and not just once, but repeatedly—even after she'd caught him."

"Yes. He did not make the best choices, it sounds like."

"No, he did not. And I still feel responsible."

Will gave her a dismayed look. "My dear Lynne. We've talked about this, remember?"

"I know, I know…but I still think I should have taught him better than this."

He reached over and took her hand, giving it a gentle squeeze. "I am quite certain, knowing you as I do by now, that you *did* teach him better than this, in every way. But he is his own person, a grown man in his thirties—he is responsible for his own actions." He shook his head. "I am not a father, but I had a father—and a mother—and while they shaped me, that shaping only goes so far. When we launch into the world, it's all up to us. For better and for worse."

She nodded thoughtfully. "I know you're right. But still. I just hate that he's done this."

"Of course you do. But it is *not* your fault."

"Right. I will keep trying to believe that." She sighed, and added, "Poor Ethan, poor Marie. But, to your earlier question, he's okay alone—I think he's even actually happy to have the house all to himself." She turned to him. "And I know you and I talked about my maybe being able to stay here the whole weekend this time. I should be able to do that, if you still want me to."

He gave her a smoldering gaze. "I would like that very much."

"I PACKED PICKLEBALL gear," she told him the next morning, as they were cleaning up after breakfast. "We do need to practice as much as we can—the tournament's in just over a month."

"Hard to believe!" he said, drying the omelet pan and hanging it on the rack over the stove. "Do you want to do some drills, or should we try to get a foursome together?"

"I know I should drill more, but it's so boring. I'd much rather play."

"Who is likely to be available? I can call Gavin."

"He's probably free—Julie will be in her shop, though," Lynne said. It was July, so Julie worked seven days a week. Everyone had finally gotten tired of telling her she should hire some staff to help out in the high season. Apparently, crazy as it seemed, Julie was content to run her own life.

"Perhaps Alicia."

"Yeah, and if not her, then Robin. I'll try Alicia first." Lynne dried her hands and pulled out her cell phone.

No sooner had she punched Alicia's number when Will's phone rang. For a moment, she thought she'd called him by mistake, but he blanched a little when he looked at his phone. "I have to take this," he said, as Alicia answered on the other end of Lynne's line.

"Hey!" Alicia said. "What's up?"

Lynne watched as Will stepped out of the kitchen and answered his call. "Oh—hi," she said, a beat or two late. "Sorry, I was distracted for a moment."

"No problem."

"So," Lynne said, refocusing, "Will and I were wanting to put together a game of pickleball—we need to get our practice in, you know."

"I do know! I'd be happy to play. I'm just sitting here playing with kittens and avoiding working on a really dull manuscript."

Lynne laughed. "Gosh, I hate to tear you away from all that."

"Not at all! Please, get me out of this perfectly lovely but rather small cabin. Fresh air, sunshine, and exercise sound like just the thing."

Lynne put the call on speaker and opened up the Playtime Scheduler app. "It looks like the morning crew is finishing up early today. I can put us in for noon and we'll probably stand a good chance of getting a court."

"Do we need a fourth? I can see if Robin is free."

"Will is calling Gavin—I'll let you know what he says. Or you could ask her anyway and we could rotate in and out."

"I'll do that. So, we'll touch base in a few minutes, and I'll see you at noon either way."

"Perfect!" Lynne hung up and slipped her phone into her pocket as she went to find Will. He wasn't in the living room, or out on the deck. She checked his bedroom; he wasn't there either. Finally, she heard his low voice behind his closed office door.

Who had called him, that he had to have such privacy to talk to them?

Or maybe he'd just wanted to not disturb her call. Well, whatever it was, she'd know soon. She went back into the kitchen and finished the last couple of dishes.

A few minutes later, he walked back in. He was smiling, but she could see worry lines on his forehead, between his eyes.

"What is it?" she asked.

He sighed, and pulled her into a hug. "That was my caretaker, down in Scottsdale. There was a flash flood overnight, and my house sustained a great deal of damage. I'm going to need to get down there and deal with it."

"Oh no! I'm so sorry! When do you need to leave?"

He nodded, still holding her. "My travel agent was able to get me on a six o'clock flight out of SeaTac, and she managed to secure the last seat on the Kenmore plane leaving here at two twenty-five. So I'm afraid I'll need to skip pickleball. In fact I should begin packing right away."

Lynne drew back to look at him, blinking sudden tears of dismay. "This is…terrible."

"I know it is. I am truly very sorry."

"Oh no, don't apologize to me—your poor house!" She shook her head. "I wish I could come with you."

His eyes widened, and he pulled her back into an even stronger embrace. "Oh, my dear Lynne," he murmured into her hair. "You have the most generous heart of anyone I've ever known. I wish you could come with me as well, though I'm afraid the trip won't be anything like as enjoyable as our proposed jaunt through France this fall."

She snorted softly, not quite a laugh. "No, dealing with flood damage doesn't sound like wine tasting in Burgundy."

He let go of her again. "I will make it up to you. But now—"

"Yes, packing," she said, giving him a gentle push toward the bedroom. "Get going. Do you want me to drive you to the airport?"

"Thank you, my dear, but no—I'll leave my car there for my return. Which should only be a few days, I hope."

"I hope so too, but you don't know that," she said, as much to manage her own expectations as anything else. She followed him into the bedroom, where he pulled a leather grip-style bag off the top shelf of his closet and set it on the bed.

"You're right; we'll just have to take it day by day. I'll know a lot more when I get there and see it in person." He opened the middle drawer of his dresser and pulled out a few neatly folded polo shirts, laying them in the bag. "Marissa, my caretaker, was quite understandably upset—very upset. I assured her that there was nothing she could have done to prevent nature's wrath, but..." He shrugged and smiled at Lynne. "I don't have to tell you about people feeling responsible for things that are entirely out of their control."

Lynne gave him a wry smile in return. "Point taken."

"I do promise to call you every day when I am gone."

"Unless I call you first!" She turned and found her own overnight bag. "I suppose I should be packing too. Unless you want me to stay here and keep an eye on things?"

"You are more than welcome to stay here as long as you like, but I imagine you'll want to get home to your son and your other responsibilities. Don't worry about this house: it is set up to be left unoccupied for lengthy periods. I can put it to bed, so to speak, in about twenty minutes."

Lynne's phone rang; it was Alicia. "Robin's in!" she reported. "Did Will get hold of Gavin?"

"Ah," Lynne said. "He—didn't get a chance. Could you call him? Will's had a change of plans and won't be able to play."

"Oh, I'm sorry. Is everything okay?"

"I don't know—I think so, mostly. I'll tell you about it when I see you."

"All right," Alicia said, sounding concerned. "I'll see you at noon."

IT HAD BEEN just over a week since Will had left. As promised, they'd talked on the phone every day—which was nearly as much contact as she'd had with him on weekdays while he was on the island. But now it was the weekend, and she was feeling his absence keenly.

Lynne told herself that it was fine; that her life had been full and meaningful before she'd met him; that she now had lots more time to see to her other responsibilities; that he would be gone all winter anyway so she might as well get used to this... but she argued back to herself just as strenuously. Now that she remembered how delightful being in love felt, she wasn't content going back to her solo life of working, community service, and embroidery.

You can't put the genie back in the bottle.

And her life wasn't even solo; Ethan was looking like he might be putting down roots, planning to stay for a while. In an ironic twist, he'd applied for a job at Island Market—the same job his friend Levon had left to take a construction job on the mainland until at least mid-summer. Ethan was likely to get the job, too; the market, like most island businesses, was extra busy during the summer and welcomed all the help they could get.

Even disgraced tech-industry artists.

She stood in the kitchen, chopping cucumbers for one of her big salads—a Greek salad this time, since she'd found some excellent tomatoes at the farmer's market yesterday. Tonight was soup group at Matt's. He was making a variation of his meatball soup, since his dad loved it so much, but he promised that Greek salad would be great with it.

Will had told her that the damage to his house was epic; the entire downstairs floor had been flooded to a depth of several feet, and would have to be gutted to the studs and rebuilt. He was still arguing with the insurance company over the particulars. They wanted the whole house torn down and a new one built in its place, but they were offering an absurdly low valuation for the work. "And the upstairs is just fine," Will had told her. "But it won't be for long; mold will take hold if we can't get the downstairs mitigated soon. So of course, the bastards are stonewalling on authorizing what I need."

Lynne knew Will had more than enough money to pay for the work himself, but she agreed with him: what is insurance for? If he went ahead without their authorization, they would consider that a breach of their contract and would never pay up. So he and his caretaker were spending all day mopping up water, moving giant fans and dehumidifiers around, hanging sheets of plastic, and competing with other flood victims for the scarce resources available for all this work.

"I would so rather be on lovely Orcas Island, in the arms of an even lovelier lady," he'd sighed into the phone last night.

Lynne sighed now in agreement, and dropped the cucumbers into the salad bowl. She tossed them together with the tomatoes, red bell peppers, and cubes of feta cheese, then covered the bowl and started on the dressing.

Her cell phone rang while she was gathering the ingredients. She hurried into the living room, finding the phone beside her easy chair. It was Kathy, the clinic's doc who had moved off island. "Hi!" Lynne said, a little breathless.

"Hi Lynne," Kathy said. "Am I catching you in the middle of something?"

"Just making a salad dressing. Thanks for calling me back."

"Oh, you're so welcome," Kathy said. "Sorry to take so long—it's been crazy here."

"I imagine. Is it good though?"

"Oh yeah." Kathy sounded relieved and happy; her joy radiated through the phone line. "I hated running out on you guys like that, but—Lynne, this is my dream job, and I *love* the community."

"I'm glad," Lynne told her, and she really was: glad for Kathy, even if her absence was making everyone's lives here harder. Nobody should stay in a job, or on an island, where they weren't happy.

"But you wanted to know about young Sara with the many children. And I'm guessing Jennifer Torrance didn't have much to share?"

Lynne sighed. "No, almost nothing. She said she only sees Sara when she's closer to her due date—it's been the same way with the three kids before this one. She's tried pushing back, but Sara insists she can't go off island for routine checkups, when she's feeling fine. And I can hardly blame her, even if she really does need to be seeing an OB, not a general practitioner."

"I know. I agree."

"So…what's the rest of her story? Do you have any insights?"

Kathy paused a moment. "I don't, really. Your message mentioned some concerns; do you want to share them?"

"Yes—she's fairly thin, but more than that, she's listless. No affect. She doesn't seem either excited or dismayed about the coming baby; just resigned."

"Yeah. I noted that too."

"I didn't see any bruising or other signs of abuse," Lynne continued. "And I did look."

"Same." Kathy gave a frustrated exhale. "Lynne, I don't know what to tell you, except that she's been like this since she became my patient—which was only the last baby, and one checkup for this one. I asked a few probing questions, but she insists everything's fine: her home life is good, she and her partner both work hard so they're tired, but the kids are healthy, blah blah. I even left a brochure out in the exam room once about domestic violence and hotlines to call, but she ignored it."

"Huh."

"I don't think you're wrong to be concerned, but…I was kind of stymied, and I'm sensing you're there too."

"I am."

"There's really only so much we can do," Kathy said. "If she doesn't ask for help…"

Lynne sighed again. "I know. I hate this."

"Me too."

They chatted a few more minutes, and Lynne thanked her again for calling back.

"Of course," Kathy said.

"And don't be a stranger!"

"You neither!" Kathy laughed. "I'm sure your path doesn't take you to Sequim very often, but if it does…"

"I will absolutely call you!"

As she finished up the dressing, she thought more about Sara. Leaving a brochure with help hotlines hadn't been a bad idea, even if it hadn't worked the first time; maybe Lynne could dig up a few more, with information about support groups for parents and the like. Perhaps it wasn't an abuse situation per se, but depression and overwhelm.

After packing the salad up to take to soup group, she peeked in Ethan's room just in case she'd missed him coming home, but he was still out somewhere. So she left him a quick note and headed out.

"Is Will coming separately?" Matt asked, meeting her at the door and glancing behind her.

Oh, right. She'd asked everyone if it was all right to bring him this time... "He had to go home to Arizona unexpectedly," she said. "There was a flash flood and his house got damaged."

"Gosh, that's awful." Matt took the salad from her. "I was looking forward to getting to know him a little better."

"He'll be back! I'm sure he'll be here by the time of the meeting at my house."

"I hope so! What a bummer for him."

In the living room, Lynne was happy to see that Robin had come with Alicia. She was well on her way to being a nice addition to their group. Gordon, of course, was delighted by the presence of another woman; he'd even given up his usual seat in the recliner to park himself between Alicia and Robin on the sofa. Julie and Gavin watched with amusement from the other side of the room.

"Hey Lynne," Julie said, coming over to give her a hug. "Gavin told me that Will had an emergency in Arizona."

"Yes."

"Oh no, is he still not back?" Alicia asked.

"No." Lynne sighed, and told the rest of the gathered group what had happened; they all expressed their sympathy.

"I think of the desert as such a dry place," Steph said. "A flash flood seems weird."

"It's because it's so dry that it's susceptible to flash flooding," Gavin told them. "The ground is parched, hard; when too much rain comes all at once, it doesn't soak into the ground like it does here."

"It doesn't *always* soak into the ground here," Matt said wryly, coming in from the kitchen with a bowl of potato chips and onion dip.

"Right, your driveway," Lynne said, remembering that he'd had to rebuild his whole driveway a few years ago after a particularly wet winter.

"It's still hard to get used to the idea of too much water being a bad thing," Julie said. "I mean, I left California years and years ago, but I still have this reflex whenever it rains. *We need it*, I think, no matter how soggy we already are."

"Tell me about it!" Alicia laughed. "I wonder if we'll ever adapt?"

"Are all of you from California originally?" Robin asked. "I know Gavin, you came from there too."

"Not everyone!" Matt said. "I grew up in the wilds of the frozen north; Dad only moved out here after Mom died, to be closer to me."

Gordon glanced at his son, looking momentarily confused. *He does remember his wife passed, I hope?* Lynne thought. She knew his dementia was advancing. It was heartbreaking when the big memories started to fade, along with the unimportant ones.

But then Gordon nodded, and turned back to smile at Alicia.

"Oh good," Robin said. "I was worried for a minute there, that I'd accidentally joined a Californians Anonymous group instead of a soup group."

"Where are you from?" Steph asked her.

"Eastern Washington. I've never lived in any state but this fine one," Robin said. "Best state in the union!"

"It just took us all a bit longer to figure that out for ourselves," Alicia said. "But we got here eventually."

Lynne grabbed a handful of chips and dipped one in the onion dip. Yum. Sometimes the classics really *were* the best.

"Oh, I meant to get us plates for that, sorry," Matt said, leaping up to hurry back to the kitchen.

She hardly felt hungry by the time they served up their soup and gathered around the table, but somehow, she managed to dig in—as did everyone else. Matt's cooking would never win any awards for originality, but it was solid and tasty.

"So," Julie said from beside her, grinning. "I was hoping to razz you and Will about how many pledges Gavin and I have, but I guess I'll just have to razz you alone."

"Oh?" Lynne raised an eyebrow and glanced over at Gavin across the table, who was watching with a smile. "We're doing all right, actually."

"I sure hope so, because our *seventy-three* pledges are pretty impressive!"

Lynne swallowed heavily, trying to keep her surprise off her face. "Well, good for you two. How much money does that come to?"

"Nearly four thousand," Gavin reported proudly.

"They're doing great!" Alicia chimed in, from down the table.

Lynne, already feeling relieved, did some math quickly in her head. "So, mostly fifty-dollar pledges then?" She gave Julie and Gavin a sweet smile. "That's just *so* nice for you. Robin is going to be very grateful."

"Uh-oh," Julie said to Gavin. "Something tells me we're not actually in the lead…"

"Oh, I hate to brag," Lynne said, and took a dainty bite of her soup. These tiny meatballs were awfully delicious. Later maybe she'd ask Matt where they'd come from; she knew he hadn't made them from scratch, but she didn't care. Busy as she was, any shortcut in the kitchen was welcome at this point.

"All right, what have you raised?" Gavin asked.

Lynne shrugged. "We don't have nearly as many individual pledges as you guys, but I believe our total is something around… hmmm, six thousand dollars?" She looked at Alicia for confirmation.

"I think so," Alicia said, pulling out her phone and opening an app. "Oh! Another one came in earlier today; you're just over seven thousand now."

"Ooh, that's a big one," Lynne said. "Who's it from?"

Alicia frowned at her phone. "Anonymous."

"Huh." She'd have to ask Will when they talked tonight if he knew who had pledged a cool thousand bucks to their little pickleball tournament fundraiser. Had he done it himself? He'd already pledged five hundred under his own name, and another five hundred in Lynne's name, though she'd tried to talk him out of it. Only because she believed in the cause—and didn't have a spare five hundred herself that she felt comfortable pledging—had she finally relented.

"This is awesome," Alicia said, glancing over at Robin, who was deep in conversation with Gordon, with Matt watching them carefully. "A lot of teams are doing well, but you two—" she nodded at Julie and Gavin, and then at Lynne "—are the top earners."

"It looks like we've got our work cut out for us," Gavin said to Julie. "If we want to pull completely ahead of Mr. Eagle Lake and Ms. Doctor."

Julie rubbed her hands together. "Game on," she said to Lynne, who just laughed. "Anything to keep my mind off stupid McLeod and his stupid commission."

"Oh no, what now?" Lynne asked.

Julie sighed, all mirth now faded. "Nothing really—just, Leslie has been looking into whether there should even have been a whole special election for the commission. At first it looked like some chicanery had gone on, but she dug and dug and, sadly, everything appears to be legit."

"Chicanery?" Steph said, looking impressed. "There's a word you don't hear every day."

"I'm still convinced McLeod is behind all the trouble you're having with the county too," Julie said, turning to her.

Steph just shrugged. "I don't know. I mean, I guess I really do need to jump through the correct legal hoops." She smiled. "Which I'm doing. It'll be fine, eventually."

Julie started to say something else but Gavin must have nudged her under the table. She glanced at him, then returned Steph's smile with a visible effort. "Right. I'm sure you're right."

Poor Julie, Lynne thought, and took another bite of soup.

Chapter 10

LYNNE

Lynne called Will after she got home, looking forward to telling him about her evening and asking about the big new pledge, but his phone rang four times and went to voicemail. "Hey," she said after the beep, "hope it's all going all right there. I'll be up for another hour or so, at least. Okay…talk to you soon."

Ethan had been in his room with his door closed, but now she heard him come out and go into the bathroom. He returned to his room a minute later, leaving the door open.

Lynne peeked inside. "Hi."

He was lying on his bed with his door open, reading something on his phone. "Hey Mom. How was soup group?"

"It was fun. How was your evening?"

He shrugged, and dropped his phone on the bed. "It was okay. I went to the Lower, shot a little pool, watched a ball game."

"With anyone I know?"

"Nah. Not even anyone *I* know. Nice people, but…" He shrugged again. "It's not the olden days, you know?"

"I do know. This is why we make new days."

He sat up and ran his hands through his unruly hair. "Are you going to bed soon, or do you want to hang out?"

"I've just left a message for Will—he might call back anytime, so I'm definitely game for hanging out if you don't mind the interruption?"

Ethan smiled at her and got up. "Sure. I'm clear on your priorities."

She gave him a gentle swat as they left the room together. "You just hush now, child."

They sat in the living room; Ethan got himself a beer, but Lynne was done putting anything more in her belly tonight. "Even without Ron Alderson, the wine at these evenings is plenty good—and plenty plentiful," she said, chuckling.

"Glad to hear it." Ethan raised his beer can toward her in a toast.

"What ball game did you watch?" she asked. "Isn't it the All-Star break this week?"

Ethan perked up. "No—well, yes, but that was earlier this week. This was the Mariners' first series after the break, versus Houston. It was a day game but they ran it again because it was so crazy."

He proceeded to give an intricate recounting of all the reasons why this particular game was going to go down in the annals of baseball history, but Lynne wasn't entirely following what happened. She understood baseball well enough, having raised a boy who loved the game; but the nuances sometimes escaped her.

Also, she kept glancing at her phone, which kept not ringing.

"And then Cal Raleigh slammed one into the right field bleachers, and the whole stadium just *erupted*!" Ethan finished.

"Wow!" Lynne said, recognizing the name, albeit barely. "Sounds pretty impressive."

"It was!" He glanced at her and smiled. "It's okay, Mom, you don't have to pretend to care."

She shrugged. "I care about you, and the things you care about. I confess, though, I am not much following sports these days."

"But you did know it was the All-Star break."

"I'm not *completely* out of touch," she said. "I'm glad you had a fun evening. That sounds better than just 'okay.'"

"Yeah," he allowed, "the game was fun. But I couldn't help thinking about how it would have been more fun to watch it with any of the old gang. Or to watch it live, maybe." He sipped his beer. "So, yeah, okay-good, I guess."

She smiled back at him.

They stayed up another half-hour, with her phone continuing to not ring. Finally, he got up and took his empty beer can into the kitchen, rinsed it, and crushed it for the recycle bin.

"You're turning in?" she asked.

"Yeah. It's late for you too, isn't it?"

"It is. You go on and take the first crack at the bathroom; I'll give Will one more try. Maybe he had his ringer off and didn't notice my call."

Ethan nodded sympathetically and headed off into the hall.

Lynne waited till she heard the bathroom door close and the water turn on before she punched Will's number again. This time, he answered after the first ring.

"Well, hello, Dr. Daniels," he purred softly. "I was just about to call you."

"Oh good!" she said, surprised at her level of relief. "I didn't mean to keep calling, but it was getting late, and…"

"I know, I know. Hang on—I'll be right back." He set the phone down; she heard a quiet sound in the distance (a door closing?), then he picked up the phone again. "All right. I'm all yours."

"Wonderful," she purred back at him, making him laugh. "How are things going there?"

He told her about what they'd managed to get accomplished that day—just more moisture-and-mold mitigation work, since it was the weekend and there was nobody from the insurance company to fight. It sounded like a long and strenuous day, and she said so.

"It was, but we're making progress."

"And your caretaker does all this work with you? She doesn't get a weekend off?"

Will chuckled. "She's terrific: so dedicated, such a hard worker. She insists that the usual work of caretaking is so minimal, that she owes me twenty-four-seven work during a crisis. I told her that's not how it works, but—what can I say? I can certainly use the help."

"She does sound great."

"She is. So, tell me about your day. How was the soup pot-luck?"

She told him all the details. Will professed to know nothing about who might have made such a big pledge today. "It wasn't me, I promise."

"Hmm. Well, it's put us well in the lead in terms of dollars raised, but Julie and Gavin are way ahead of us on individual donors."

"The cash raised is the important part, though, isn't it?" he asked. "I don't mean to sound crass, but the whole point of this is to help make up a budgetary shortfall for Robin's center."

"True," Lynne allowed. "But since it's a community center, it seems to me that increasing awareness and the involvement of as many people as possible on the island is also a good thing."

"That's a good point. So it sounds like we're both winners."

"Everyone's winning with this." Lynne smiled. "Well, I don't want to keep you up, and I do need to get to bed myself."

"I wish I was there to tuck you in," he said softly.

"Oh, me too. Well, goodnight."

"Pleasant dreams, my dear. We'll talk tomorrow."

ON THURSDAY, WHEN Lynne arrived at the clinic, Dr. Leland Park met her in the hallway. "Do you have a minute?" he asked, nodding at his office door.

"Of course."

She sat in his guest chair as he settled in behind his desk. "Do we have a new doctor yet?" she asked, unable to resist the question. She knew he'd interviewed two candidates last week.

"Not yet, sadly. I hope I'm not scaring them off by telling them the blunt truth about what it's like to live and work here, but both applicants withdrew their applications earlier this week."

Lynne sighed. "God, I'm sorry. But you do have to be honest with them. Otherwise we'll just have another Kathy situation."

"Yes." He shook his head. "I'd rather not invest that much time training and getting to know and like someone, only to have them leave. It's better that they have a clear sense of what they're getting themselves into."

"Yeah. Well, the right candidate will come along sooner or later."

"I certainly hope so." He glanced down at his desk, at a piece of paper that Lynne couldn't see.

"So, what's up?" She didn't want to rush her boss along, but she did have a full day of patients ahead of her, and a bunch of pre-charting she hoped to do.

Leland looked back up at her. "It has come to my attention that you are involved in a fundraising event for the Junior Center—a pickleball tournament?"

"Yes, but—I'm doing that on my own time, it's not interfering with my—"

Leland laughed. "Oh! Lynne, that's not where I'm going at all. I just wanted to let you know that the word spread throughout the clinic, and all your co-workers are one hundred percent behind the effort. In fact, everyone has been mentioning it to their patients as well." He picked up the piece of paper and held it out to her, grinning. "Between your colleagues and an impressive number of patients, we've already raised nearly five thousand dollars."

Lynne took the paper and stared at it, stunned. It was a list of new donors and the amounts they'd pledged, and it was huge.

Not only that, but none of these were pledges she'd already known about. *Ooh, now we're ahead on both money* and *individual donors.* Finally she looked back up at Leland. "Wow. This is… completely unexpected! Are you sure it's kosher to hit up our patients for something like this? It sounds a little unprofessional."

"Not at all! Nobody's putting any pressure on anyone. It actually started when Jason had a flier with information about the tournament in the exam room, and a patient asked about it. Then it sort of took off from there."

"This is amazing," Lynne said, still taking it in. "Wow. I mean, just, wow."

Leland looked so pleased with himself. "I think it's a wonderful idea. I just wish I played pickleball myself—I'd love to help in a more concrete way."

"Well, I'd be happy to teach you how to play," Lynne said. "It's a lot of fun."

"Sounds like. This fellow you're partnered with, Will somebody?"

"Hamilton."

"I don't know him, I don't think. Is he a full-timer here?"

"Part-timer, and I know what you're fishing for, Leland." She smiled at him. "He's my boyfriend." What a foolish term for people in their sixties, but she didn't know a better one. They weren't really partners…not yet, anyway—at least not anywhere off the pickleball courts.

Leland's smile grew even bigger. "I had wondered. Well, congratulations, and I won't keep you any longer, but I just needed to share that with you."

"Thank you. I can't wait to tell Will about this." Then she frowned. "He's off-island right now, though, dealing with an emergency at his other home—a flood."

"I'm sorry to hear that." Leland got to his feet. "Good luck with everything, to both you and Will."

"Thank you!"

"How MUCH LONGER do you think you'll need to be down there?" Lynne asked Will that evening, hoping she didn't sound needy. But it had been nearly two weeks, and it sounded like the work was nowhere near under control.

Did he really have to be there personally for all of it? Couldn't his caretaker, well, take care of some things? Wasn't that her job?

"I really couldn't say, my dear," he said, sounding quite regretful. "We're just trying to take it day by day." He sighed. "This is certainly not how I wanted to spend my summer."

"Me neither!" She sighed back. "I'm not going to keep nagging about the tournament, but we really do need more practice together."

"I hope you're finding time to play on your own, at least," he said.

"Well, some. But it's not the same." Actually, she'd been so busy, she'd only gotten out to the courts once. And she'd kept thinking that Will would come back any day now…so it was easy to put off trying to drum up a foursome.

Lynne frowned and shifted in her chair, settling the phone more comfortably against her ear. All the warm feelings from telling him about what her colleagues had done were quashed now under her discontent—with his absence, and with her own neediness about it, despite how she was trying to hide it.

"I confess I haven't gotten out to play at all here," he said. "There's just been far too much to handle, all day every day."

"And I imagine the weather isn't really conducive to playing there in the summer."

"The weather?" Will sounded puzzled, then chuckled. "Oh, no, all the courts are indoors here. It's hardly ever good pickleball weather in the Sun Belt."

Indoor pickleball courts! What will they think of next? "Gosh," Lynne said. "I've never played indoors."

"It's one of the things—the many, many things—I love about Orcas Island: playing in the fresh air and sunshine, without getting fried like an egg."

"That's right," she said with a chuckle. "You're never here in the winter, are you."

By the time they exchanged their sweet nothings and said goodnight, Lynne was feeling better about the whole situation.

But she still wished he'd get on back up here, where he belonged.

TIME PASSED. WILL didn't come back to Orcas. The insurance company proposed another settlement, which was a little better than their original offer but still far from acceptable. The water was all cleaned up, but now the ruined carpet had to be removed before it damaged the subfloor and the foundation. Lumber and other building materials continued to be in short supply, as did labor; it had been a widespread flood, with hundreds of houses impacted. Will expressed his frustration and regret every time they talked, but reiterated that he really needed to be on site.

Then it was time for Lynne's soup group. Will had been gone nearly three weeks. He'd promised—okay, he hadn't *promised* exactly, but nearly so—that he'd be back in time for the dinner at her house, but that was tomorrow night, and he hadn't booked a flight.

He's not coming, she told herself early Saturday evening, as she sat in the living room working on a new piece: one of the commissions, at long last. *Just stop holding out hope, because you're only going to continue being disappointed.*

Ethan was out tonight, as he often was on the weekend nights. His work at the grocery store was very physical, so he came home weeknights as exhausted as Lynne was. But, being young, he bounced back for the weekends.

After their one big conversation about it, he'd been pretty closed-mouth about the situation with Marie…and Lena. Lynne didn't even know if he was communicating with either woman. He did seem to be making new local friends, which was good.

And it left her alone with her embroidery, which used to be plenty for her.

She was largely ready for her dinner tomorrow. She was going to make silky butternut squash soup, with pureed pears and a touch of curry. She'd made this years ago, when the soup group was first morphing from a book group; everyone had loved it, but then she'd kind of forgotten about it. It had taken her a while to even dig up the recipe, which was simplicity itself: cube and cook the squash and pears in chicken broth, add seasonings, blend until smooth. The others were on board to bring bread from the bakery in town, and dessert, and drinks; Steph was going to bring a rice dish that she thought would go well with the curried soup.

I really wish Will were here, Lynne thought, for the fourteen millionth time.

She glanced at her phone. It was several hours too early for their goodnight call; he was probably busy working on the house. But she missed him. Maybe she'd call him early, just to hear his voice.

Before she could talk herself out of it, she picked up the phone and touched his number.

A woman answered: "Dr. Daniels?"

"Uh...who is this?" Lynne asked.

"Marissa," she said, sounding confused. "Why is Will's doctor calling him on a weekend? Is something wrong?"

Lynne laughed. "Oh, I'm not his doctor, I'm his—" Then she caught herself, something telling her to step carefully here. *Why is Will's caretaker answering his phone and interrogating his callers?* "I'm a friend of his on Orcas."

"You are?" Marissa didn't sound confused anymore; now she was annoyed, even angry. "A *friend?*"

"Yes, a friend," Lynne said forcefully. "We're playing together in a benefit pickleball tournament in a couple of weeks...that is, if he's back here in time. May I speak with him?"

"Are you the one he talks to every evening?" Marissa asked.

Then the phone switched to speaker; Marissa's voice took on that echoey, hollow sound. "Hmm...yes, looks like you are. Interesting."

What the hell? Lynne thought. Was she scrolling through his calls? "We do speak on the phone with some frequency, yes. And I need to ask him something now. Could you please get him for me?"

"He's not available right now," Marissa snapped, taking the call back off speaker. "I'll tell him you called. Again."

Lynne heard Will's voice faintly in the background. "Is that my phone?" Even in the distance, he sounded upset.

Then it sounded like Marissa covered the phone with her hand, though not completely; Lynne could still hear her muffled voice. "Yes, and a woman is calling, a doctor, says she's your *friend.*"

"Marissa, I—" Lynne heard, and then the line went dead.

Lynne sat in her chair staring at her phone. Was that what it sounded like? If Marissa was his "caretaker," she was way overstepping her bounds.

But if she was a girlfriend...or something even more...

She certainly didn't act like a caretaker. She acted like someone who had just caught her man in a lengthy, profound deception.

Lynne set the phone down and got up, wandering into the kitchen without even being aware she was doing so. Running the past few weeks over in her mind. How Will always wanted to talk late in the evening, at their usual "goodnight time;" how he murmured softly into the phone, intimate as a kiss; how their calls always lasted no longer than fifteen minutes.

How he couldn't tell her when he was coming back.

She found herself staring out the kitchen window at her driveway, and Steph and David's house beyond, down a little path between the shrubs that divided their properties. *I don't want to be alone right now*, she thought. *Because...I think I am actually alone right now...far more alone than I had realized.*

The phone rang. It was Will—or, at least, his name appeared

on the caller ID. After a brief debate with herself, Lynne answered, tonelessly: "Hello."

"I can explain," Will said, his voice low and anxious.

"I'm not sure you need to," Lynne said. "I think I have a pretty clear idea of what just happened there…and what it means."

"It's not what you think!" he whisper-shouted. "But I can't do this now—can I call you later, at our usual time? Or maybe a little later?"

"Is Marissa your girlfriend? Your *wife*?"

"Lynne—please," he said, sounding desperate. "It's not exactly like that—"

"I'm pretty sure it is exactly like that."

"She's crazy! I don't know why she's being like this—"

Lynne had heard enough. She hung up.

He called back immediately, of course. She switched the ringer off, then left the phone on the kitchen table and went back out into the living room, and straight out the front door.

In thirty seconds, she was ringing Steph's doorbell.

"Hey," Steph said when she opened the door, with a puzzled smile. "Is everything okay?"

"Will has a girlfriend in Arizona—at least a girlfriend, maybe a wife, I don't know. She lives in his house. Oh god. I'm so *stupid*. What was I thinking? A man like that isn't going to be single. What a moron I am!"

Steph stepped aside. "Get in here." She turned and called down the hall, "David! Emergency brandy time!"

STEPH FED HER, and David plied her with brandy and then wine, and then brandy again, and then Steph fed her some more, and they both listened and made sympathetic sounds, and eventually, Lynne stopped feeling stupid and started feeling angry.

Really, really angry.

"He said he was going to take me to France!" she cried, waving her arms around. "He said he'd never met anyone like me. He said he was long divorced! He said his wife never liked to come to Orcas Island!"

"Do you think he's married to this Marissa?" Steph asked.

"I don't know! Maybe? She isn't his ex; that was Maggie." She took another sip of brandy, which David had refilled when they'd moved to the living room. "Marissa could be his fifth wife for all I know! He told me she was the caretaker! He's been lying to me since day one!"

"What an ass," David said quietly, shaking his head.

"Thank god I never said *I love you*," Lynne said. "God. I was close—I certainly have been feeling it. What a narrow escape."

"Did he..." Steph started, then frowned.

"Did he what?"

She shook her head, then continued. "If you guys weren't at the *I love you* phase yet, maybe...he didn't think he needed to commit to exclusivity?"

"Don't defend him!" Lynne nearly shouted, then added, "I'm sorry. I'm yelling at you, because the one who deserves to be yelled at isn't here. But—no, he had plenty of opportunities to tell me we weren't exclusive, if that's what we were doing. He could have called her his girlfriend, partner, side piece, whatever. He did no such thing." She took a breath. "She certainly seemed unhappy about *me* calling."

"That...does sort of look bad, yes," Steph allowed.

"Oh my god, I need to do a whole STD panel," Lynne realized, feeling her cheeks flush as she said it. "God knows who else he's been sleeping with."

Steph reached over and took her hand. "I'm so sorry."

Lynne blew out another breath, trying to get a handle on herself. "I'm sorry too. I'm ruining your evening—I just barged in here, ate half your dinner and drank most of your wine, and I didn't even ask if you had other plans."

David chuckled sympathetically. "Other than Steph wondering if she needed to redo the pilaf for tomorrow, we had no plans."

Lynne turned to Steph. "Redo the pilaf? What's wrong with it?"

"Oh David," Steph chided him, then said, "Nothing's wrong with it. I just...the flavor profile wasn't what I was envisioning, to go with sweetness and curry. I was going to freeze this batch for some other time and start over."

"You can still do that!" Lynne got to her feet, swaying only slightly as the wine and brandy made itself known to her head. "Not that you need to, on any of our accounts, but I know how you like to get your cooking right—to your own satisfaction."

"Sit, sit," Steph said, patting the sofa. "I can work on it tomorrow if I'm still unhappy with it." She shrugged. "Maybe the flavors will mellow overnight and it'll be just the thing."

"Maybe—" Lynne started, and the doorbell rang.

For a bizarre moment, she imagined it was Will, somehow magically teleported from Arizona to Orcas Island. But of course it couldn't be.

"I got it," David said, getting up.

Steph patted the sofa again, and Lynne sat back down as they both listened.

"Hey," Ethan's voice came up the hallway. "Is my mom here?"

"Oh jeez," Lynne muttered, putting her face in her hands.

Steph patted her shoulder. "It's fine."

"Mom!" Ethan cried, hurrying into the living room, David behind him. "I didn't know where the heck you'd gone!"

"I'm sorry," she said, getting up and giving her son a hug.

"I got home and your car was there but you weren't, and your phone was on the kitchen table with the sound turned off and a ton of missed calls from Will, and—I just didn't know what to think."

She squeezed him tighter, then released him. "I didn't mean to worry you. I just...I should have left a note or something, but I didn't think of it, I just rushed over here."

"Did you and Will have a fight?"

Lynne looked helplessly at Steph, then back to Ethan. "He has a girlfriend. His 'caretaker'. In Arizona."

"Oh no." Ethan looked horrified, and something else—frightened? Guilty? "Oh god, that so totally sucks." He sank into a chair. "Mom, that's the worst."

"It is," she said softly, studying her son. This must be bringing up all his own stuff, but so what, she couldn't take care of him right now.

Ethan shook his head, looking pale. "I did *not* see that coming."

"I don't imagine anyone does," Lynne said, perhaps a little more tartly than she'd intended. Ethan blanched further.

"I'll grab another snifter," David said, and headed for the kitchen.

In a few minutes, Ethan was sipping brandy, and his color had improved a bit. Lynne had refused any more; she'd already had more than was advisable, especially the night before she was hosting a dinner party.

Oh god. "Tomorrow's soup group and I'm going to have to tell everyone," she moaned. "They're all expecting him to be there."

"Do you want me to send an email around?" Steph asked. "To cancel, or just to give everyone a heads-up?"

"I don't know. I don't want to cancel."

"I can tell them what happened, at least; do you want me to tell them you don't want to talk about it?"

"I don't know," Lynne said again. She leaned her head against the back of the sofa and closed her eyes for a moment before looking back at Steph. "Honestly, you guys are my best friends— all of you. If I can't talk about it with the group, who can I talk about it with?"

"And we're a pretty supportive bunch," Steph added. "Remember how everyone rallied around Matt last fall, and Alicia now."

"True." Lynne laughed sourly. "What is it with us all these days? Is everyone's life falling apart?"

Steph and David exchanged a warm, private glance.

"Okay, not everyone," Lynne allowed. "But almost."

"Yeah," Ethan said, taking a generous sip of his brandy.

Lynne looked at her son. "Finish that up, and then we should get home. I've already imposed enough on Steph and David."

"You're fine," Steph said, but Lynne knew it was time to go. Now she wouldn't be going home to an empty house, at least.

"Go ahead and send the email around," Lynne told Steph, as they were heading to the door. "Just let everyone know what happened. But tell them I'm fine talking about it, if anyone wants to. I don't need to be tiptoed around."

"Got it." Steph hugged her at the front door as David turned on the porch light. "Take care, and call if you need anything. Or if you change your mind about canceling."

"Will do."

As Lynne and Ethan stepped out onto the porch, Steph added, "I'm glad you came over."

"I didn't even think about it," Lynne admitted. "My feet just carried me here."

"That's perfect."

Back at their house, Lynne slumped into her chair after pushing aside the unfinished embroidery piece. "I guess I should go to bed, but maybe I should drink some water first." How much wine and brandy *had* she drunk? Far more than her usual, that was for sure.

"I'll get you a glass," Ethan said, already on his way to the kitchen. He returned with a full glass in one hand and her phone in the other. "Here, and...what do you want to do with this?"

She took the water and drank it halfway down before setting it on the table beside her. "I don't know—I can't leave the ringer off or I'll miss other important calls, but I will not, I cannot, talk to that man."

"You can block his number."

Lynne looked up at her son. "Oh. That's a good idea." He started to hand her the phone, but she said, "I don't actually know how to do that, though."

"You *don't?*"

She shook her head. "It's never come up. Nobody calls me who shouldn't be calling me."

"Wow." He tapped the screen and said, "You don't even have a passcode on this phone?"

"No—I've never needed that either."

Ethan only looked mystified—bewildered at the bizarre ways of the older generation. Then he tapped a few buttons, switched the ringer on, and handed her the phone. "There you go. He's blocked, and you have a phone again."

"Thank you." She set it on the table beside her water glass. "Not that I'm ever going to need to know this, because I am never, ever speaking to that man again, but can numbers be unblocked too?"

"As easily as blocking them," Ethan assured her. "And who knows? Never say never. You might want to talk to him again, someday. If he, um, apologizes." He colored, but soldiered on. "If it was maybe a misunderstanding or something. If..."

"Never. Not if he was the last man on earth."

Ethan just nodded, and mumbled something about hitting the hay.

Chapter 11

LYNNE

Steph was the first to arrive for soup group. "David sends his love," she said, kissing Lynne's cheek, "and pleads introvertism, but says if you need him, he'll come right over."

"He doesn't need to come. I'm just happy he's willing to share you with the rest of us."

Steph chortled. "Oh, he has very little choice in the matter." She followed Lynne into the kitchen and set her rice dish, in its pretty covered casserole pan, on the stove.

"Did you redo it after all?" Lynne asked, sniffing the air. "Is that curry I detect—above and beyond what's already perfuming this kitchen?"

"You know I did," Steph said with a grin. "I finally realized I was trying to be too clever by half. If I just used the same spices as your silky butternut squash soup, but in a different medium, they'll go together beautifully without this feeling like a boring copy."

"Sounds good to me." As if Steph was capable of cooking anything boring.

Matt arrived next, bringing the loaf of hearth bread from the bakery that everyone had fallen so in love with.

"I'll toss that in the oven," Lynne said, taking the bread. "Just to warm it up."

The sound of another car in the driveway alerted Lynne to Alicia and Robin parking behind Matt's car.

"Oh crap," Lynne said, watching Alicia get out and grab a bag from the back seat. "The tournament."

"What are you going to do?" Steph asked, following her gaze.

"I don't know. I wonder if it's too late to find another partner?"

"Don't look at me," Matt said. "You want to win, don't you?" He got himself one of Ethan's cans of beer from the fridge.

Steph shrugged, and poured two glasses of wine, handing Lynne one. "Let's talk to Alicia about it. She might have ideas."

Alicia swept into the house and said, "Oh Lynne!" She pulled her into a big hug. "I'm so sorry about what happened. What a turkey. And he seemed so nice!"

"I thought so too," Lynne said wryly.

Alicia drew back and looked at her as Steph poured wine for her and Robin. "What about the tournament? You guys are our best team, you're killing it on the fundraising!"

"I know," Lynne sighed. "That's what I was going to ask you: is there anyone looking for a partner?"

Alicia frowned. "Not at this late date. I had a few people who asked me to find them someone to play with, but they're all matched up now."

"I suppose we actually have to play in order to collect the pledges," Lynne said glumly, looking at Robin.

"Hey, don't worry about me," she said bravely. "Even if your team has to drop out, we're already way ahead of where we would have been before Alicia had this awesome idea."

Lynne shook her head. "No, Alicia's right: we're the team that's raised the most, by far. We can't let you down this badly; we have to play."

There was a tap on the door, and Julie walked in; Gavin was off at another meeting tonight, and had sent his regrets. "I was in the shop all day so I only saw Steph's email before I drove over just now," Julie said, coming to Lynne for a hug. "Damn, that's bad news."

"I know. Thanks."

Julie accepted a glass of wine from Steph. "Is this all of us?"

"Yes, I think so," Lynne said. "The soup's just hanging out, and the bread is warming; we can sit down for a few minutes."

In the living room, talk returned to the tournament. Nobody would hear of Robin's protests that the Junior Center would be fine without Lynne and Will's fundraising. But no one else could think of a solution. Even if a substitute player was found at this last minute, would the pledges that had come from Will's friends—not to mention Will himself—want to support the new team? Despite all the pledges from her coworkers and patients, Lynne was still pretty sure that well over half the amount raised had come from Will's people. Maybe even three-quarters.

He did, after all, run in a different crowd than she did.

Julie finished her first glass of wine, set in on the coffee table in front of her, and turned to Lynne, holding her gaze. "You know."

"What?"

"You don't have to be speaking to somebody to play pickleball with them."

"Are you crazy?" Lynne cried. "Sure you do. Even if you just say 'I go' or 'yours,' you have to talk to them."

Julie shook her head, looking fierce. "All right, game communication only. Play with him, earn all the sweet, sweet dollars you can from all his rich-guy friends, and then never speak to him again."

"Julie. That's cold."

"I kinda like it, though," Steph said slowly.

"What?" Lynne exclaimed. "You're both crazy!" She turned to look at Alicia and Robin, sitting side by side, and then at Matt. Nobody looked even the slightest bit incredulous. Alicia was even nodding her head thoughtfully. "No!" Lynne went on. "You're *all* crazy!"

"It's actually the best way of getting back at him," Julie said.

"How in the world is that any kind of way of getting back at him, much less the best?"

Julie leaned forward, warming to her topic. "Right now, he's wronged you so badly—the slimy cheater was trying to have his cake and eat it too. And you're rightfully furious with him, and furthermore, you don't want to give him the satisfaction of letting him know how much he's hurt you."

"Okay…" Lynne nodded.

"So you don't show him that. You play with him in the tournament, you speak *only* pickleball-specific words, you guys come in second place, collect your money for the Junior Center, and you never communicate with him again after that."

"Excuse me, what?" Lynne said, now holding Julie's gaze. "*Second* place?"

Julie gave an evil laugh. "Aha! You do want to play. I can see it in your eyes."

Lynne took a big sip of her wine. "I don't think I could pull it off. I'm still too…emotional."

"This just happened yesterday," Julie argued. "The tournament's not for two weeks. Don't make any rash decisions right now; at least give it a few days."

Lynne leaned back in her chair. "Maybe."

"I don't know, I think it's brilliant," said Ethan, from the hallway door leading to his bedroom.

"I thought you'd already gone out!" Lynne said, as the other, equally surprised members of the group greeted him.

He shrugged and smiled. "I…fell asleep, actually, and now I'm not really feeling a drive to town." Looking around the room, he said, "Is it okay if I stay for soup group?"

"You want to hang around with the oldsters tonight?" Julie teased him.

"I sure do," Ethan said, and headed into the kitchen. "Hey!"

came his shout, a moment later. "Who's drinking my beer!"

Matt laughed and mimed hiding the can behind himself in his chair.

"You can call it *your* beer when you're the one buying it!" Lynne yelled at him, and everyone laughed.

STEPH OFFERED TO help stay and clean up after the meal, but Lynne shooed her home. "You've done quite enough, my friend," she told her. "Go home to your sweet man, who would never court one woman while he was living with another one. Besides, I've got my strapping young son here to help."

"No way!" the son in question protested, but he was smiling, so she didn't have to swat him with her dish towel.

"I'm glad I didn't cancel the dinner," Lynne said, a few minutes later, as they were well into the cleanup. "I feel…well, not better, entirely, but less heavy. Less hopeless."

"I'm glad." Ethan rinsed plates and bowls and loaded them into the dishwasher; Lynne moved dishes closer to the sink as he made room for them on the sideboard.

They worked quietly and efficiently for a while longer. Eventually, Ethan said, "Do you think *I'm* a slimy cheater? Trying to have my cake and eat it too?"

"What?" Lynne asked, but she was buying time. She knew exactly what he was talking about. "I mean…no, of course not. The situations are entirely different. Besides, those were Julie's words, not mine."

"But you didn't disagree with her. That is how you're feeling about Will, right?"

"I…well, yeah, kind of."

"And how are the situations different, anyway? I was living with Marie and sleeping with Lena."

"Well…" Lynne shook her head, thinking. *Because you're my son and I love you and I know you're a good person who just made a very stupid mistake* wasn't really the watertight logic that it felt like, emotionally. "Lena knew about Marie, at least. You weren't trying to lead a whole secret other life or something, and hiding it from them both."

"Does that make it better?"

Lynne put down her dish towel and sat at the kitchen table. "Sit down," she told her son. He did. "What's brought this on?"

He nearly rolled his eyes. "Duh! Man cheats; woman is righteously pissed. Isn't it obvious?" He huffed out a half-laugh. "If I were the kind of guy who thought the whole world revolved around himself, I'd think the universe had cooked this all up just to show me how it feels."

No, that would be if someone cheated on you, *silly boy,* she didn't say, because she took his point. And it was a pretty sweet and thoughtful point, if she were being honest with herself. "Well, I guess I'm glad this is making you think, at least," she said.

"Oh, I'd already been thinking."

What the heck, she was just going to ask. He wouldn't have brought it up if he weren't willing to talk about it. "So, have you talked to Marie at all?"

He shook his head. "She has my number blocked. And before you can ask: Lena does too, or at least she did the one time I tried."

Lynne just nodded.

"I try Marie every few days," Ethan went on. "But it just rings and rings, so."

"I'm sorry."

"Yeah." He glanced away, then back again. "But this really brings the whole situation into a kind of perspective for me." He looked at her, clearly weighing whether to say something more.

"Out with it," she said.

He gave a crooked smile. "Never can fool ole Mom," he muttered. "It's just, the other thing is, you don't even know exactly what's going on here. Right? It does look bad, as Steph and them all said; but you haven't let Will explain. Not that I'm saying you should, not right now!" he added quickly, putting up his hands as if warding off a blow. "But just...I think the idea of letting it all percolate for a few days isn't a bad one. And then seeing how you feel."

Lynne watched him, thinking at least as much about his unaccustomed maturity as his actual advice. Was her little boy finally growing up? Well, adversity had a way of doing that to you. "I don't really see what choice I have," she finally said. "So much of this is out of my hands. I don't even know if he is willing or able to come back to the island in time for the tournament."

"So just wait, and think about it, and see what happens next," Ethan said. "And let me know if you want me to teach you how to unblock numbers."

"Never, not ever," she said.

ON FRIDAY, A letter arrived postmarked Scottsdale. Lynne brought it into the house and set it on the kitchen table without opening it.

In the five days since soup group, Lynne had worked an extra-full week at the clinic; she had run a full STD panel on herself and it had come back clean; she had wept, raged, felt blank, felt weirdly fine, and fantasized about driving out to Eagle Lake and setting Will's house on fire; she had talked variously with Steph, Julie, and Alicia; she had finished one of her commissioned tapestries and then, unhappy with everything about it, unpicked half the stitches again; she had eaten ramen for dinner three of the five nights.

It was eight days until the pickleball tournament.

By now, she was feeling closer to the "weirdly calm" side of the equation, more often than not. In fact, the whole episode, starting from the night of her gallery opening, was starting to seem like a strange alternative reality. Maybe even a possession, a haunting: being occupied by the ghost of her teenage self. All emotion, no thought.

The love-endorphins part of the haunting had been fun. The *I'm a goddamn idiot* part, not so much.

Now she went to the fridge, pulled out a bottle of white wine, and poured herself a hearty glass. She brought the glass back to the table, sat down, and stared at the unopened letter.

She was still there a half-hour later when Ethan came home from his shift at the grocery store. "Hi Mom, how was—oh hey, what's that?" he asked, noticing the letter.

"What does it look like?" She took another sip of the wine.

Ethan picked up the letter. "You're not gonna open it?"

"I haven't decided yet. Do you think I should?"

He shrugged. "I would."

"Why?"

"I'd be curious to see what he says."

"You're the one who showed me how to block numbers on my cell phone," she pointed out.

"No but see, Mom, this is different. If he calls and you answer and listen to what he has to say, that's all in real time. You have to respond right then, or hang up on him, or whatever. With a letter, you can read his words and think about it and answer whenever—or never."

"I can also ball it up and throw it in the fireplace."

"Or that." He grinned. "But, after you read it, okay?"

"Whose side are you on here, anyway?"

"Yours!" He fiddled with the letter. "You're not the tiniest bit curious?"

"I am," she admitted. "That's why it's not already in the fireplace."

He set it back down on the table in front of her. She did not pick it up.

Ethan got himself a beer out of the fridge and sat down with her. "Do you want me to open it? Let you know if you should read it or not?"

Lynne laughed. "Ah crap, I'm a coward, aren't I?"

"You're not! You're just—being careful. Which is smart."

"Nothing about any of this is smart," she grumbled, but she picked up the letter and slit it open with the letter opener she'd been fantasizing about plunging into Will's chest. Just briefly. Tiny, teensy fantasy.

With her medical training, she'd know exactly where to plunge it.

Inside the envelope were several thick sheets of fine stationery, covered in a man's neat handwriting.

"Wow, lots of words," Ethan said, peering over her shoulder. She pulled the letter to her chest and Ethan leaned back. "Want me to give you some privacy?"

"Please."

Ethan kissed her cheek, then grabbed his beer and got up. "I'll be in my room. Holler if you want me."

She waited till she heard his door close to begin reading.

My dear Lynne,

I throw myself upon your mercy.

I have no excuse for the situation we find ourselves in, only an explanation, poor and inadequate though it may be.

When I met you for the first time last fall, on the pickleball courts, and you joined Gavin and me for beers afterward, I found you charming and interesting, and hoped vaguely that we might become friends. I left for the winter soon thereafter, and gave the whole afternoon very little further thought.

When I met you for the second time, the night of your art opening in May, the situation could not have been more different. From the moment I caught sight of you across the gallery, standing beneath your exquisite artwork, resplendent in your cornflower-blue silk and hand-embroidered blouse, I was enraptured. I had to talk to you, spend time with you. Know you.

I could not believe my luck when it seemed that you felt the same way.

I do not have to describe these past few months to you—the happiest months of my life. You were right there with me. Sometimes it felt like a dream we shared—a dream I fear I have dashed beyond repair.

Again, I have no excuse, but here is the rest of the story. I will understand if you don't want to read it, but I have to hope that you will.

I have been single a long time, as I told you when we were sharing our life histories. During the many years since Maggie and I divorced, I have on occasion dated, but I have also spent long stretches of time focused on other interests—travel, work, even pickleball. During one of those "non-romance" times, I hired Marissa to live in and caretake my Scottsdale house for the half-year I spend on Orcas. She would then move out when I returned to Arizona. It was a well-functioning business arrangement, suitable for us both.

Five or six years ago, Marissa's situation changed, and she asked me if it would be possible for her to live at my house year-round. Again, strictly business; she offered to continue to take care of the routine maintenance for a reduced salary during the months when I was in residence, and that seemed like a mutually beneficial arrangement to me, so I agreed. My house is quite large; the caretaker's apartment has its own entrance, and is fully equipped with kitchen and laundry facilities; we could continue to live here together without ever seeing each other, should we choose.

Marissa is a pleasant woman, smart and capable; I would not have hired her otherwise. We have always liked each other. After she moved here full-time, occasionally I would invite her to join me for dinner—it can be sad, cooking and eating alone. We became closer, but always respecting the employer-employee boundary.

Then one night, two winters ago, that boundary was crossed. I will tell you the details if you wish to hear them—I hereby vow never to betray your trust again, either with an outright untruth or an omission of anything you have every right to know—but I will not burden you with any knowledge you do not want to hear. Suffice it to say, our relationship shifted.

We spoke of it, briefly, at that time. She made it clear to me that she was not interested in me as a potential life partner—this was not love, nor did it look likely to become love. She is a generation younger than I am; we are very different in many ways. But she found my company agreeable, as I did hers; without speaking of it further in any detail, we shifted to what the young folks today might call a "friends with benefits" arrangement.

And that was where the situation stood when I asked you to dinner on the night of your art opening. Both before and after the shift in our status, Marissa and I rarely communicated when I was on Orcas except on matters concerning the house and its needs, or my plans for returning to Scottsdale. The vast majority of her private life is opaque to me; once you and I started seeing each other, it no more occurred to me to mention you to her than it would for me to tell her about what I had for lunch on a given day, or what my doctor said about my latest cholesterol test.

As for me telling you about her, as I am sure you are wondering right now? Yes, that was a grave, dishonest omission on my part, for which I have no excuse. Again, I throw myself on your mercy. I plead only—despite the instant spark of attraction that first night—the slow accretion of my true understanding of what I feel for you, and my long habit, as a single man, of living my life as if I had no one to answer to, no one's feelings to consider.

This was wrong. Let me be clear. And I believe I understood that it was wrong long before I began even consciously struggling with the idea that I needed to tell you about Marissa.

Sadly, by the time this struggle became fully conscious to me, it already felt far too late to tell you without hurting you deeply. Even then, however, I should have; but I was frightened of losing you, so I did not. I told myself that we had not made any commitments to one another—yes, I know that was disingenuous, that I was lying to myself as well as you in that. I told myself that I would break things off with Marissa when I returned for the winter, and then there would be nothing to tell. But what I mostly did was avoid thinking about it, because it was much more delightful to focus on you, our time together, how much I enjoyed your presence in my life, how much I craved to spend every waking minute with you.

Then came Marissa's call, and I needed to rush back down here months ahead of schedule. The work of dealing with the flood was all-encompassing, and at first neither of us made any mention of our prior arrangement. We worked every day from dawn till long past nightfall, then fell, exhausted, into our separate beds, only to get up and resume the work early the next morning.

But one night, a week or so into the crisis, she came to my bedroom. I am ashamed to tell you that I panicked, and I did not tell her that our arrangement had already changed without her knowledge; instead I told her I was tired, and that I wanted to be alone. (You may remember the night when we spoke a little later than our accustomed time.)

A more astute, or less willfully blind, man might have noticed at that point that Marissa's feelings toward me had shifted. But I was still avoiding dealing with a situation that had already gotten far out of control. At the very least, I owed her an explanation. I did not give her one. I simply continued putting her off with vague excuses.

The situation came to a head, as you know. She took my phone without my knowledge, and answered your call. Then she understood why I was avoiding our former intimacy, and she was—rightfully—hurt and angry. And you are, also rightfully, deeply hurt and angry enough to, apparently, block my number—or at least ignore my repeated phone calls, my attempts to apologize and explain myself.

And so, my dear Lynne, who I never wished to hurt in any way, the ball is in your court, so to speak. I will be returning to Orcas Island on Monday the 10th. The insurance company has, at long last, agreed to cover the full cost of the necessary repairs; my continued daily presence here is no longer necessary. I know my return is less than a week before the pickleball tournament; I would be willing, even delighted, to be your partner and follow through with our obligations. I of course wish for so much more than that, but I would entirely understand if you wished to have nothing more to do with me—either before or after the tournament.

I will say one more thing. We have not yet said "I love you" to each other, though I have certainly been feeling it and, before this incident, I imagined, hoped, prayed that you were feeling the same. So let me say it now: Lynne Daniels, I love you. I want to be with you, and you alone. If you will give me another chance, I promise never to deceive you again. My life is pale and flavorless without you. I miss you, I adore you, I love you.

I await your response.

Love, and hope,

Will

Lynne set the letter down on the kitchen table. She stared into space, letting it all percolate. Then she picked up the letter and read it again, more slowly this time.

It was a good apology, as far as it went, but she still had questions. What was going to happen with Marissa? Would he fire her—or would she quit? Was part of the reason he was coming back to the island now the fact that living with Marissa had become unpleasant, untenable?

Was any of what he had written even the truth, or was it another tale he'd constructed when his last one fell apart?

Had he truly not slept with Marissa for the entire month he'd been down there?

Did Lynne want to play in the tournament with him? She still really, really hated the idea of letting down Robin and her center, not to mention all the friends, colleagues, and patients who had pledged their support.

She thought about what Julie had suggested, and how the rest of the group had seemed to ratify the idea. Could she pull it off, though? It really wasn't in her nature to freeze out even a casual acquaintance, much less a man she cared about so intimately... perhaps even loved.

Did she love him? *I was thinking so*, whispered a small voice inside her.

Do I still? she asked that voice.

No answer.

She picked up the letter but did not read it a third time; instead, she folded it neatly and tucked it back into the envelope. Then she sipped her wine, and sat for another few minutes before getting up and going across the small house to Ethan's closed door.

He answered her soft tap by opening the door and peering out at her, love and concern on his face. "You okay?"

She smiled and nodded. "I think so."

"You want to talk about it?"

Lynne shrugged. "Not just yet. But, can you tell me how to unblock a number?"

"Mom!" he said, unable to hide his grin.

"I'm not ready to talk to him yet!" she rushed to add. "But...I want to send him a text. Let him know I got his letter."

Ethan reached out for her phone. "You can send a text without unblocking him, actually. He just won't be able to answer."

"Really?" She thought about it. "No, that feels unfair. And, I don't know, a little childish."

"You sure?" He still held her phone, waiting.

"Yes. He's coming back to Orcas on Monday. I want to let him know I'm thinking about my response, but if I wrote a letter, it wouldn't get there before he left."

"Okay." Ethan woke up her phone and turned the screen so she could see it. "So here's your blocked numbers—well, number—and you unblock it just like this." He showed her.

"That seems pretty simple."

He smiled at her. "It is."

"Thank you." She took her phone back. "I know you're curious about the letter, and I will let you read it, but…not just yet, okay?"

"Whatever you need, Mom."

She pulled her son into a hug, and held him for a long moment. "Okay," she said, releasing him. "I'm going to go send a text."

Back in the kitchen, she sat down and opened up the text function.

Will, I've read your letter. Thank you for the explanation. It has given me a lot to think about. I have unblocked your number, but please do not call me just yet. I will call you when I'm ready to talk— probably after you're back on Orcas. Lynne.

She hit *send* before she could overthink it.

Thirty seconds later, her phone chimed with a text: *Thank you. I will await your call.*

Chapter 12

LYNNE

Lynne spent all weekend redoing the commission piece. By the time she was done the second time, on Sunday evening, she still couldn't decide whether it was any good, but this time she simply set the piece aside, promising herself she would look at it when her head was clearer.

Ten minutes later, she pulled it out again, photographed it from several angles under several different lights, and sent the photos to Kate.

Oh my god, Kate texted a minute later. *That is stunning: I need to see it in person. Is it too late for me to come over? I'll bring wine.*

Lynne laughed and wrote her back. *Come on over.*

On Monday, Lynne found herself at the shared desk in the clinic's back-office area, pulling up the Kenmore Air website to find out when their scheduled flights were landing. Even if Will had left Scottsdale first thing in the morning, he still wouldn't have been able to make the morning flight. But he could conceivably catch the midday flight, and he could certainly make the four p.m. one.

You can text him and ask when he's landing, she told herself. *Or you can just finish your workday and call him then, like a grownup.*

Assuming you're ready to talk to him, that is.

She logged out of the computer and stepped into the hall to go see her next patient. *Apparently I am ready*, she thought.

THAT EVENING, HOWEVER, she found herself deep in the second-guessing once more. She still had all the same questions she'd had after reading his letter. *So call him and ask him the questions*, she told herself. *But how will I know he's telling the truth?* she countered herself. *Nothing in this or any world is certain* she answered herself, gnomically.

"Oh, for crying out loud," she said, and picked up her phone.

He answered after the first ring. "Lynne. Oh, Lynne."

"Hello, Will." She tried to keep her voice steady, but his voice did things to her…unfair things, sweet things, cruel things. "Are you home? On Orcas, I mean?"

"I am home. On Orcas." He drew a breath. "I never realized how much this house—and your presence in this house—had come to feel like home to me."

She cleared her throat. "Um. Well."

"Forgive me," he rushed to add. "I do *not* mean to presume. I just wanted to tell you…before I met you, the house in Scottsdale always felt like my real home, and Eagle Lake my vacation home…yet that switched, this summer, without my even noticing it. I did not say that in the letter—it was already far too long—but I wanted you to know that."

"Okay. Thank you." She tried to recenter herself. "It…it was a very nice letter. Thank you for writing it, and sending it."

"I didn't know what else to do. My phone communications were…not getting through, and I could not let what we had just slip away without at least trying to fight for us."

"Yes. I did block your number. It's unblocked now."

"Yes. You mentioned that," he said, his voice soft and kind.

"Right." She took another breath. "So—I'm still processing everything. I will have questions, and everything is going to take time, but, well, we only have a few days until the tournament, and I really *do* want us to play in it—we've made so many commitments and raised so much money and I don't want to let Robin down, or anyone who contributed—so, let's play, even if everything is still unresolved, and then over time we can…continue to talk." Whew. "I mean. If that works for you."

"Oh Lynne," he said, sounding so full of love that she thought her heart would crack open right then and there. "Of course that works for me. Anything you need."

"Okay." She nodded, though she was alone at the kitchen table. "So."

"So," he echoed her. "It's Monday; the tournament starts Saturday. Do we want to practice together at all this week? Make sure we're ready? I know you must have a busy schedule at the clinic."

"I do, but yes, we should practice." She thought a moment. "I can see if Julie and Gavin are up for a game after work on Wednesday maybe?"

"That works for me," Will said. "If you'd prefer, I could call Gavin and set up the game."

She almost insisted that she could do it, but then caught herself and said, "You know what? That would be great. Thank you."

"What time? It stays light till all hours, as you know."

"Six should be safe. I can do any remaining charting after we play."

"Sounds good." He paused a moment, and then added, "Shall I text you after I've gotten hold of him?"

"Yes, please."

"Will do." After an even shorter pause, he said, "Thank you, Lynne. For giving me another chance."

"Well, I don't—"

"I don't mean at our romance, though I certainly have hopes for that. I just mean reading my letter. Talking to me." He chuckled. "Playing pickleball with me."

"Okay, right, that." She smiled. "Well, of course."

"No, *not* of course," he insisted. "You would be well within your rights to never speak to me again. I didn't mean to deceive you, but I did, and I let it go on far too long. So, thank you."

"You're welcome," she said, and meant it.

THIRTY MINUTES LATER, she was cooking dinner for herself and Ethan when her phone chimed with a text. Thinking it was Will with news on whether Wednesday evening's game was on or not, she picked it up.

But it was Julie. *What the ever-loving what? Did I miss something? Are you guys talking to each other? What happened?*

Lynne started to type out an answer, but then set the phone down, turned off the burner, and sat down and called Julie. "I'm taking your advice," she told her.

"My advice was to play in the tournament with him while not speaking a non-pickleball-specific word! This, this, this *practice session*—this feels a lot like mission creep to me! Again: what did I miss?"

"Well, after you and I talked that last time, I came home and found that he'd written me a letter…"

"Tell me everything."

LYNNE CHANGED INTO her pickleball clothes in the staff bathroom at the clinic, annoyed at how nervous she felt. *The ball is in your court*, she kept telling herself, like a mantra. She had only agreed to play in the tournament with him, and to this one practice session. *You don't need to see him ever again after this weekend if you don't want to,* she told herself. *He has no power here.*

Oh, but he did. Somehow, without her ever becoming quite aware of it, Will Hamilton had gotten all the way into her heart…the very heart that was galloping with excitement, and nerves, and anticipation, and trepidation, as she got ready to see him again.

And anger. Still plenty of anger.

She'd talked about all this with Julie on the phone the other night. "How *old* am I?" Lynne had laughed, when she'd confessed how jumbled-up she was.

"That's what I kept asking myself when Gavin and I were working ourselves out!" Julie had told her. "I think that's a good sign."

"So you think I should give him another chance after all?" Lynne had asked. "Not just confine him to pickleball-only words and then never speak to him again?"

"Now, I didn't say that. The man still definitely has some 'splainin' to do. All I'm saying is, he's made a good start on that."

Lynne closed the toilet lid and sat down on the seat to tie her shoes. Then she stood up, studied herself in the mirror, sighed, and headed out to her car.

It felt a little ridiculous to drive the equivalent of one city block from the clinic to the pickleball courts, but she didn't want to have to walk back and get her car after they were done playing.

Actually, if she were being entirely honest with herself…she also wanted the ability to quickly leave, should she feel the need to.

She pulled in and parked next to Gavin's car. Will hadn't arrived yet: good, she could continue to collect herself. Julie and Gavin were warming up on court one, Julie aiming drop shots across the net. Lynne got out of her car and got her gear bag from the trunk.

"Hey!" Julie, called, waving with her paddle. "Come on in."

Lynne joined them, taking the side next to Julie. "Do you want to—oh, here he comes," Gavin said, as Will pulled in.

Lynne turned to Julie, apparently with a panicked expression, because Julie said, "You've got this."

"Thanks." She gave her friend a quick grateful smile as Will got out of his car, looking altogether too good to be real…or fair.

Julie patted Lynne's arm and then jogged over to the other side of the net, joining Gavin as Will entered the courts.

He had eyes only for Lynne. "Thank you," he said quietly, as he walked up and held out his paddle. "It's so good to see you. You look beautiful."

Lynne touched his paddle gently with hers and nodded. "I…"

"I know," he said at once. "But I promised to be entirely honest with you, so I couldn't not say it."

She looked up at him as he flashed his adorable smile. "Um." She cleared her throat. "So, do you need to warm up, or should we play?"

Will chuckled, and then finally glanced across the net, to where Julie and Gavin were pretending not to avidly watch this awkward, uncertain reunion. "Hi, you guys," Will said. "Thanks for coming out."

"Our pleasure," Gavin said. Julie only nodded at him, looking fierce and formidable. Lynne felt a surge of affection for her friend. Whatever happened, Julie had her back.

"I'm ready to play," Will said.

"Great!" Julie said. "Let's do this."

Will and Lynne were on the Bainbridge Island side of the courts, so they served first. Knowing Will preferred to be the second server, Lynne took the ball. Keeping her focus completely on the game and *not* the gorgeous man three feet to her left, she stepped behind the baseline, called out "Zero-zero-start!" and gave the ball a whack.

Gavin returned it deep, but Lynne was ready for that. She got behind the ball, planted her feet, and dropped it just over the net on Julie's side. Julie never had a chance.

Lynne and Will switched sides. "Good one," he murmured to her as they passed each other.

She only nodded, clinging fervently to her focus. *I can't look at him*, she thought. *I'll lose it.* "One-zero-start," she called, and served.

And suddenly, they were up five points, and Julie was starting to look worried. On the next rally, one of Will's shots set Julie up for the kill. She took full advantage.

"Ouch!" Lynne said, reaching down to rub her shin where the ball had stung her on its way by. "Good shot."

Julie grinned at her. "Can't let you pickle us."

Gavin and Julie managed to score three points before handing the serve back. "At last," Will said, taking the ball. "I wondered if I was going to get to serve at all this game." He flashed Lynne a smile as he stepped behind the baseline. "Not that we need me, the way you're playing."

She found herself giving him a tentative smile back. "Thanks."

He just nodded before calling out the score.

They played four games before Gavin wiped his brow and said, "If we all play like this during the tournament, scouts are going to be fighting over us. We're all going to get sponsorship deals! Invitations to play in the Olympics!"

Lynne laughed. "I'd like to see that!" But still, she was pleased—because though of course he was exaggerating absurdly, he also wasn't wrong. Something about being so wound up must have kicked her into a higher gear. She had never played so consistently well, making shots she'd been sure were past her reach, her focus laser-sharp on her game.

And, she had to admit, she and Will did play exceptionally together. Whatever was wrong between them, it did not touch their rapport on the court.

Each team had taken two games. Under normal circumstances, this would have been a fun evening, full of teasing jibes and relaxed banter. But Lynne felt suddenly exhausted, even though they'd played just over an hour.

"I'm done," Julie said, echoing Lynne's thoughts. She took a big drink from her refillable water bottle. "I didn't get much lunch today—I need a big dinner, stat."

"I can help with that," Gavin said, snaking his arm around her waist. "Mijitas maybe?"

Lynne glanced over at Will, who was looking at her politely

but keenly, a question in his eyes. "Not tonight." She shook her head. "This was nice, but...I can't. I'm going to go home."

"I understand," he said at once. "I'll just say, again, thank you for today—for even giving me this much of a chance."

"You're welcome," she said.

Everyone walked out to their cars together. "Should we do this again later this week, or are we good, do you think?" Gavin asked.

Julie shrugged and looked at Lynne.

"I have a crazy schedule in the clinic," she said, before she could let herself second-guess it. "I think I'd be better served by getting enough rest."

Julie nodded enthusiastically. "Me too—I can't believe the tournament has to happen during the busiest time of year. I don't think I got to sit down all day."

"It's probably smart not to jinx ourselves," Gavin said. "We should take this excellent practice session as a clear sign that we are more than ready."

"Then we shall all meet again on the field of battle," Will said, smiling at everyone, his gaze lingering on Lynne before he stepped over to his car. "And may the best team win."

As she drove home, Lynne replayed the session in her mind. Will had looked good—very, very good. Tanned and healthy, so obviously his time in Arizona had not been spent entirely indoors. He had not overstepped any boundaries, except maybe that little comment right at first, about her looking beautiful. Then again, she hadn't exactly announced any boundaries: just that she wasn't ready to talk about their issues yet.

For the most part, though, he was clearly following her lead on this.

Which was good. Right? *Yes, right*, she told herself. He'd made his statement—page after page of handwritten words.

Now it was up to Lynne to figure out how to respond.

What do I even want? she asked herself as she drove out Crow Valley Road toward West Sound. That was easy: she wanted his betrayal, his dishonesty, to have never happened. She wanted to return to their earlier, more innocent days, when they were just falling in love with each other, and nobody else was inside their relationship. She wanted their connection to grow as effortlessly and delightfully as it had before he went away, leading to a happily-ever-after.

Lynne sighed. *What do I want that is actually possible?*

But she was not any closer to knowing the answer to that than she had been before she'd seen him this evening.

SATURDAY DAWNED BRIGHT and clear. The gusty winds that had blown through the islands on Thursday and Friday had died down; the day promised to be exceedingly pleasant. It might even get hot in the afternoon, so it was good that play was set to begin at eight a.m.

Lynne was more of a lark than an owl, but this was early even for her, especially on a weekend. She'd had to set her alarm for six, in order to eat (and digest) a decent breakfast with sufficient caffeine, and drive all the way to town…leaving enough time before she set out to dither about what to wear, like a teenager.

Now she stood by the registration table in front of the courts, studying the tournament bracket for their division—the somewhat absurdly named Advanced Recreational. All four courts were filled with players warming up; people in pickleball gear and holding paddles milled around the crowded parking lot, drinking coffee, greeting each other, and stretching.

"We're seeded," came Will's voice in her ear.

Startled, Lynne turned; Will smiled and took a half-step back.

"I'm sorry," he went on, "I didn't mean to scare you."

"That's all right—I was just trying to figure out how it works. Last time I played in a tournament, it was round-robin, and we just waited to be called for our next games. This looks more like some sort of basketball thing."

"Apparently, they had enough sign-ups to do a real bracket,"

Will said. "That should make for more orderly play, and a better outcome."

Lynne looked back at the diagram. "What does seeded mean?"

Will was still smiling. "Not much of a sports fan, then?"

"You know I'm not." Even this oblique reminder of all the time they'd spent together this spring and summer made her wince. She coughed to cover her discomfort.

Will pointed at their names, at the top of the chart. "That's us, and our first match is against Ellen and Sam Howard, at eight."

"I see that."

Will nodded, and moved his finger down to the very bottom of the chart. "Julie and Gavin are down here, and they'll play at the same time, against Ken Jones and Sarabeth Maravillosa."

"Right...?"

"So, somebody has been very clever about putting this together. When we win our first match—"

Lynne chuckled when he said *win*.

"—we'll advance and play the winner of this match here, at nine." He pointed. "Same with Gavin and Julie, down there. Which means—"

"We won't meet them till the finals," Lynne said, suddenly getting it.

"Assuming they make it to the finals," Will said with a wicked smile, and a little too loudly, the reason for which was apparent a moment later.

"Assuming *you* make it to the finals," Julie said, swaggering up to join them in studying the bracket, Gavin just behind her.

"Which aren't even till tomorrow!" Lynne realized, looking closer at the sheet. Five matches would be played today, with the remaining three on Sunday.

"You didn't realize this tournament went all weekend?" Gavin asked, looking worried.

"I did," Lynne said, "but—"

"Of course it ends at any time for *losing teams*!" Julie said, with rather too much glee.

Lynne was saved from having to come up with a clever riposte by the public address system crackling to life. "Good morning, Orcas Island picklers!" Alicia's voice boomed over the loudspeaker, ending in a feedback screech. "Oops, sorry."

Glancing around, Lynne spotted Alicia at the other end of the row of long tables set against the tennis court fence. She was holding a microphone away from herself and talking to a young man who was helping her adjust something.

"Okay, that's better," Alicia said a minute later, at a much more tolerable volume. "Welcome, everyone, to the First Annual Orcas Island Invitational Benefit Pickleball Tournament! We have an amazing lineup of talent here today…"

Alicia spoke for a few minutes, thanking all the individual donors as well as the business sponsors, explaining how the order of play would go as well as the special tournament rules: matches would be best two out of three games, with only the tie-breaker needing to be won by two points. She pointed out the snack table, the porta-potties, the raffle table, and the first-aid van. "And sponsorships are not closed!" she finished, grinning at the large and still-growing crowd of players and audience members. "Anyone who wants to pledge some more, come see me anytime!"

"Shameless!" someone called out from the audience, laughing.

"You bet I am!" Alicia called back to them. "I am shamelessly delighted to be a part of raising so much money for such a worthy cause. Let's hear it for the Junior Center!" Loud applause and cheers rang out. Standing near Alicia, Robin shook her head, but she was grinning.

"All right!" Alicia said, after the accolades had died down. "Unless anyone has any questions…?"

A murmur of *No, not me* rolled through the crowd.

"Then let's get started!"

"I think we're on court six," Will said to Lynne.

"Court six? But there's only—oh, the tennis courts."

They headed over to the two tennis courts, which had been taped to become four pickleball courts, with temporary nets on flimsy little stands. "Ugh, this is confusing," Lynne said, looking at the jumble of painted and taped lines, trying to visualize where they were supposed to play.

"It'll all make sense soon enough," Will said. "At least we're all in the same boat."

Their opponents showed up then, and after introductions and polite paddle-tapping, the match began.

It was a little before eleven, and Lynne and Will had won their first three matches. Not handily, but decisively enough. Their third match had gone quickly; afterwards, Lynne had found the porta-potties, and then took a seat in the stands to watch an Advanced match on court one. She could see Julie and Gavin playing a match over on court four, but there was no seating there, and she could use the rest.

She sipped her water, watching the experts play. Gosh, they were good. It was fun to watch them, how fast they moved, how close to the kitchen line they played. How quickly they reacted.

Will walked over from the snack table, munching on a protein bar. He held up another one: "For you, if you want it."

"No thanks," she said, but gave him a smile. "I don't want to put anything in my belly until we're done for the day."

Will nodded, and glanced at the empty spot next to her. "May I?"

I should tell him no, she thought, but found herself saying, "Sure." *What the heck,* she told herself. *I'm not Julie.*

"I can already smell the hot dogs grilling," Will said.

"Me too, and it's driving me crazy," she admitted, apparently completely incapable of avoiding un-pickleball-related conversation. But maybe what and when to eat counted? She sighed, and took another sip of her water.

Beside her, Will shifted on the bench. "It's going well, so far," he tried. "You're playing at least as well as you did on Wednesday."

"Yep," she said, and after a slightly too long moment as she realized how curt that sounded, she added, "So are you."

"Thank you."

The game they were watching ended, with the younger couple victorious. Everyone tapped paddles across the net, then they switched sides.

"I guess that wasn't the match, then?" Will asked.

"It's going to game three," said a white-haired woman sitting on the other side of Lynne. "Horace and Louise took the first game."

"Good for them." Will smiled at her. "Us old folks have to stick together, show those young upstarts who's boss."

"Those young upstarts are their kids, actually," the woman told him.

Now that she knew that, Lynne could see the family resemblance. "Oh, that's great."

The tie-breaker game started up, and Lynne leaned forward to watch, both because it was even more interesting knowing that the players were all family, and to avoid having to look at the gorgeous, impossible man next to her. He even smelled good, after nearly three hours of exercise.

Which only reminded her of how he smelled after other forms of exertion they'd enjoyed together...

She stifled a sigh and stole a glance at him. He was finishing his energy bar and apparently fully absorbed in watching the match before them.

After the younger couple took a quick five-oh lead, Will said quietly, "No matter what the future may hold, I am happy to be here with you right now."

Lynne turned to look at him; he gave an embarrassed smile.

"I'm sorry," he said. "I know this isn't the time or the place—"

"It's okay," she said. "I'm just...I'm still pretty mixed up about everything."

"If I can help in any way…answer any questions…"

"What's happening with Marissa?" she blurted, to her own horror. "I mean right now. Does she still work for you, is she still in your house?" She covered her mouth with her hand to stop herself from going on.

Will took a breath and held Lynne's gaze. "The question of her employment is undecided. Our more intimate arrangement is over—definitively, permanently."

Lynne must have looked skeptical, because he went on.

"No matter what happens between you and me, it is clear to me—and to Marissa as well, I believe—that that arrangement was untenable. It was unprofessional, and a mistake. Even if I hadn't met you, it was inappropriate for me to cross that boundary with an employee."

"Okay," Lynne said. "Is she…" She stopped, unsure what she even wanted to know at this point. Was Marissa angry? Clearly—that had been plain when Lynne had spoken to her on the phone. Was she heartbroken? "I don't actually want to know any details, really, except—you said in your letter that it seemed that her feelings had changed, and, well…"

Will smiled. "Will she hunt you down and threaten to kill your pets? No, you're safe."

Lynne felt her eyes widen. "That's not what I meant! I don't even have any pets." *Jeez, he knows that, it was a joke*, she told herself. "I was thinking," she hurried on, "that if she'd fallen in love with you, she might be really hurting right now."

The smile didn't leave Will's face, but its texture and depth changed. Suddenly, Lynne found herself looking into the face of the man she'd fallen in love with: that tender, thoughtful, kind and generous man. "Oh, Dr. Daniels…" he murmured, reaching out to touch her arm briefly before drawing his hand back. "Only you would be concerned for the feelings of a romantic rival."

It should have sounded diminishing, even mocking. It did not.

It sounded awed, loving. Humbled. It sounded like something a man who really knew her—and loved everything about her—would say.

He's always been good at saying the right thing, a tiny, cynical voice inside her head reminded her. *Maybe even too good. Don't let him muddle you.*

"*Is* she a romantic rival?" she asked.

Will looked suddenly horrified. "No! My god, I didn't mean it that way. I only—"

"I know," she said. "I did read your letter—more than once. I just…you really didn't sleep with her, your whole time down there?"

"I did not." He held her gaze. "I was not even tempted. When she came to my room, I…I could only see your face." He shook his head. "I told you I'd known this was all wrong—my keeping her a secret from you—but that I wasn't letting myself think about it. That was the moment when the scales fully fell away from my eyes, and I realized how miserably, how horribly I'd screwed up." He took a breath. "I even promised myself I would tell you everything once I saw you again, but then events overtook me and, well, here we are."

She looked into his eyes, their jade flecks shining. *I want to believe him*, she thought. *I really do.*

Around them, the bleachers erupted in cheers and whoops. "All right!" the woman next to Lynne shouted. "Go, Louise! *Get 'em!*"

Lynne and Will both turned their attention back to the game as the older woman called out the score: "Ten-five-one!" She wound up and served the ball low and fast across the net to her son.

Who smacked the ball straight into the net! "Aww jeez!" the young man cried, throwing his arms into the air. His sister dropped her paddle to the ground, then quickly picked it back up and jogged to the net, where she and her brother tapped their parents' paddles.

"What a comeback!" the woman next to Lynne said. "That was incredible!"

Lynne smiled at her, embarrassed. "I guess I missed it." How long had she and Will been talking? It had seemed like only a few minutes.

"Horace and Louise *dominated*! They won the serve back and never looked back! They just *mowed those kids down!*"

The woman looked altogether too happy about this, Lynne thought. *Sports fans are weird.*

"How DID IT go?" Ethan asked, when Lynne dragged herself into the house at five that evening.

She smiled through her exhaustion. "We won all our matches. So that means you get to come see us play tomorrow."

"All right!" He grinned and patted her on the shoulder. "I knew you would."

He'd worked all day at the grocery store, only getting home a few minutes before she did, but he'd already started a pot of water boiling for pasta, she was happy to see.

Lynne dropped into a chair at the table, too tired to even get herself something to drink.

Ethan turned from the stove and looked at her. "Water, or wine? Or both?"

"Water first. Then wine."

He got her full glasses of each and set them on the table. "How did the rest of it go?" he asked, delicately yet pointedly.

Lynne drank the entire glass of water and then took a sip of the cool, crisp wine. "It went...all right, I think. Will and I talked some."

"Oh?" Ethan sat down across from her.

"He's broken it off with Marissa—and he promises they didn't sleep together while he was down there—but she still works for him, for now."

"How do you feel about that?"

"I don't know. It's not my place to tell him to fire somebody he had working for him long before we ever met—"

"No, Mom, you totally can tell him that," Ethan insisted. "You can set any condition you need that makes you feel more comfortable with him, *if* you're considering getting back together at all." He peered at her. "Are you? Considering it, I mean?"

"I don't know." She took a bigger sip of her wine. "I mean, I was quite certain I never wanted to lay eyes on him again, but…" She shrugged. "He seems…open, honest. Contrite. My heart wants to believe in him, but my brain is still telling me to be careful. The bottom line is, I'm confused."

"Tell me more, while I cook." Ethan got up and opened the fridge, pulling out a bunch of vegetables and some chicken. "I mean," he added, glancing over his shoulder, "if you want to."

Lynne chuckled. "I do have girlfriends, you know."

"I do know, and what advice have they given you? To basically throw the guy off a bridge without even giving him the opportunity to make it up to you, to prove he's changed his ways!"

Lynne studied her son, who had grabbed the chef's knife. As he chopped up an onion, she said, "Well, you do have some sympathy for his position."

His shoulders rose a bit as he continued chopping. "Of course I do. But Mom?" Now he turned around, setting the knife on the cutting board and meeting her gaze. "What I really see is that you guys had—have—something real. You love him." Her mouth fell open, but before she could say anything, he went on. "I've known you longer than any of your girlfriends here, and I've never seen you like this before. After Dad died, and you eventually started having the occasional boyfriend…some of those guys were nice and all—I thought Terry was actually pretty great—but you never loved any of them. You and those guys had fun together, but it was so obvious they weren't Dad, none of them. I mean, that's what I thought then: you'd had your one great love of your life, and now he was gone, and that was that. I was actually kind of relieved when you stopped dating."

"I...didn't realize you paid that much attention to my dating life," Lynne said.

Ethan laughed. "How could I not? You're my mom!" He shook his head, smiling. "I want you to be happy. I always have, even when I was being a little shit as a teenager."

"You were never a little shit!" Lynne protested.

"Oh, yes I was. But this isn't about me: it's about you. When you got so serious so fast with Will, I was kinda worried. I told Marie—" He cut off abruptly, glancing away for a moment, his eyes hooded. "When you told me about how much time you were spending with Will, I thought, What's his deal, what does he want?"

"I thought you liked him—you met him that first night at my opening, same as I did, more or less. You and Marie were both thrilled that I'd had a date."

He gave her a pained smile. "Yeah, at first it just seemed sweet and fun, after you'd been alone so long; but then, like I said— you really seemed to fall for him fast. I wasn't sure that was a good idea. But as the time wore on...it was just more and more obvious that it was real, and good. And mutual. So I was coming around to seeing this as a good thing. I'd never seen you this happy before." He shook his head again. "Now, he may be a lying piece of crap, and maybe even this whole handwritten letter-apology-good behavior thing is some sort of game...but what if it's not? What if he genuinely loves you, and he made one really big stupid mistake, and he's going to make sure this never happens again, and you guys live happily ever after?"

Lynne snorted softly. "Is that what you think is going to happen?"

"I don't know!" Ethan tossed his arms in the air. "But you won't either if you don't give him another chance." He turned back to the cutting board and picked up the knife again. "And that's all I'm gonna say. It's your life, and you get to be the decider about it."

"That's true," she agreed. "He certainly does seem sincere," she added, more softly.

"Hmm," Ethan said, still chopping.

She picked up her wine glass, surprised to see that it was nearly empty. She set it back down and got up to refill her water glass. "I'll…think about everything you've said." And she would, she realized. It was rather sweet that her son gave her love life this much thought.

"Good. I love you, Mom."

"I love you too." She looked at the great collection of veggies overflowing the cutting board. This was going to be quite the dish. "Do you need any help with that?"

"No, I've got this. You relax—you've got another big day tomorrow."

She wrapped her arms around her son and pulled him close in a hug. "Thank you. Come get me in the living room when it's ready."

"You bet."

He wouldn't let her clean up after dinner, either. "Just go to bed, you're exhausted."

"I'm okay—and I'm too full to lie down right now," she said. "I'll work some more on my needlepoint while I digest."

Fifteen minutes later, she heard the sound of the dishwasher starting. "Thank you for all that," she told Ethan as he stepped into the living room.

"My pleasure."

"Do you want to watch something on TV together?" she asked, setting down her fabric.

"No thanks, I've got some things I want to do in there." He nodded toward his bedroom. "We should probably both turn in early."

"That's fine. Sleep well."

"You too."

A minute later, however, he was back. "Mom?"

"Yes?"

"Do we have any blank paper?"

"What kind?"

"Um, like, stationery?"

"We should; you can check in my desk."

He crossed the room to her small desk under the window and began looking through drawers.

"What do you need stationery for?" she asked, though she was pretty sure she knew.

He turned around to look at her, his cheeks flushed. "I'm, um, going to write Marie a letter."

"Ah." Lynne smiled. "That's a nice idea."

He shrugged. "Should have done it weeks ago, but I'm slow."

"Let me know if you'd like me to look it over before you send it."

"I will." His blush deepened. "Thanks, Mom."

"You're welcome. Good luck with your letter."

"Thanks," he mumbled.

Chapter 13

LYNNE

Ethan wasn't up yet Sunday morning when Lynne had to leave for the courts, so she wasn't able to ask him about his letter...or anything else. But she smiled again to think of it.

Men writing heartfelt letters to try and win their ladies back, she thought, as she got into her car. *What will they think of next?*

The courts, and the parking lots around them, were even more packed than yesterday. People had set up folding chairs to either side of the bleachers; someone had erected a very professional-looking shade tent over much of the seating.

Which was a good idea: it promised to be an even warmer day.

Lynne was lucky to find a parking spot at all, way over by the dog park. She ran into several people she knew on the way to the tournament desk to check in. Everyone wished her good luck, and asked if she was having fun, and exchanged pleasantries about the weather, the competition, and the quality of the snacks.

The island really needed this, she thought, as she waited in line.

"Hey!" Alicia said brightly, looking up from her laptop when Lynne reached the table. "How are you feeling?"

"A little old for such exertions," Lynne said with a laugh. "But ready to go again."

"Great!" Alicia touched a few keys on the computer. "You're all checked in, and Will's already here—I think he's over at the coffee stand." Alicia peered down the long row of tables, trying to see past the crowds.

"I'll find him," Lynne said.

Alicia lowered her voice. "How's it going?"

"Fine, actually." Lynne glanced back at the ever-growing line behind her. "We can talk about it later—not that I've got much to say just yet. I'm still reserving judgment."

"That seems wise." Alicia nodded. "Well, you look good, for what that's worth."

"Thanks!"

Lynne stepped away and headed for the coffee stand, where she did indeed find Will waiting in another long line, chatting with an older man and woman. *Oh, who am I kidding, 'older'?* Lynne chided herself as she got closer. *They're my age—our age.*

"Hi!" Will said when he caught sight of her. He stepped back to make room and said to the couple, "Okay if my partner cuts in line? I'm buying her a coffee either way."

They both laughed. "In that case," said the woman, "cut away!"

Lynne smiled at them both; Will introduced them as Max and Shirley, neighbors of his out in Eagle Lake. "And, incidentally, team sponsors of ours," he added.

"Oh! Wonderful to meet you, and thank you!" Lynne said, shaking both their hands. "Are you also playing?"

"No, gosh, no," Max said with a chuckle. "Far too much exercise for us."

"We're excited to watch y'all though!" Shirley said.

Will was good as his word, buying both their lattes. They took them over to the bleachers, barely finding two seats together where they could perch for a minute to drink them.

"How are you this morning, Dr. Daniels?" Will asked, when they'd gotten settled. "I hope you rested well?"

"I did—after Ethan cooked me a delicious pasta dinner, full of protein and vegetables."

"Clearly you raised that boy right."

More or less, she thought. "And you? Ready to face our first opponents of the day in—" she glanced at her watch "—barely twenty minutes?"

"You bet." He lifted his paper cup up to touch hers in a toast. "Drink up, then we should find a court where we can hit a few balls around, loosen up these tired old muscles."

Their first match was a tough one, made all the more challenging by the fact that it was held out on the retaped tennis courts. Not only was it a lot harder for anyone to watch them there, but there was also more of a breeze today, coming straight through the chain-link fence to the west. Lynne hadn't realized how much the tennis courts blocked the wind from reaching the pickleball courts.

Still, they pulled it out in two close games.

"Whew," Lynne said to Will, after they'd congratulated their opponents, a couple in their thirties from San Juan Island. "I'm glad that didn't go to a tie-breaker."

"We would have taken them," Will said with a grin.

"I hope so. But these are only going to get harder and harder. Since we're seeded and all."

Will's grin widened. "You're picking the lingo up fast, for not being a sports fan."

Lynne laughed. "It's not *that* complicated."

Their second match, however—the semi-finals—was surprisingly easy. They faced one of Lynne's patients and a friend of hers who both seemed in a bit of awe of Lynne. Or maybe it was that Lynne and Will played together like a well-oiled machine, reading each other's body language expertly, communicating as needed, backing each other up like they'd been playing together for years.

It also helped that this game was on court one in front of the bleachers, and seemingly everyone that Lynne knew on the entire island was in the stands, cheering them on. Ethan sat in the front row next to Matt and his dad; they all waved madly when Lynne spotted them.

Lynne and Will took this match eleven-four and eleven-six. When they came off the court, Ethan ran up and hugged his mom. "I'm sweaty!" she laughed.

"And you're a winner!" he exclaimed. "That was amazing!"

"On to the finals," Matt said with a grin.

"Ugh, don't remind me!" Lynne said. She turned and caught Will gazing at her.

"We've got this," he said, and the look in his eyes... *So help me, I believe him*, she thought.

"Hey, Julie and Gavin are going to a tie-breaker over here in their semi-finals," Steph called from the other set of bleachers. "There's room if you want to squeeze in next to me!"

"Ooh, I don't think I can watch them," Lynne said.

"We have to check out the competition," Will told her, as Matt and Ethan both nodded. "Whoever wins that match, we'll meet them in the finals."

"Nope, nope, nope," Lynne said. "You guys watch if you want. I'm going to the snack table."

"I thought you didn't like to eat between games," Will said, looking concerned.

"Changed my mind!" Lynne cried, and turned away, trying to cover the sudden attack of nerves. "I need all the help I can get right now," she called over her shoulder as she walked off.

Nobody followed her, so nobody had to watch her down two snack-size bags of Cheetos and a can of Coke. Then, weirdly feeling much more settled, she wandered back over to the courts. There was no longer any room in the bleachers, or even standing room with any view of the game.

Good. She'd meant what she'd said: she didn't want to watch their future opponents, either team. Besides, she knew it would be Julie and Gavin across the net in the finals.

IT WAS JULIE and Gavin across the net in the finals.

They both looked at least as sweaty and exhausted as Lynne felt, which was some consolation. They were only a few years younger than Will and Lynne, but right now Lynne was feeling every one of her years, and wishing she could give a few of them back.

Or to Julie. Even better.

"All right!" Alicia announced, standing in front of court one holding her microphone. The crowd quieted; even all the other courts were silent, as the finals for the other two divisions had already been played. "Okay, everybody!" Alicia said with a huge grin. "It's the moment we've all been waiting for: the finals of Division Two!"

Right, the most anticipated match of the entire tournament, Lynne thought, though she kept her snark to herself. *How do the Division One folks feel about that, I wonder?* She glanced around, seeing at least as many Advanced players in the audience as Beginners, everyone sticking around to watch this one last match. She shook her head in wonder. If she'd thought everyone she knew on the island had been here to see the semi-finals, she'd been sorely mistaken. This felt like everyone she'd ever known in all her life. *Oh can we just get started already?* she thought, hugging herself around the waist, trying to tamp down her nerves as Alicia went on about the two teams, the money they'd each raised, and what felt like three hours' worth of announcements.

At last, Alicia pulled a quarter out of her pocket and said, "Coin toss to determine the starting serve!" She turned to Lynne. "Heads or tails?"

"Tails," Lynne said, and Alicia flipped.

The quarter landed on the cement walk in front of the fence, bounced, and nearly rolled under the first row of bleachers. A dozen people bent down to look at it. "Tails!" someone called out, and the crowd broke into applause.

Will grinned at Lynne. "Good omen," he said, his white teeth shining in the sun.

She just nodded, and they all stepped onto the court.

Alicia followed them on, handing Lynne a brand-new ball. "You've got this," she whispered.

"You're not rooting for me over Julie?!" Lynne said, a little appalled.

"I'm rooting for *all* my friends!" Alicia smiled at her. "That way, I'm always happy."

Lynne just shook her head as Alicia left the court, but she had to smile as well.

And then it was time to serve—no need for warmups. She looked across the net. Julie stood ready to receive; Gavin was up at the kitchen line. They both looked relaxed and determined.

"Zero-zero-start!" Lynne called, and served one low and fast across the net.

Julie returned it solidly, and Lynne fell into the zone as the game was on.

THE SCORE WAS tied at eight when Julie called a time-out. She had been about to serve when she suddenly stopped, dropped the ball, and lifted her arm and paddle into a T-shape. Her expression was hard to read, but she did not look happy.

Gavin stepped quickly to her, and they had a huddled exchange. He put his arm around her shoulder; she shrugged it off but kept talking to him, shaking her head.

Will sidled over to Lynne. "Did she hurt herself?"

"I don't know," Lynne said, frowning. "I didn't see a stumble or anything."

"Maybe it's a cramp."

She looks mad at him, Lynne thought.

Time-outs were technically supposed to be thirty seconds, but nobody was holding them to that. It was probably closer to a minute before Julie made an angry gesture and stepped away from Gavin to pick up the ball.

"Eight-eight-one!" she called, and even from here, Lynne could hear the quaver in her voice. She looked very upset.

"Time-out!" Lynne called, raising her own arm and paddle.

Julie just stared back at her as Lynne walked up to the net, gesturing for Julie to approach.

"What's wrong?" Lynne asked, when her friend finally met her at the net. She had clearly been crying—the streaks on her face were not just sweat.

"I...just..." Julie could hardly get the words out. This was anger, Lynne realized: pure and volcanic. "I cannot *believe* the gall of that man," she finally spat. "Asshole!"

"Who—Gavin?" Lynne asked, stunned.

"No!" Julie practically yelled, then lowered her voice as she snuck a glance at the bewildered audience. "Stinker Face McLeod. He has the nerve to show up *here*! During the freaking *finals*! Why can't he leave me alone, what is *wrong* with him?!"

"Is everything okay?" Will asked, meeting them at the net. Gavin had also come up and put a tentative arm on Julie's back; she didn't shrug him off this time.

"No it's not!" Julie seethed. "The man who's single-handedly trying to ruin my business, and my life, has come to lord it over me!"

"Sam McLeod," Lynne whispered to the puzzled Will. "He's a vacation rental developer..."

But Will was breaking into a smile. "Oh hey!" he said, turning and waving to the very man himself. "Hi Sam!"

Lynne, Gavin, and Julie all stared at Will. He didn't notice at first, because Sam was waving back at him.

Then Will turned back to them. His face fell. "What is it?"

"You *know* him?" Lynne asked.

"You *like* him?" Julie added, aghast. She wheeled on Gavin. "Did you know this?"

"Whoa, no, wow," Gavin said, taking a step back under the intensity of Julie's dismay. "Will, seriously?" he asked his friend.

"Sam McLeod?"

"I…what's going on here?" Will asked carefully. "What's wrong with him?"

"Are you shitting me?" Julie snapped, and took a few steps away from the net, as if not trusting herself to stand so close to Will.

"Yes, I know and like him. We're in similar lines of work, and…" Will started, but regrouped. "Okay, there's obviously something I'm missing here, but this isn't the time or the place—"

"Hey, guys," Alicia said, stepping onto the court. "Everything okay? This is a pretty long time-out…" She glanced meaning-fully at the crowd, which was growing fidgety. She clearly hadn't picked out Sam McLeod. "Can we get back on track?"

Gavin looked at Julie, who gave an exaggerated shrug, as if forcing tension out of her shoulders. "Okay. Yeah. I can do this. I have to do this. Sorry, Alicia."

"Are you sure?" Lynne asked her.

"We'll talk about it later," Julie said. "All of us." She gave Will a dark glance; he nodded sorrowfully at her, still confused but clearly getting the gist. "I've got this."

"Okay!" Alicia said to her, and turned to the audience. "Here we go! Sorry for the delay, everyone!" Then she hurried off the court, latching the gate behind her.

As Julie headed back behind the baseline, Will and Lynne re-turned to their positions. "He's our big anonymous donor, and a really great guy," Will said softly. "I had no idea…"

Lynne just shook her head, unable to even process all the ram-ifications of this right now. "Later."

Julie picked up the ball and her paddle, and took another deep breath. With grim determination, she served.

EVERYONE TRIED AS hard as they could to hold it together, but Julie had clearly been deeply rattled. Will and Lynne took the first game eleven to eight.

Lynne tried to check in with Julie again as they switched sides and took a two-minute break, but Julie just said, "I can't. I have to focus." She didn't even talk to Gavin, or drink any water, or look at the audience; she just paced behind the baseline until it was time to serve.

Julie played like a woman possessed during game two—a woman possessed by the spirit of an Olympic-level pickleballer, at that. The crowd ate it up, whooping and cheering her amazing, almost superhuman moves. It was no surprise when she and Gavin took the game, eleven to three.

"I'm just glad we got those three points," Lynne muttered to Will as Alicia walked back onto the court for a coin toss to determine the starting serve for the tie-breaker. "It wasn't a complete humiliation."

"I wish…" Will started, but stopped himself, and squared his shoulders. "We'll take the next one."

"I wish I had your confidence," Lynne said with a sad chuckle. Her heart ached for her friend.

"It's not confidence," Will said. "Merely observation: she gave it everything she had in that last game, and now she's hanging on by a thread. We'll be the tortoises, you'll see. Slow and steady wins the race."

"Heads or tails?" Alicia asked Julie.

"I don't care," Julie said.

"Heads," Gavin said.

Alicia flipped, and everyone bent over the coin. "It's tails!" Will called, and handed Lynne the ball.

She gazed across the net at Julie, whose expression was stony yet determined. Then she called out the opening score, and served.

"I TOLD YOU SO," Will cried, sweeping Lynne off her feet in a strong hug before coming to his senses and setting her back down.

She found herself reluctant to let go of him.

The crowd was cheering and shouting all around them—it was deafening. In another minute, a dozen people had stormed the court, patting Will and Lynne on their backs, hopping up and down with glee.

"Unbelievable!" someone cried.

"What playing!" someone else said.

"What a comeback!"

"I've never seen anything like it!"

"Wow," Lynne said to Will, trying to take it all in.

Ethan was there, and he too picked up Lynne and twirled her around. "Mom! You rocked!"

She laughed. "Thanks."

"Age before beauty!" a man called out.

"Hey now," Will said, looking offended on Lynne's behalf. She shook her head and smiled.

Gavin and Julie had taken an early lead, but then it seemed that Will had been right: Julie had used up all her fire in game two. She flubbed easy shots, and nearly tripped over her own feet more than once. Even so, it had been close, but Will and Lynne had pulled it out, eleven to nine.

"Congratulations to our big winners, and our champion fundraisers as well!" Alicia announced into the microphone, putting her arms around Lynne and Will and drawing them to her sides. The crowd whooped and cheered all over again. "Thank you everyone for making this tournament such a smashing success— and the most fun ever had on Orcas Island!"

Amid the cheering, Lynne looked around for Julie, not seeing her. Then Alicia swept Lynne and Will out of the court and over to the registration table, where three big shiny trophies were lined up, flanked by smaller trophies. "Gather round for the awards ceremony, followed by the raffle winners!" she announced.

Lynne just wished she could fully enjoy it all. She still wanted to find Julie, make sure she was all right, but it seemed she and Gavin had slipped away. Which was probably for the best. Gavin would take care of her.

Thank goodness she had him.

Lynne told herself she owed it to Alicia, and Robin—not to mention all the friends and patients and colleagues and fans who had contributed to the cause, and cheered them on—to not only stay and accept the accolades, but pretend like she was as uncomplicatedly excited as they were.

"Did Sam do something to Julie particularly?" Will asked her, when everyone's attention was on the raffle drawing. "Or does she just not approve of developers in general?"

"He did—he's still doing it, it seems," Lynne whispered back. "He's put a lot of effort into squashing her business, and probably making her lose her home in the bargain." She shook her head. "At first, we thought she was overreacting, seeing trouble where there wasn't any, but I'm no longer so sure…"

Will shook his head. "That's not the Sam I know. Maybe it's just a misunderstanding?"

Alicia's voice came over the loudspeaker again. "Lynne and Will—please join the other winners for the group photo!"

"Later," Lynne said to Will again, and put on her smile.

THE FESTIVITIES ROLLED straight into lunch, a generous barbecue feast cooked by members of the families helped by the Junior Center—including many kids—and served on a bunch of long folding tables that had been brought in and set up in the unpaved parking lot by the courts. It was delicious, and Lynne found herself feeling a little better about everything.

Or maybe she had just been hungry.

I'm so glad I had the foresight to take tomorrow off work, she thought, stuffing a big bite of pulled pork into her mouth. She could already feel her muscles stiffening up. *I haven't gotten this much exercise in…I can't remember how long.*

Ethan sat with her and Will, along with Steph, and Matt and his dad. Alicia was still busy running around taking care of everything, and obviously having a wonderful time doing so.

"So, this is your lovely lady?"

Everyone turned at the voice. Sam McLeod stood behind Will, grinning down at him.

Will shot Lynne a careful glance even as he stood up and shook McLeod's hand. "Hi, Sam," he said. He smiled, but Lynne knew this wasn't his relaxed, unguarded smile. "This is Dr. Lynne Daniels, yes."

"Pleasure to meet you!" Sam boomed, reaching a hand down to shake Lynne's.

After only the briefest hesitation, she shook his hand back. "Nice to meet you too," she said, keeping her voice even.

"What a great event!" Sam said, gesturing at the whole scene around them. "Pleasant day, great community spirit—too bad the facilities are so decrepit."

"I'm sorry, what?" Lynne asked. She got to her feet as well. *I'm not going to let that man loom over me.*

"The pickleball courts are cracking—the parking lot is a dust bowl—the tennis courts are a disgrace, with that pitted surface and shabby fence," he said, shaking his head. "This whole place is a dump!"

"I don't know," Lynne said, between clenched teeth. "We like it."

Ethan got up and stood beside his mother, but Sam ignored him. From the table, Steph and Matt and Gordon were watching the whole exchange, wide-eyed.

"Will," Sam said, "I see an opportunity here. I'm so glad you asked me to sponsor you in this tournament and its little charity thing, but it's obvious that we can do much more." He turned and scanned the area again. "What happens in the winter? This dust will turn to mud, and no one wants to play out here in the rain and snow! I see a whole unified facility, stretching into that field there—" he pointed at the historic cemetery just beyond the courts "—with indoor courts as well as outdoor, a rec room, changing rooms, obviously a snack bar—oh, we can brainstorm it." He grinned at Will. "What do you say, my friend? We can build a first-class facility here. My business manager tells me pickleball is the next big thing, and having seen this little shindig today, I believe it. There'll be a waiting list a mile long to get into our club."

Is he kidding? Lynne thought, too aghast to even speak. She turned to look at Will.

But he wasn't looking at her. He stared straight at Sam McLeod and said, "No, Sam, I think you're wrong about that."

Sam's smile barely cracked; he cocked his head as if he didn't understand. "About what? I can show you the numbers. Pickleball is growing in leaps and bounds! We can charge whatever we like for memberships, the island's economy can bear it. We'll make a fortune!"

"I'm not sure you heard Dr. Daniels a moment ago," Will said, taking a step away from Sam and closer to Lynne and Ethan. "'We like it,' I believe she said." He looked at Lynne, a question in his eyes. "Meaning there's nothing wrong with the courts just as they are. Isn't that right?"

"That is right," she agreed, and before she could second-guess the impulse, reached out to take Will's hand. He squeezed her hand and stood a little taller. "We like our crappy little courts," she went on, turning back to Sam, "and we like our town's sidewalks without parking meters too!"

Will shot her a puzzled glance before shrugging and telling Sam, "There you have it. I don't know what-all you've been up to around here, Sam, but it doesn't look like you've made yourself very popular with the locals."

Sam gave a dismissive snort. "Oh, parking meters—there's always going to be a disgruntled little coven of old-timers who are opposed to progress—to change of any kind. When it was put to the voters, the measure passed resoundingly."

"It passed because you snuck it into a mid-winter special election under deceptive language!" Lynne retorted.

Will squeezed her hand again and drew her another step closer to himself as he said to Sam, "Again, I don't know everything, but I've heard enough. This conversation is over. My friends and I are going to enjoy our lunch now." He turned to Lynne and indicated the table, where their food was growing cold. "My dear?"

"Thank you," she said, turning her back on Sam McLeod and sitting down.

"Wow, Mom," Ethan whispered in her ear as he sat beside her.

She smiled at him and snuck a glance at Will. Joy and peace settled inside her. *Yes. Wow.*

"I'VE MISSED THIS view," Lynne murmured to Will, as they snuggled on his couch before the picture window.

"Me too," he murmured back, gazing into her eyes.

She chuckled. "I mean out there." She waved at the golds and pinks of the lowering light on the water, the last rays of the sun hitting the hills of the mainland beyond.

"Oh that," he said, not taking his eyes off her.

There was nothing for it but to lean forward and kiss the man.

A luscious while later, she sipped her wine, then set the glass on the coffee table.

"Hungry?" he asked.

She thought a moment. "Not really. That lunch was huge; I think this little spread is all I need. What about you?"

He had set out fancy crackers and fancier cheese, big fat grapes, exquisitely ripe figs, and chocolate-covered pistachios. They'd been nibbling, sipping, and cuddling since she'd gotten here... after driving to her house, taking a shower, and packing an overnight bag.

"I am perfectly satiated as well," he said with a grin.

"*All* your appetites?" she teased.

He kissed her again. "Well, if you put it *that* way..."

She chuckled, and kissed him back.

A minute later, he said, "So. I know there are many things we need to talk about..."

"Yes and no," she said. When he looked a question at her, she went on: "I need to tell you the details of what Sam's been doing around here, but you already have the general idea: that he's been trying to impose his big-city ways on Eastsound, and damn anyone who stands in his way."

"I knew he could sometimes be a bit of a bull in a china shop," Will mused, "but I didn't realize it was anything like this bad. I've known him for a few years, but not very well, obviously."

"I'm glad to hear it. If he were one of your best friends…" Lynne gave an exaggerated shiver.

"Not at all." He picked up her hand and kissed the back of it gently. "But I didn't mean Sam, when I said we have things to talk about."

Lynne nodded. "I know. And, we will talk—a lot, I hope. For years."

His eyes lit up. "Do you mean that?"

"I do." She smiled at him. "I'll start: so much has changed for me this year—in the months since we met. Some of it wasn't easy." He nodded, glancing downward briefly, not interrupting her. "But all of it has led us here." She picked up their joined hands and held them to her heart. "Here," she emphasized.

"I do not want to be anywhere else," he said softly.

"Neither do I." She paused, gathering her thoughts—ideas that had been coalescing over the last few weeks, ripening into something she thought she could articulate in the last few days, and finally bursting into bloom as she'd watched Will tell McLeod to take a hike. "About the changes. When we met, I knew who I was. As well I should have: I'm sixty-two years old, I've had a satisfying career, I've raised a son, I am a member of this community, with a number of excellent friends—I knew my place and my purpose." She held his gaze, making sure he understood. "But when you and I hit our rough patch, it felt as though I'd failed at everything—not just romance, which was bad enough. But I felt that I didn't know myself at all. I'm a doctor, sure, but I'm overwhelmed, overworked, and failing at retiring. I'm a mother, but my only child is mired in a life crisis entirely of his own making. Even my little personal embroidering hobby got away from me—no, hear me out—that art show has led to a frankly terrifying amount of attention. The number of commissions alone—I don't know if I can fulfill them, especially given my work schedule. And when I sit down to work on them, half the time I can't find the muse at all."

Will held her hand and nodded at her, waiting for her to continue.

She took a deep breath. "But I realized something this week. I think I had to fail at all that stuff...in order to discover who I *really* am."

"Oh?"

"Yes. I *am* an artist—I'm only having such trouble with the commissions because suddenly my art has commerce attached to it. Other people, and their expectations. There have always been projects that got started and never finished, and plenty of times I've been dissatisfied with how pieces turned out. It just never mattered all that much before, when no one was looking." She shrugged. "I have to learn how not to let it matter now, when they are looking."

"I know you can do that."

"Thank you." She smiled. "I also realized I am a lover, and not a failed one at that. Our rupture hurt so badly for that very reason: what we have is real, and it grieved me when I thought I'd lost it."

His eyes shone; he squeezed her hand.

"Ethan said something to me last night that really resonated: he told me that he was worried about our relationship, yours and mine; especially at first. How quickly we'd gotten so close."

"He was?" Will looked puzzled.

"Yes. He hadn't seen me care about anyone the way I did Charles—his father—until you came along. He, too, knew who

I was, and all of a sudden I was somebody else. But then he came around. He said he'd never seen me this happy." She looked into Will's eyes. "I'm not giving us another chance just because my son wants me to…but it does make me feel very good that he approves of us."

"It makes me feel wonderful," Will said. "And honored."

Lynne nodded. "The doctor-failing-to-retire thing: I'm going to have to work on that one."

"I know you aren't asking for my advice, but I will point out, nobody is forcing you to work."

"I know. But I do care—about the patients, and about the clinic and my fellow docs. I would not feel good about leaving them in the lurch."

"I see no failure there, Dr. Daniels," Will said. "I see a loving, generous, caring person who helps countless people."

"Thank you." She smiled. "Thank you for understanding."

"Oh, I do."

"Good. There's only one more piece." She felt an embarrassed grin stealing across her face, but damn it, she was going to say it. "I've never been any kind of an athlete, even when I was younger. I believe in exercise because it's good for our health, and it can be fun. But this week, I realized…I'm a damn good pickleball player. And I love it."

Will laughed, and pulled her into his arms. "You are an amazing pickleball player, and I adore you."

The conversation shifted to a more nonverbal phase for another luscious while. Before it could go all the way to awkward sofa sex, Lynne pulled away and said, "Actually, there is one more thing I wanted to say to you."

Will, his hair uncharacteristically mussed and his face flushed, said, "Yes?"

"No more secrets, ever."

"I promise that, my dear Lynne, with all my heart."

She smiled. "Even things that don't seem important—if this is going to work at all, we have to tell each other everything."

"Absolutely everything. What I had for lunch, someone tailgated me all the way to town, what I dreamed last night, I stubbed my toe in the bathroom…"

Lynne giggled. "I know, I know. This is going to take some practice, for both of us," she admitted. "I've been living alone for a very long time; I'm as unaccustomed to sharing my whole life with someone else as you are. But I am eager to give it a try."

"Not half as eager as I am, my love."

"For now, however…" she said.

"Yes?" His eyes shone.

She leaned closer. "No more words." Then she kissed him, in case it wasn't clear what she'd meant.

Will was a quick study, however. He did not miss the point.

AFTER A LUXURIOUS night and a lazy morning in bed, Lynne sat propped against a stack of pillows at his headboard, sipping coffee. "This is the life," she said. "I could get used to—"

Somewhere in the room, inside her purse, her cell phone rang.

Will looked over at her from his own nest of pillows. "Shall I fetch that for you, milady?"

She groaned. "I want to say no, but…"

He was already out of bed, and handing her the phone before it could go to voicemail.

She took it and looked at the caller ID. "It's the clinic," she said, wanting to groan again, and louder this time. Could she *never* get a moment to herself? She swiped to answer it. "Dr. Daniels," she said, crisp and professional.

"Lynne," said Leland Park, "I'm so sorry to bother you on your day off—"

"That's okay," she hurried to assure him, already calculating how long it would take her to get home and grab some work clothes—unless it was a true emergency, in which case nobody would likely mind her showing up in casual dress. "What is it?"

Oddly, Leland chuckled. "I just thought you'd like to hear the news as soon as it was official: Dr. Danielle Westerbrook will be joining our team. Her first day is next Monday."

Lynne gasped, and felt Will tense beside her. "Oh my god that's wonderful!" she cried, turning to Will. "She accepted the offer?" Now Will smiled tentatively, but still looked a little bewildered.

"She did, and she's eager to jump right in," Leland said. "In fact, she'll be on-island by Wednesday, and would love to start shadowing you right away."

Lynne leaned back against the pillows, feeling tears of joy filling her eyes. "I'm free! I can retire!"

Will grasped her hand—the one not holding the phone—and squeezed it. All his confusion vanished, replaced by joy.

"Well," Leland said, "we do hope you'll consider continuing our previous on-call arrangement…"

"Of course," Lynne said. "I just hope you don't need to call me in very often."

"I hope we don't either. In fact, I plan to leave the job posting live. If we get a second good candidate, I won't turn them away."

"Can we afford to hire two new docs?" Lynne asked.

"We'll find the money," Leland assured her. "All right: that's all I wanted to tell you. I'll let you go enjoy your day off now."

"Thank you!"

"What are you up to—making more beautiful artwork?"

Lynne chuckled. "Something like that."

After she hung up, she clicked the ringer off on her phone, tossed it onto the plush carpeting at the foot of the bed, and turned to Will. "Come here."

He did.

~ o ~

READ ON FOR A SNEAK PEEK OF

Toil and Water

Book 4 in The Island of Second Chances

COMING SOON!

Chapter 1

MATT

Matt saved his work, pausing yet again to make sure the whole set of files had fully updated on the external hard drive, as well as the cloud and his computer's hard drive. Then he had to find his mental thread again before moving to the next page. The client had asked for "only small tweaks" to this page—but, like, thirty of them. Matt sighed, and pulled up her email again to be sure.

"What in the world is wrong with the blue," he muttered, rolling his eyes at her suggestions. "If I change it to dark magenta, you won't see the illustrations at all."

Still, the customer is always right, and yada yada blah blah blah.

He made the change. It looked terrible. He saved the file, and double-checked that it all went to the external drive, the cloud, his machine. Becca was only going to make him change it all back again when she saw how bad it looked.

But, he still had to go through the process.

He'd made about six of the thirty-some changes and was just starting to question whether he needed to go through the lengthy save process quite so often when the lights flickered. Matt sighed again.

Ah, the joys of working on an island on a blustery October day...an island whose electrical grid was connected to the mainland by what amounted to a huge extension cord.

Of course Matt had a surge protector and battery backup for his computer array—he could hardly call himself a professional web designer if he were carelessly losing work right and left—but all technology fails sooner or later. His belt-and-suspenders approach was the best he could do.

And saving his work constantly, particularly on windy days.

He'd just started on the next change when the lights flickered again, for longer this time. Outside, the wind seemed to pick up in response, howling in the trees, pushing branches against his window.

Matt saved the file again and sat, waiting to see if he needed to go start the generator. It was a pain to fire it up and use it, but better than being without power. While he waited, he heard his father's slow shuffling footsteps in the hall coming his way.

He got up and went to his office doorway. "Hey, Dad," he said. "What's up?"

Gordon looked up at Matt with a frown. "Something's wrong with my bed."

Before Matt could respond, the power went out entirely. Well, that answered that. "I'm right here, Dad," Matt said, reaching out for his father's hand in the semi-gloom.

Gordon's hand was cool, despite how warm he kept his room. "The power went out!"

"Yes, it did; we seem to be having a bit of a windstorm," Matt said gently. "I'll get the generator turned on in a minute. What's wrong with your bed?"

"It's flat."

It took Matt a moment to parse this. "Oh, right—when the power flickered, it probably reset itself. We can raise your head and feet up again as soon as I start the generator, okay?"

"Why is the power out?"

"Because we're having some weather. Do you want to come sit in the living room while I get the generator going?" Matt tugged on his dad's hand gently.

Gordon planted his feet, resisting Matt's guidance. "It's dark in here."

"Yes, I know. Probably a tree fell somewhere, took down a power line. Come and get comfy in your chair in the living room, and I'll get the lights back on." He wanted to pull again, but when Gordon got confused, he got even more stubborn, which led to more confusion…it was important to interrupt that cycle before it could get under way. "I'll get you some of your juice if you just come sit down, okay?"

Gordon hesitated another moment, but then let Matt lead him to the living room and park him in his easy chair. Which of course would not recline, because that needed power too.

"Just sit in it like that for a minute, Dad," Matt said. "I'll get your juice, and then we'll get the lights back on."

"It's cold in here."

"Heat too, coming right up." Matt hurried into the kitchen before his dad could ask him why it was cold.

By the time he'd gotten Gordon his juice, and answered a dozen more questions (sometimes two or three times), and made it out to the garage with a flashlight, the power of course had come back on again. Matt checked the generator anyway—this would have been the first time this season he'd used it, though he'd made sure to keep the gasoline in his five-gallon container fresh. The generator started right up, thankfully. Matt let it run a minute, then shut it off.

"What was all that noise?" Gordon asked when Matt went back inside.

"I was testing the generator, like you taught me to, Dad," Matt said, going and sitting across from his dad. "Remember? Back when we lived at the North Pole."

Gordon gave a disbelieving snort. "It wasn't the North Pole, it was…um…"

Matt waited a moment, then prodded, "You know where."

"I don't remember."

"Smallest county seat?" Matt prompted.

"Ivanhoe!" Gordon cried, breaking into a grin. "Ivanhoe, Minnesota!"

"That's right!" Matt grinned back at him. "I knew you remembered."

Gordon smiled for another moment, then frowned again. "Why don't we still live in Ivanhoe? I liked it there."

"I know you did. But you moved out here a while after Mom died, to be closer to me." Matt watched his father closely when he said *Mom died*. Usually Gordon remembered losing his wife, but sometimes he got confused when Matt referred to her as "Mom," thinking he was talking about Gordon's mother.

Gordon just nodded this time, still frowning. "But why were you living here and not at home?"

"I went away to college in Seattle, and then I got a good job after graduation and stayed." *And I never ever ever wanted to spend another minute of my life in The Smallest County Seat, Minnesota*, he added silently. "Eventually, I came up to Orcas Island on a weekend, and realized that this is where I wanted to live."

"Even though the power goes out all the time?"

Matt barked out a laugh. "Only in the winter, Dad." He got to his feet. "So, let me go see if I can get your bed back how it should be."

IT HAD BEEN a trying day all around. Not just the stupid annoying job or the second, longer power outage after the first one, or even Gordon's increasing confusion and crankiness (he really did not do well with anything out of the ordinary). It had just been one of those days when it seemed like everything that could go wrong, did, along with the overwhelming sense that it had always been this way and it was always going to be this way.

Matt knew that wasn't true, in either direction. His dad had only moved in with him a couple years ago, when his dementia made it inadvisable to live even semi-independently. And, well, nothing lasted forever, Matt knew. It would be sad to lose his father, but he was already losing him, little by little.

Dementia was a cruel disease.

Now, dinner and dishes were all done, Gordon was bedded down for the night, and Matt was ready for his reward: the best part of his day. He and Megan didn't talk every night—they were not dating, they each had separate independent lives, they had no responsibilities to each other, they were both very clear on this—but they did talk frequently, and he felt it keenly when for one reason or another, they didn't connect.

And he was pretty sure she felt the same way.

So why *weren't* they dating? There were all the usual barriers: distance (she lived in Portland, he was up here); prior commitments (Matt's father; Megan's job); and the fact that, when Matt first met Megan last December, he was only a few months out of a serious relationship and not at all over it.

They both held out hope that things might change in the future, even though those changes would inevitably mean loss and a certain amount of upheaval. But, the best things in life always came at some cost, didn't they?

Meanwhile, they had their frequent phone calls, and extremely occasional visits—mostly when she came up here to visit her mom, Matt's friend and fellow soup group member Julie. It worked. For now.

Matt poured himself a finger of single-malt and settled in Gordon's chair, pushing the button to recline it slightly and raise the footrest. Then he pulled out his phone and punched Megan's number.

"Hey!" She answered after one ring, and his heart warmed. She was always cheerful, it seemed, but she sounded even perkier tonight. "How was your day? Mine was amazing!"

Matt chuckled. "Then you should tell me all about it, because mine was dreadful."

"Oh no! In that case, you *have* to tell me yours first. What happened?"

"Well, nothing, really; it was just death by a thousand paper cuts. You know?"

"I'm *sooo* sorry." She sounded like she wanted to reach through the phone line and give him a hug. God, how he wished she could. "You should still tell me about it. It might make you feel better."

"No, it wouldn't. It was just—work and Dad and the power grid and too boring to even go into. I want to hear yours: *that's* what will make me feel better."

"Hmm," she said, sounding dubious all of a sudden. "It's... well, it's exciting news, but you're maybe not going to like it so much."

"Oh?"

"Yeah." She took a breath, and then launched ahead: "Remember how Jacob was off in Italy looking at this ginormous old house that he thought GoodTilth should buy and make our first overseas office?"

"Yes," Matt said, wondering where the *I'm not going to like this* part was. Jacob was Megan's boss at the environmental startup she worked at and loved...except for a few of her more nincompoopish coworkers and most particularly her ineffectual boss himself. "Is he back, then?" Megan, as de facto second-in-command, had been much happier while he'd been away.

"He is...and he did buy the house. It was like eighty thousand euros, which is not even a hundred thousand dollars!"

"That's kind of crazy," Matt said. "But you guys had the money in the bank, right? You got that grant for expansion a few months ago."

"We did—enough to not only buy it but to do a bunch of much-needed repairs and upgrades. Like, all new wiring, and the place needs a new roof, and all that. Oh," she laughed, "and some-body has to get rid of the turkeys living on the ground floor."

"Turkeys?!"

"Yeah. I'll send you some pictures." She switched her phone to speaker, and texts started coming through on Matt's phone, so he did the same.

"Wow," he said, after scrolling through a few of the shots. Indeed, a bunch of large white birds with bright red wattles wandered around on stone floors, past ornate fireplaces and antique furniture, with deep-set windows looking out onto a cute courtyard. "Cool place though."

"It is!" Her initial enthusiasm was back. "Once we clean the turkey shit out, it'll be even cooler."

We? Matt thought.

"So here's the thing," Megan went on in a rush. "Jacob's wife actually hated the little town, so she put the kibosh on them going to live there while the whole thing is getting put together—the remodeling, the business licenses and all that, everything—so he asked me if I'd be willing to go and do it."

Matt stared at the phone, speechless. Finally, he cleared his throat. "Um." He took another breath. "What did you tell him?"

"I, uh, told him I'd think about it—but Matt! What an opportunity! To live in Italy for a year, without having to leave my job or pay rent or anything! You know I've always dreamed of living abroad. And you can come see me!"

"I…would love to do that," he said, hating how wooden he sounded. "But I'm not sure how that would work…"

"I know. Your dad." She sighed. "Maybe, I don't know, Ramona could come stay or something?"

"Maybe." They were both silent for a minute. "So, a year?" he asked, already trying to tell himself that this was all going to be all right.

"That's a guess. Maybe less…maybe more. We'll have to see how it goes, once it gets underway."

"Right." He tried to swallow a lump in his throat. "So, um, this is great, Megan."

"It's not," she said, sounding dismal. "I'm sorry—I know it's so far away, and it's just jerky of me to be so excited about this...I knew this was going to be hard for you, and I don't mean to be insensitive—"

"You're *not*," he cut her off. "You were right: this is an amazing opportunity, and you would be an idiot to pass it up. And I can't know how my life is going to go—how long I'm committed here." *When my father will die.* "And this will mean you don't have to work in the same office with Jacob, right? If his wife doesn't want to be there?"

"Right," she said. "I'll get to pick my own team—two, maybe three people to take with me."

"It's a no-brainer, then," he said. "You have to say yes."

"I'm going to keep thinking about it, and you should too. I told him I'll tell him next week."

"You *have* to say yes," he repeated.

She chuckled. "We'll keep talking about it. Anyway, I need to go now—I told Mom I had news, and she's already texted me three times wondering why I haven't called her with it."

"All right. Say hi to her for me."

"I will." She paused. "Matt. I'm sorry."

"Don't be! We'll...we'll figure this out."

"We will."

He smiled at the phone, even though she couldn't see him, as they said their goodnights. Then he sat in his father's chair for a long time, holding the phone against his chest.

He was going to lose Megan, before they'd ever even kissed.

Notes and Thanks

As I MENTIONED previously, these books are set on Orcas Island, but it's an Orcas that's not entirely contiguous with the one we know out here in the real world. There are real businesses in the books, and then there are made-up ones. I again played with some geography for the sake of making the story work. And, of course, so far as I know, there are no plans in the works for parking meters...or other, more heinous intrusions on our peaceful rural beauty.

Thanks once more go to Kathia Zolfaghari for the astonishing cover—she really knocked it out of the park this time. Even more embarrassingly gushy thanks go to Spencer Ellsworth for his smart and thoughtful editing—and for all the fun and funny comments I found sprinkled throughout the manuscript. Thank you to Marcela Barrientos for all the "inside real estate" information about the island, and for taking hours of her time to show me around the Eagle Lake development even though I made it clear I'm not in the market for a new house. (And apologies to Marcela as well for my not finding a place for an evil realtor in this book, even though I promised—maybe the next one!) Many thanks to Dr. Robert Wilson for his time generously answering my many questions about what it's like to be a doctor here. Any mistakes or misrepresentations are my fault, not his.

Thanks *always* to Darvill's Bookstore for their eternal love and support! Thanks to Watermark Bookstore in Anacortes for enthusiastically jumping on board the "soup group" train.

And thank *you*, dear reader, for joining me on another fictional journey!

Shannon Page
November, 2025
Orcas Island, Washington

About the Author

Shannon Page lives on Orcas Island, with her husband, author and illustrator Mark Ferrari. The island is an amazing place to live, and to write. She's a versatile writer (which sounds much better than saying she can't make up her mind!), publishing novels of fantasy, cozy mystery, romance, and science fiction, as well as personal essays; for her "day job," she's a freelance proofreader and copy editor. She also loves to edit anthologies. In her spare time (haha), she cooks, gardens, plays pickleball, and takes *lots* of pictures of frogs. Visit her at www.shannonpage.net.